PROPHECY FULFILLED

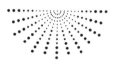

TAMAR SLOAN

JESS CONNORS
PUBLISHING

To Noel, Pat, and Tricia.
For maintaining the momentum.
xoxo
Oh, and Sean...

CONTENTS

PART I
EDEN

CHAPTER ONE

"READY?"

I look up into summer sky eyes, full of the warmth of sunshine and love. Noah's lips are tipped up. Hasn't this moment been centuries in the making?

"Ah, not really." I glance nervously at the trees behind me. I appreciate that Noah took me for a walk to calm my nerves. He would have sensed how much this evening has unsettled me. It's just that it didn't really work. "Are you sure there are no surprises?"

"Very sure. Your Were-in-law wasn't allowed within a Glade's-width of the preparations."

That has me smiling. Tara, proudly bonded to Noah's twin, Mitch, is also the Alpha of our neighboring pack. They have their hands full with the Channons. And their mutineers.

"And I think they finally found something that actually holds her focus."

Being newly bonded didn't keep Tara occupied for long. The prospect of college after the holidays certainly didn't. Even an unsettled, divided pack wasn't enough to keep Tara from organizing anyone in her orbit. But the discovery that she's carrying Mitch's child? Now that did the trick.

"Who knew Tara would take up knitting and take it to a whole other level?"

Noah chuckles. "After she painted the nursery walls in a forest diorama." He pulls me in close. "But you're changing the subject."

"You changed it. I just ran with it."

"Happy birthday."

I blush. A month bonded and you'd think I wouldn't every time Noah's voice dips like that. It's a voice that captures the life we've forged. The future we're facing. The nights we've discovered. "Thanks. What's that, forty-eight times now?"

"Hey, when half of the Prime Alpha pair reaches eighteen, it needs to be acknowledged."

I arch a brow. "Consider it acknowledged with the flowers, the cheesecake and the all-vegetarian family lunch."

"So you don't want your present?"

"What?" I glance around the clearing we stand in. This grassy opening protected by trees is the Phelan land we'll build our house on one day. It's the place close to the family who has accepted me with hearts as big as Wyoming. It's the place where a future I never imagined will set its foundations. It's the place I'll live, laugh and love with my bonded mate. "You've already given me everything, Noah."

Noah's hand is in his pocket, that soft, sexy smile tipping up his lips. His eyes never leave mine. "Well, I want you to know…"

His hand tugs up and a fine gold chain is wrapped around his fingers. I gasp when I see the matching gold pendant swinging from the fragile links.

My hand comes out to grasp it as the sun catches the edge, light glinting and refracting. The wolf outline, a head thrown up in a howl, is identical to the one that is imprinted on Noah's chest. And every other Were in existence. "It's beautiful."

"Eden." I look up and my breath evaporates at the warmth and sincerity in those blue pools. I wonder if he notices his hand brush his chest, touching the mark that I've indelibly changed. "You have my heart, my love, my life. Now you have a part of me."

I'm never sure what I've brought to Noah's life. Sure, I'm a Changeling. A part-Fae who can connect with animals, but it's also a heritage most Weres will never know about. All that creates is complications and tension as Weres discover the leader to lead all leaders isn't one of them.

"Thank you." My voice is breathy and a little choked.

He takes the chain and lifts it and I raise my hair as he clasps it. The wolf, golden and fragile, settles on my chest. It's warm and cool and full of promise.

"You're one of us now, Eden."

The kiss that graces my lips demolishes any trace of doubt that had considered germinating. The warmth, a glimmer of the heat I've discovered we create, a fulfilment of the connection I can't live without, envelopes me. My arms rise and clasp his shoulders. He's given me something that shows what his mark had already become even before we had bonded. Noah belongs with me.

And I belong with Noah.

As we pull away, all too conscious of how new our passion is, how easily it gets carried away, a wry thought adds itself to the reality of our connection.

We just need to convince Weres of that.

Noah rests his forehead on mine, and I breathe in the spiced sandalwood weaving through the emotion we're cocooned in. "I love you Eden, more than love you. What I feel for you is so much bigger…deeper… stronger…than that one little word."

"I know. It's always been more."

"Let's show them what more can mean."

I smile, a genuine one. This has got to be the reason we were chosen as Prime Alpha. Noah, the boy who couldn't change until I was threatened. Me, the girl with a secret identity that connects to Weres in a way they'll never know about. Our connection is so binding, so deep, it shows the potential that partnership can mean.

Noah steps back, pride and love practically bursting from him. "We'd better get going to the Glade. Don't want to be late."

I pull in a breath. And then another.

It's time.

The short walk back to the Phelan house is quiet. There's a breeze that is trying to gain some momentum, and it blows my hair back. I lift my face to it. With our hands held, I can feel everything Noah is feeling. The nervousness and uncertainty I can relate to. The anticipation, the low buzz of excitement I cling to. Those are the emotions that speak of hope and faith.

Back at the house I realize Noah's walk had more than one purpose. Because in the time we were gone, a truck has parked in the Phelan driveway. A big, shiny new truck. A big, shiny, silver truck with a whopping red bow on it.

"Noah, you can't afford this!"

Noah shoves his hands in his pockets. "Not on Prime Alpha wages," he jokes.

There's a pause, and I drag my astonished eyes away from the gleaming metal hulk to find his brief smile falling away.

"But your mother can."

My head swings to the truck then back to Noah. "Alexis bought this?"

Noah nods, watching me carefully. Maybe a little cautiously. "For your birthday."

I settle my gaze on the truck. "Why would Alexis buy me a car?"

"A top of the range, brand new car."

Moving in with Noah seemed to shatter the final, fragile column which was holding up my relationship with Alexis. I've been living with the Phelans a month now and she hasn't visited.

Hasn't called once. The appearance of this truck has been the first contact from her.

"She contacted you?"

Noah purses his lips. "She rang me and said she wanted it to be a surprise."

"What did you say to her?"

"I asked her why now."

"And?"

"She didn't answer. I told her she could bring it over, but you'd make your mind up about what to do with it."

Anger, firing fast and hot, has me stepping away. I don't know what Alexis is trying to say, probably trying to buy, but I'm not willing to find out. "I don't want it."

Noah has 'I thought you'd say that' resting between his furrowed brows. He understands the relationship I have with my mother. He's seen the distance between us. He knows he's never heard my name pass her lips. "What do you want to do with it?"

I cross my arms. He knows she's the one person I can't stop being angry at. "I'm going to do with it what I've done with every other overpriced, unnecessary piece of pseudo-parenting she's ever given me."

"Shove it in your wardrobe back at the Inn?"

I feel my lips twitch. "Give it back."

The front door of the Phelan house opens and my best friend's voice reaches me a moment before she does. "You could give it to me."

My smile breaks free as Tara loops her arm through mine, the breeze playing with her red hair. "You don't want this truck."

Tara takes in the gleaming silver, the tires that have barely done the rounds. I look a little closer. The leather seats. "I kinda do."

"You really don't."

Tara sighs. "Are you sure?"

"You'd have to thank the benefactor for their generosity. Probably be indebted for a very long time."

Tara drops my arm, frowning. "I suppose grey is the color of haggis."

Noah slips his arm around me. "Or whales."

Tara shoots hazel darts from her eyes. "Or dead people."

Mitch joins us, wrapping his arms around Tara. She melts into him, her hand coming up to caress her gently curved stomach. He throws his twin a don't-poke-the-bear glare over the top of her head. Tara is synonymous with emotional and impulsive. Pregnant Tara is volatile.

Noah grins but raises his hand in a conciliatory gesture. Their dad, Adam, strides past, his gaze saying 'smart move.'

Beth comes to stand beside me. "This is going to be amazing."

I glance at Noah's mother, a smile belying my nervousness. They're all looking at me and my nervousness dials down a notch. I'm surrounded by love and acceptance. I'm surrounded by faith. It's a novel feeling I still marvel that I was lucky enough to bond into.

I take a deep breath, wrapping one hand tightly around Noah's, the other coming up to clasp the wolf pendant. "I'm ready."

Tonight, the eve of the full moon, we run for the first time as Prime Alpha. It's momentous. It's intimidating. It's inevitable. By now, every Were knows we exist, they know of the fateful day when Tara's younger sister, Dana, had me surrounded by wolves with death in their eyes. If the crowd that had amassed hadn't seen me subdue them and Noah strip a Were of his power, then the phone calls long into the night would have made sure they knew about it.

But tonight we show what the Prime Alpha is. A massive white wolf. With a human girl riding on his back.

A human has never joined a run, never seen it.

Tonight we make history in more ways than I would have liked.

Like he knew my thoughts were starting to be weighed down by the seriousness of this all, Caesar comes rushing out. He throws his great big German Shepherd body at me, tail wagging.

Bracing myself, I bend down to rub his head. "We've been over this, big boy. You can't come."

"I wish I was going to be there." Tara is leaning back a little, hand on the small of her back. It's the classic pose of a pregnant woman...if she had any more than the gently sloping belly Tara is lovingly caressing.

Apparently Weres can't shift once they're pregnant.

I rub her arm. "There'll be others."

"But gob dash it, it's your first one," Tara wails.

Caesar looks up at me, like he agrees with what she's saying.

Mitch rubs her back too. "You could come, stay at the Glade."

It's about the only way a Were could be human at a run.

Unless it's me.

Tara turns, indignation straightening her spine. "We talked about this, Mitch. Who knows when the cravings could hit!"

Noah snorts. "Now there's a scenario none of us are equipped to face." He shrugs. "Unless we bring the cheese stuffed pretzels."

Tara punches him in the arm. "I can't have them cold, you gooseberry."

Noah arches a brow. "What was I thinking?"

I place my hand on Tara's arm to distract her from the murderous thoughts she's obviously entertaining. "Look on the bright side. Were babies grow faster, so you'll be joining us sooner than you think."

Like a bomb, Tara instantly diffuses. She rubs her belly again. "That's true, I'll just stay here and work on growing Jellybean."

I glance at Mitch. Jellybean? He shrugs as he grins. It seems their child has been named for the moment.

I glance at Caesar. *See, you need to stay home and keep her company.*

Thankfully, Stash takes that moment to come out and join us. Caesar's tail is already wagging before the Phelan's Labrador has joined us. Patting them both, I send them inside. They'll park themselves at the door, making sure Tara doesn't even notice she's alone.

Not one Were will raise an eyebrow that she won't be joining us. Weres can smell a pregnancy almost as soon as it's conceived. Since they discovered their Alpha is carrying an heir, her pack has been too busy celebrating.

Tara's smile is the smile of the content. "You kids go. I want to hear about it when you get back."

I step forward, walking past the brand-new truck to Noah's familiar, beaten one. "Let's run."

CHAPTER TWO

When there's no response, I turn back. Everyone—Adam, Beth, Mitch and Tara have frozen. Noah is the only one to move as he slides closer to me. Mitch is next as he tucks Tara behind him.

Then I hear what their Were senses had already registered.

Roaring, wild and loud, hurls through the trees. It's a sound of fury looking for prey. Noah and I glance at each other before our gaze returns to the tree line. If whatever is making that feral sound is coming this way, we need to know about it.

Tense muscles tighten even further as the sound undeniably gets louder. Whatever it is, it's coming toward the house.

When a massive bear breaches the trees, my pack moves.

Adam steps forward, the Phelan Alpha taking his protective stance. Mitch moves squarely in front of Tara, his broad body shielding her small frame. When Noah steps forward to be with his father, I join him. I can feel the power of the Prime Alpha surging through his veins. Through mine. Adam is our protector, but we are his, and all Weres'.

The bear notices the movement and his trajectory goes from wild and stumbling to focused and deliberate. Another roar, rage powering through it, is directed right at us. His anger has found a target.

The smell hits me before I see it. They all would have noticed it before I did. Coppery and strong, blood coats the front of the bear.

He's injured. Seriously injured.

Judging from the raw gashes on his chest and abdomen, fatally injured.

Another smell tickles my nose, this one more subtle but just as dangerous. Metallic and ominous, I know the Phelans are planning on shifting.

To protect Tara. And to protect vulnerable me.

There's no time to question why an injured bear is so close to the house. Although the reserve isn't far away, wild animals stay clear of the Phelans. They sense, scent, the part-time predators who live here.

I keep my voice low. "Tara, go get Adam's shotgun."

Tara's startled eyes fly to mine, but I figure what we need to do is obvious. The bear needs peace from pain. Quietly, she blends back and heads to the house.

Noah and Adam step forward, Mitch and Beth flanking them. I can feel Noah's steely determination to meet this roaring, angry animal in the clearing behind the house. The bear's head shakes with fury, it stumbles then rights itself. I can feel its pain.

I move forward to join them and feel Noah's surprise. They would have heard my words to Tara, probably assumed I would have stayed back where it's safe. Noah's hand comes out and I step forward. It wasn't to stop me; it was to hold me. I try to tell him that it's going to be fine through our connection.

Then I release Noah's hand, losing the anchor that was helping keep the fear at bay. But I know what I need to do.

I break away from the steadily moving front of Weres and move to the head. In two confident strides I move in front of them. Without looking over my shoulder I give them a stop signal.

Noah's surprise morphs and deepens, concern weaving through it, but he doesn't stop me. Of the Weres behind me, only Mitch and Noah know of my Fae heritage. But all of them have seen what I can do with animals. They were all there when I was surrounded by four wolves ordered to kill me, and watched them surrender at my command. They all know this is the only way the bear won't experience more pain.

The bear sniffs the wind, still angry, but aware something has changed.

As I move closer, the damage to his body is unmistakable. Blood, thick and dark, oozes from multiple tears. I feel the pain dominating the bear's mind, the fury at the violation. The desire for retribution.

There's no danger here.

Even though I no longer need the tune, it begins to swirl through my mind. Soft and soothing, I use it to calm myself as much as the wounded animal.

The wind gusts again and I wonder how the bear is still standing. His body sags, the loss of blood draining his anger.

We can help you.

When the bear drops onto four paws I take another step forward. I only need a few more feet and I can calm him completely, allowing Adam to end his pain humanely.

Another step and there are only feet between me and the bear. His pain hits me like a wave and my eyes mist. How did this happen to such a powerful animal?

The wind gusts, once again changing direction. It buffets me from behind, blowing my hair in my face.

The roar that discharges this time is like a sonic boom. The rage that had dissipated is back, this time propelled by the power of something I don't recognize. Frantically, I push the hair out of my eyes and look up. Wide eyes take in the bear, back on his hind legs, sniffing the air Mother Nature just threw at him.

I feel his fury spike, reaching a new level, but I don't have time to diffuse it. The bear drops, his massive bloody body launches forward. There's no time to move, no place to hide.

"No!"

Noah's voice punctures my fear; it's a sound laced with inevitability.

I brace myself as the bear crashes into me, see the gleaming teeth that are so close, smell the blood. I pull in tight, bracing myself, as hundreds of pounds of furious animal bowl through me. Over me. I cry out as pain tears through my leg.

The sound of an angry pack, one growl crashing over the other, is all I hear as the world turns black.

CHAPTER THREE

EVERYTHING IS QUIET. QUIET BUT BRIGHT.

The light tells me it's day, but the quiet is unfamiliar. Living with the Phelans means quiet is nothing but a part of my past. There's Tara and her over-the-top joy at being pregnant. There's Mitch and his power tools screeching in the shed. There's Adam's booming Alpha voice telling Stash and Caesar to stop hogging the couch. There's Beth and her cooking. There are everyone else's groans of despair at the prospect of Beth cooking.

Then there's Noah's voice, telling me this is exactly where I belong. Even the nights are no longer silent thanks to the amazing new life I have. I lie in bed, listening to Noah's deep, regular breathing reminding me I'll never be alone again.

My eyes fly open. Noah. Where's Noah?

"Hey, beautiful."

A strong hand clasps mine and warmth filters up my arm and I instantly relax. When consciousness finally catches up with me I realize two things. First, I'm in a hospital. Second, I'm here because of the pain in my leg. I go to shift it and gasp. The significant pain in my leg.

"Sh, you're better off keeping still."

I turn to look at Noah. He's mussed, eyes smiling now, but the remnants of tension remain in his strained brow. And then consciousness brings memory with it. "The bear!"

I go to push myself up only to find a wave of dizziness is triggered. The bright white room all of a sudden feels a little less stable.

Noah is on his feet, pushing me back down. "The doctor thinks you might have concussion. Lie back and rest, I'll tell you everything."

I fall onto the pillows I'd barely left, waiting for my vision to catch up.

I look to Noah, already knowing what happened after I was knocked over. "He didn't calm."

Noah's lips thin, the strain creeping back into his features. "No, he didn't. He went straight through you to get to us."

Noah seems to know what's coming next because his hands are already on my shoulders. "Everyone's fine."

I relax, the Phelans weren't hurt.

"Well, everyone but you. You've got a handful of stitches in your calf thanks to his rush to get past you. And you knocked your head when you hit the ground."

That would explain the burning pain and the dizziness.

"What about the bear?"

Noah sighs. "We took care of him."

Four Weres would have been no match for an injured bear, no matter how wild with anger he was. I don't ask, but I hope it was quick.

I push myself up, slowly and gingerly, grateful that the dizziness seems to have passed. Noah is watching me carefully, probably trying to sense how I feel.

I rub my brow, confused. "I don't know what happened. I could feel that he was calming down."

"Maybe a wild animal in pain was too big an ask."

My gaze flies to Noah. The strain in his voice, the doubt I feel from him has me pushing up. "Noah, we had to try."

Noah doesn't reply as his hand tightens on mine, so I do some of my own sensing. He's concerned, I know what seeing me in danger means to Noah. The same it would mean for me. But there's a sense of contemplation, and I'm not sure what that means. Maybe he's wondering some of the same questions which are just starting to form in my mind.

"Why was there a bear so close to the house?"

Noah frowns, and I know he's wondered this. "We don't know."

"How was he hurt?"

His gaze shifts to our clasped hands. "There was no way of telling how he'd been injured by the time we were done."

I watch Noah's thumb stroke the back of my hand. The bear would have been nothing but shreds and tears, and they wouldn't have been able to get a vet involved, the injuries would have raised too many questions.

Is he wondering the same question I am? Why couldn't I calm him?

That question I don't ask out loud. There's still so much we don't know about my Fae heritage. What it means. What is doesn't. Nor do I want to remind Noah of my vulnerabilities. As the Prime Alpha mate, he needs someone strong by his side.

Noah's hand comes up to stroke my cheek, the warmth settling me. "How are you feeling?"

I shift my leg, controlling the grimace. "Pretty good."

Noah arches a brow. "Right."

I smile. We both know lying isn't my strong suit. Noah's smile is genuine, but a little strained. "You'll probably need an extra night after I tell you what I need to say."

I sit up straighter, the dizziness gone, my leg forgotten. The bear is dead, those who have come to mean the most to me are uninjured. What else could there be?

"Your mother's coming to see you."

"What?"

"Dad rang her. He thought she should know seeing as you lost consciousness and the doctors want to keep you in overnight."

My head falls back onto the pillows and the world barely swirls. The dizziness seems to be settling down. The car, then this? The world feels like it's changing too fast for me to keep up with.

"You could pretend to be asleep."

I look at Noah, liking the sound of my get out of jail free pass, but then sigh. "No, I won't let you face her alone."

"It'll be scarier than the rabid Weres."

My smile twitches. "Well, they had emotions."

Noah snorts and my smile blooms. Together, we've conquered the past, crafting a future that is unknown, but one I want.

"Plus, my parents are down at the cafeteria—Tara needed a top up—so I doubt we'll be alone."

So this is what a pack feels like. Unquestioned support you can rely on.

A nurse pokes her head around the corner. "Ah, you're awake. You have a visitor."

My chest tightens. "Thanks."

The nurse smiles. "I'll let the doctor know you're up."

Noah grasps my hand. This will be the first time I've seen my mother in over two months. I left with angry words between us and nothing has been resolved. What does she have to say?

The blond hair that walks through the door isn't what I am expecting.

"How's my favorite little sister?"

I push myself up a little as a thought strikes me. Am I Orin's only sister? We don't speak about our father; Orin has said it's a moot point that there's no use discussing. But he has a mother, just like I do...

"Pretty good."

"Wonderful." Why do I doubt I've managed to fool him either? "What did the doctor say?"

"They're keeping me in overnight, but tomorrow I'll be back to normal."

I add the last little bit for my mate's sake. No need to make this a bigger deal than it is.

Orin sits on the edge of the bed, his Fae smile wide. "So, what did we learn from our little incident?"

I slide a glance at Noah. "That some bears are crankier than others."

Orin's smile slides down a little. "You didn't calm him?"

I'm not sure anyone has ever considered hitting a Fae. From what I can tell, they're the embodiment of Mother Nature's serenity. But Orin just pushed Noah's protective button, and that's not what I need right now.

"He was calming."

Orin returns to his calm and silent demeanor, but I can already feel Noah's worry. I throw my brother a 'thanks' look. Orin smiles, either clueless or unruffled. Most probably unruffled. "I need to go away for a little while. We will talk when I return."

My guess is we'll be talking about the bear I couldn't calm. "You're going away? Where?"

I want to ask more, see if I can get a straight answer out of my brother, but Noah clears his throat. "Alexis is on her way."

Orin's blond brows perk up a little. "Oh."

"Yes, oh."

Just like Weres cannot know about my look-alike brother's existence, neither can Alexis. This is the reality of my diverse heritage. Humans don't know Weres exist, and Weres don't know Fae exist. Part of navigating that tight rope is keeping the parts of me separate. I could just imagine my mother would...what? What would Alexis do if she saw Orin? Living proof that my father, the man she had a child to, probably still exists no matter how much she's tried to strike him from her memory. I realize I have no idea. I've spent my life with my mother being a distant, cold, mystery.

Orin arches a brow. "Good thing Fae have invisibility powers."

"They do?"

"No."

I shake my head. "Then you need to get going."

Orin leans over and places a gentle kiss on my forehead. His calmness and love wrap around me like a hug. "I'll see you when I return and recommence our lessons."

Orin has spent this last month teaching me about the heritage that I relish, that I have to keep hidden. I've learned that Fae are deeply connected to the earth in ways I have yet to understand. We aren't many, but Fae believe in the power of a few.

I flush. I bet a Fae has never been injured by a bear, no matter how angry it was.

"No one can see you."

"We have existed for millennia beside humans and Were. I think I can manage it."

With a final smile, Orin is gone. I don't even get a chance to turn to Noah before my mother strides through the door. I sit up in shock. In part because Alexis' dark complexion and flurry of busy movements are like a slap after Orin's peace and calm. But mostly because, surely, she must have seen him in the hallway.

"I don't have time for your shock."

I feel Noah bristle, but for some reason I'm not taken aback by Alexis' curtness. Is it because I'm used to it?

"I didn't expect to see you, Alexis."

"Adam rang me." She crosses her arms. "You wouldn't have told me otherwise."

I avoid that question-turned-statement. "I'm fine."

Alexis waves a hand, as if to swat my words away. Great, I can't even lie to my absentee mother. "Tell me."

"I have a few stitches in my leg, but it barely hurts. And the dizziness is almost gone now."

The last part I say for Noah's sake, I can still feel his worry.

"Dizziness?" Alexis has gone from tense and tight to tenser and tighter.

Noah steps in a little closer, a movement which has my mother narrowing her eyes. "Eden was knocked over when she stepped between the two fighting dogs at the vet center. She blacked out for a little while."

Seems likely enough.

"Were you dizzy beforehand?"

I frown, having no idea where this is going. "No."

Alexis scans me from my head down to my sheet-covered toes. "That's good."

Noah and I glance at each other, both puzzled. I can almost feel the shrug he would be pulling if she wasn't here. I look back, and my mother is clutching the strap of her handbag, the leather scrunching between her too-tight grip. She's watching me very closely. I glance away, not wanting to know what the scrutiny means, nor wanting to care.

"You received my gift?"

I look back, mouth opening. How do I tell her I don't want that truck without having an argument? Noah isn't going to stand here quietly for much longer, especially if her stubborn side comes out.

A flurry of movement from the doorway punctures the silence. "Eden, you've got to try these cheesy chips with chives."

"She probably isn't very—whoa." Mitch stops right behind Tara, who's frozen a few feet inside my room. She's only met Alexis a couple of times, but she knows who she is.

Adam and Beth entering completes the picture.

Beth steps forward, smiling at Alexis. "Lovely to meet you, Alexis."

My mother looks around, taking in the people who have stepped in and surround me like petals on a flower. "I hope you're taking good care of her."

Beth's smile widens. "Of course. We love having Eden with us."

Alexis nods once, short and sharp. "I raised her to be a strong, independent woman."

Noah is practically growling beside me. As I squeeze his hand, I notice that Adam and Mitch are also staring at Alexis with steely focus.

Adam nods once. "She's an amazing young woman. You should be proud."

Alexis narrows her eyes at him. Her hand hasn't left the strap of her handbag. She turns and heads to the door. She looks angry, but then again, my mother always does.

At the door she turns, her hand releasing the bag to grip the doorframe. "I think we should talk when you get out."

My fists twist in the sheets as my new pack seem to contract around me. "I'm pretty busy." Which is true. Noah and I have a Prime Prophecy to figure out. "But I'll try to stop by."

With that, she's gone. Noah seems to unwind and my head falls back. That was more painless than I expected.

Mitch lets out a pent-up breath. "Does she even know what your name is?"

A smile trips up my lips, looking to ease some of the tension. "Maybe she didn't name me?"

Noah snorts and Tara giggles. The tension dissipates and I relax back into the mattress. It felt good that I could face Alexis on my own. It felt better having so many loving souls backing me up.

Adam sits on the end of my bed, blue eyes assessing. "How are you feeling?"

I smile, noting that the dizziness seems to be all gone. "Better by the minute."

Adam glances at Noah before looking back at me. "Are you up for a talk?"

Adam's voice is full of layers. I don't need to sense Noah's stillness to know this is serious. Adam's steady gaze and tense face say it all.

"Sure."

"Because of the incident with the bear, the run didn't happen."

Noah would already have thought this. My brain has yet to catch up.

Oh no. There was no Prime Alpha run. No statement of leadership, of a common direction. And now it's going to be another month before that can happen.

A lot can happen in a month.

I look at Noah as our connection prickles with unease. Adam hasn't said it because Tara is here and Kurt is her father. But a month is a lot of time for Kurt to be manipulating and planning. He'd been working to undermine and plot revenge the whole time we assumed he had accepted his banishment. Instead, he was gaining supporters.

A month is too long.

I straighten and Noah stands beside me. The alarm winding around my veins echoes the sensation I can feel in him. "What are they saying?"

"Well, something happened."

I feel Noah's surprise at that statement. That means he doesn't know about this either. We wait. I'm not sure what Noah's thinking, but I'm hoping this isn't ground shaking news.

"The run didn't happen, but not only because you weren't there." He pulls in a breath and holds it like he's bracing himself. "The Precept Rock has changed once more."

My head swims again, the room spinning and contracting, but

I'm pretty sure it has nothing to do with the bump to my head. The ground didn't just shake, there was a tectonic shift.

We wait some more, and I realize that Adam was bracing himself for a reason. Things aren't just moving, they're rearranging. The future is deviating in a new direction, and no one knows what the destination is supposed to look like.

Adam's face is the only thing that's still in this maelstrom. His eyes are grave, his broad Alpha shoulders tense. "It had already changed when we got there. It's grown in height, it's almost as tall as me."

Noah's hand tightens around mine, and I mirror the action. This is big.

"And another precept appeared. My guess is this is the last one."

Mitch and Tara glance at each other as Tara rubs her belly protectively. Beth has rested her hand on Adam's arm.

Noah is tense and taut, his hand a solid anchor. "Dad, if you could get to the point, that'd be good."

"It said 'united we conquer.'"

United we conquer.

My world contracts, narrowing to become just Noah and me, looking at each other, trying to process the implications of those three words. It seems the Prime Prophecy has clearly and irreversibly spelled out its intentions.

We stay there for long moments, processing this individually, but also as one. It feels like a great unknown has just been answered, along with a gazillion questions being born.

Tara pops a cheesy chip into her mouth. "In some ways it's nothing new. We kinda figured that's what you guys are all about."

Mitch nods as he slips an arm around her shoulder. "In other ways, it's another puzzle, with quite a few moving pieces."

In a flash, I'm dizzy again. I pretend it doesn't happen, but

Noah notices. "Eden and I are going to have to talk about this." He looks up. "In the morning though."

Adam nods and stands. Beth smiles in understanding. "Get a good night's rest, honey."

I thank them as they file out the door.

They leave behind a host of unknowns.

Noah leans down to rest his forehead on mine. "United we conquer, huh?"

I can't help a smile. "Seems straightforward enough."

"Well, look at what just the two of us have managed to create."

I feel the love pouring from this mate of mine, and my smile grows. "It's more than I could ever have dreamed of."

I push up, touching my lips to his, my own love flowing freely. These feelings have always been bigger than us, we just need to find out how much bigger.

CHAPTER FOUR

I GLANCE AROUND, I'M PRETTY SURE I HAVE EVERYTHING. IT'S NOT like there's much to get together after an impromptu overnight stay.

I grasp the wolf pendant resting on my chest. In just twenty-four hours the world of Weres has changed, and changed significantly. I was rushed in unconscious and now I'm leaving to a world which is even more unsure than the one I left. I just have to believe that as long as Noah and I are together, then we can do whatever it is we're meant to do.

United we conquer.

It would be nice to know what that actually means.

A wave of light-headedness washes over me and I hold myself still. There's no way I'm mentioning to Noah or the nurses that those annoying little ripples haven't completely disappeared. They'll hopefully be gone by tomorrow, and right now we don't have time to find out they probably mean nothing. I decide to grab a bottle of water from the vending machine in the hall, just in case I'm looking pale or something when Noah arrives.

As the bottle clunks into the chute, I hear a male voice hurl from the room next to mine. "That's because it was stolen!" A beeping sound within picks up tempo.

"Mr. Davenport." A placating female voice, a nurse I'd say, sounds like it's starting to lose its patience. "Now isn't the time to address that. You need to rest."

"Easy for you to say, young lady. You didn't lose something you've been working years to find." There's a pause, and the sound of something clunking. "Stop tucking me in, damn it."

"Harold, you recently had quite a scare. You need to remain in bed."

I step back, realizing I'm eavesdropping. Noah will be here soon. I need to get ready for the next stage of being Prime Alpha.

"I will not. There was a photo of a scarlet warbler on that camera, and now it's gone! And now I'm stuck in this bed and can't go find it."

A scarlet warbler? I can't help myself as I step forward again, this time in the direction of Harold's doorway. The scarlet warbler is one of the rarest birds in the park. In fact, they were assumed extinct. Peering inside, I see an older man, lean and mostly bald, trying to push back the sheets and stand up. The nurse is gently but determinedly keeping them in place.

"I'm sorry, did you say a scarlet warbler?"

The man stops and looks up. "Yes, I did."

I step in the room a little. "Everyone thought they were extinct."

In all the times Orin and I have wandered the woods, animals and birds and insects greeting us and surrounding us, I haven't seen the bright crimson markings of a scarlet warbler. The presence of another endangered species in that glorious forest would be useful information.

"I know." He glances at the nurse. "That's why that camera is so important."

The nurse straightens, eyes pleading. She wants me to come

in? Only a few feet from the bed I stop. "How did you manage that?"

The man sits back, now busy tucking himself in. "Years of work. Bird-watching takes patience, young lady."

That has me smiling. "Yes, it does. What a wonderful achievement. Where were you?"

The man's eyes narrow, assessing me. "I went west from Fitz's Hill."

My eyebrows shoot up. "That's quite a hike. But the lodge pole pines there are quite thick, which is the warbler's ideal habitat."

It's also quite a distance from the visitors' center, heading in the direction of the Phelan house in fact.

"Exactly." He squints pale blue eyes at me. "What's your name, young lady?"

"Eden. Sorry for interrupting, I just overheard—"

He waves an impatient hand. "It's nice to meet someone with some knowledge about our natural world."

The nurse steps back, finally able to tuck him in without a fight, eyes surreptitiously rolling.

I can't help but smile at this cantankerous bird-watcher. "I have a friend who hikes around the reserve quite a bit. Maybe I could get him to have a look out for it." Orin would definitely spend some time looking for the camera or the bird if it meant proof of scarlet warblers in the park. Oh, except Orin has gone away...

Harold harrumphs. "It's too late for that."

"Why do you say that?" I'm about to ask where he lost it when the monitors beside Harold start beeping.

The nurse peers at them, then pushes Harold back onto the pillows. "Taking it easy, remember?"

Harold's hand comes up to massage his chest, face suddenly looking pale. "I might rest now."

I'm already walking backwards toward the door. "I think that sounds like a great idea."

The beeping slows as I leave the room, and I wonder if I was actually helpful. I decide to tell Orin about the scarlet warbler and keep an eye out for any sightings. Heading back, I sit on the bed, glancing at the clock. Noah will be here soon.

I'm sitting on the edge of the bed when Dr. Martinez enters, eyes scanning me. "All ready to get going?"

"I just need your tick of approval."

She comes over as I pull up the leg of my pants. A white gauze is all that covers the handful of stitches. "How's the pain?"

"It aches a bit, but I haven't needed to take anything for it."

She throws a sharp look my way. "Good. Any more dizziness?"

I slip my trouser leg back down again. "Nope."

Dr. Martinez makes some notes on her clipboard. "Eden..." Something in her tone makes me look up. "We did some routine blood tests that I'd like to talk to you about."

What? I wait, wondering how many times I'll have to hear that serious tone directed at me. It can't be anything too major, I've been feeling fine until yesterday.

Dr. Martinez glances down again. "How old are you again?"

"I'm eighteen."

"So young," she says to the pages she's flipping through. "And your boyfriend?"

I shift on the white sheets. This conversation is getting odd. "I'm not sure where this conversation is going, Dr. Martinez."

With a sigh, the doctor lets the clipboard drop. Her steady brown gaze is directed straight at me, and for some reason I know I'm not ready to hear what she has to tell me. "Eden, we're going to have do some more tests to confirm, but it looks like—"

There's a rap on the door before it pushes open. Noah, handsome and smiling, strides in, then stops. "Ah sorry, didn't think I'd be interrupting anything."

My smile is reflexive—it's like everything in my world becomes okay when Noah is here. "Of course not." I reach out my hand and he comes to stand beside me, our hands winding together. "Dr. Martinez was just giving me a clean bill of health."

The doctor closes the chart, never missing a beat. "Yes, everything seems to be in order. The leg should heal fine."

I can feel Noah's relief. "And the dizziness?"

Dr. Martinez glances at me. "Perfectly understandable considering what's going on."

I let the gratitude wash over me, knowing Noah would understand this emotion. There's too much going on for me to process whatever Dr. Martinez was about to launch into. We've got enough on our plate as it is.

I stand, ignoring the twinge in my leg. Right now, I just want to get home. "Thanks, Doctor. I appreciate it."

"Don't forget, though," now her brown eyes bore into me, "I'll need to see you in a few days."

I smile up at Noah. "To get the stitches out."

Noah nods, sensing my need to be out of these white walls. I suspect this is why I was never good in cities. I need to feel connected to Mother Earth.

Out in the parking lot I take a deep breath. The air smells of city; grey car exhaust, black bitumen, and someone smoking nearby. But underneath it all, Mother Nature is there; in the clear air that fills my lungs, the reminder of the cold to come. It settles and invigorates me.

"Better?"

Noah is smiling at me, watching me reconnect with the thread we all carry. "Much. I can't wait to get home."

He pulls me into his arms. "I missed you."

I wrap my own around his shoulders. Our first night apart since our Bonding. Why does it feel like we've always been together? "It was lonely without you."

"It just shows you, it takes a rabid bear to keep us apart."

I tuck my head into Noah's chest, hearing his heart, feeling the warmth of his wolf tattoo. "But we'll always come back together."

His lips brush my hair. "Always." He opens the truck door for me. "We need to talk before we get home. Are you up for it?"

I roll my eyes. "It was a cut and whack to the head, not a near death experience."

His lips twitch. "Sorry, protective Were needs to calm down, huh?"

"My wonderful, amazing protective Were. But yes, I'm fine."

Noah sighs as he turns on the ignition. He pulls out of the parking lot before he speaks again. "Okay. So what do you make of the latest Precept?"

United we conquer. "I'm not sure. Like Tara said, the united bit we already figured."

Noah is watching the road as he thinks. "Yeah.

"It's the conquering bit which sounds tricky."

"Yeah. And like it's not going to be easy."

I stare straight ahead. Conquering sounds so…forceful. Is it the peace-loving Fae in me or the nervous human who feels intimidated at that thought?

But then I think of Kurt, and what he's done, and what he wants to do. There is no way he's going to let go of that without a fight. "But the Precept rock has always been the one that reveals the truth."

"It does seem to know what it's talking about."

I can't help but smile. "Which means we need to unite. It's just the how we need to figure out."

Noah rubs his lip. "I've been thinking about that. Kurt has had to have been moving around, looking to gain supporters."

"Talking to other packs?"

"Exactly. And feeding them his twisted truth. That's what he did with Daniel Tate."

We pull up at a red light. I'm staring out the windscreen when it hits me. "He wants Weres to conquer."

Noah's shocked face turns to mine. "He's been trying to unite them."

Oh god. The last Precept is only going to fuel that belief...for him and every Were he speaks to.

Noah's fist thumps on the steering wheel. "And the Prime Alpha run didn't happen."

I bite my lip. We knew that run was important, that Weres needed so see us together.

My hands tighten into fists. They needed to see me.

Instead I was rushed off to hospital after fainting. What a fragile human thing to do, not to mention there's no speedy healing for me.

But what Kurt has yet to realize is that things have changed. I'm not the nervous, hesitant human that he tried to attack the first time. I'm also more than the Changeling who subdued his supporters as they tried to kill me.

I'm all that now and more.

"I think that's what we do too, then."

Noah glances at me as we pull onto the dirt road which takes us to his home. Our home. "What?"

"We talk to the packs. Show them what the Prime Prophecy really means."

Noah's smile is slow. Slow but heart-stoppingly beautiful. His whole face is a glowing mixture of pride and inspiration and possibly a little excitement. "That's exactly what we need to do."

I push forward, my seatbelt digging into my shoulder but I don't care. "We'll travel around the state, showing them that the Prime Alpha is about more than just the strength of Weres. Showing them what uniting is really about."

We reach the house and Noah pulls up in the drive. His hand comes out to clasp mine. "You're amazing."

I shake my head. How could he not see this? "I'm everything because of you, Noah."

"I'm nothing without you, Eden."

This kiss is lightweight and loving, yet weighted and wonderful. With each day we are closer, and stronger.

With each day our challenges become bigger and more intimidating.

We pull back and I gaze into those summer-sky eyes. Noah looks so sure as he asks me, "Let's do this?"

I nod. "Let's do this."

It's time we became Prime Alpha.

CHAPTER FIVE

THE FOLLOWING MORNING, AFTER TALKING AND PLANNING LONG into the night, I'm wishing I could have bottled that sense of I-can-do-this. Today we get organized to go on our Prime Alpha road trip because it seems we have the not-so-small task of uniting all Weres.

As we stand in the driveway again, I ignore the dizziness which swirls around my head. Obviously the late night didn't agree with me. Caesar leans into my leg, and I'm glad he can't talk. Noah doesn't need to know that the dizzy spells are still here.

Tara comes to stand beside me. "I wish I was going with you."

Mitch slips an arm around her shoulder. "Only because you love Ned's Nachos."

Tara pats her belly. "One. Ned was smart enough to place a restaurant in almost every town between here and the border. Two. They're Jellybean's favorite."

I frown. "I thought Penny's Pancakes were her favorite."

Mitch's arm tightens around Tara's shoulder. "He," Mitch's brows come down, "has a healthy appetite."

Tara rests her head on Mitch. "Yes, she," she elbows him playfully, "does."

Noah comes from around the house. My guess is he was on the thinking chair with Adam, going over what we'd agreed on. We'd poured over the map of Wyoming, identifying where each pack lived, who would be pleased to see us...who may not be. We'd mapped out our trip, the one that starts tomorrow.

"You ready?" he asks.

Ah, loaded question much? "Let's do this."

Noah's smile is full of love. It makes me feel like we can do anything, including the daunting task before us.

We head around the house and come up against my mother's birthday present. Crap, I'd forgotten about all that. We both stand and look at it. Caesar wanders over to it and I send him a warning glare. This car isn't his personal fire hydrant.

Noah nudges a shiny black wheel with his shoe. "It would be a more comfortable ride for the road trip..."

I arch a brow. "Yes, it would be. And you'll owe Alexis for. The. Rest. Of. Your. Life."

Noah retracts his foot. "But my trusty old truck is certainly up for the miles."

"I thought you'd say that."

Noah steps around. "We'll do something with it when we get back."

Whenever that is. Who knows how long this is going to take. I don't even know if we'll be back in time for college to start.

"Actually..." I wait for Noah to turn. His eyes ask the question I'm about to answer. "Maybe I should do that today."

"You want to bring it back?"

I sigh. "I'd prefer to deal with it before we leave."

Noah is back at my side, his hands cupping my hips. "Are you sure?"

Now that the idea has been born, I'm realizing it's what I need to do. I need to tie off these loose ends before we embark on something that could be bigger than either of us are expecting.

"Yeah. I need to do this. Do you mind?" It will mean Noah will have to do the supply shopping without me.

"I'll be fine. You sure you want to do it on your own?"

I nod. "It's better that way. We need to get organized." I shove him a little. "Plus she seems to get defensive when you're around." Even more so when there are more Weres acting like my protectors.

Noah's shoulders rise and drop on a huff. "Good. She's learning you've got back up."

With a lingering kiss we say goodbye. It's a kiss that says we don't want to part, but responsibilities are calling.

Noah is just about to climb into the car when Mitch comes jogging over. "Thank the gods of sanity I caught you."

Noah frowns. "What's up?"

Mitch is already heading to the passenger side. "We need pickles."

We're both smiling at the urgency in Mitch's voice. Noah opens his door. "I can get them. No need to come."

But Mitch is already climbing in. "No way, bro. She said she was going to clean to take her mind off the missing ingredient for the banana split."

Caesar glances at me in alarm and I shrug a sorry. Within a blink, he's disappeared around the side of the house.

Noah is chuckling as they click themselves in. I'm kinda glad to be going out. Tara takes cleaning to possessed levels. Craving and nesting at the same time is a dangerous mix.

I wave goodbye as they leave, then glance at the gleaming grey truck. It's time to return this sucker to who it belongs to.

As I drive to the Inn I realize Noah's right; the truck is a pleasure to drive. It quietly purrs, accelerates discreetly and powerfully, the leather interior all cool and matching. But I don't care. I'm not accepting any more of my mother's gifts.

There's no car in the driveway when I arrive, but that doesn't mean much. Alexis parks in the garage. Considering it's morning though, she's likely to be at work, which is just what I need. I'd rather not deal with the icy anger at what I'm about to do.

I knock on the door, going through the motions. No one can claim I didn't try. To say my jaw slackens when I hear laughter from the other side would be an understatement. My hand flops to my side, wondering who's in there.

When the door opens, the shock has my mouth snapping shut. I take a step back, knowing my eyebrows are somewhere in the stratosphere as my mother stands before me. I quickly school my features to match hers.

She scans me from head to toe, like she always has. Her cool expression doesn't change. Then she notices what I've parked in the driveway. A manicured brow spikes up. "So you've received it."

I cross my arms, no longer intimidated by her arctic manner. There's nothing my mother has that I want anymore. "I'm returning it."

Alexis seems to tighten, her chin pulling in a little. "You'll need your own transportation."

"Noah's truck does the job fine."

"You're tying yourself to him. You need some independence."

I was tied to Noah before we were born. Plus, thanks to her, I've had enough independence to last me for the rest of my life.

"I'm fine." I can't help the sarcastic snipe that slips out. "Thanks for caring."

Alexis sucks in a breath, and I'm surprised the barb seems to have hit. Not that it matters; I'll be leaving tomorrow. It's time to call Tara and get a lift back.

"Who is it, Alexis?" A male voice, smooth and cultured, carries from behind her.

Alexis turns and steps back as a tall man comes to stand before her. Well groomed, as I'd expect anyone in Alexis' house to be, he tugs on his suit as he smiles at me. He's familiar. I know I've seen him somewhere before.

"Ah, the star of Alexis' winning promotion. How wonderful to finally meet you, Eden."

The marketing awards last year. This is the English dude who came second after Alexis' winning ad, the one that sold me out.

I remember the laughter that tinkled out as I knocked. It seems my mother is entertaining some hot shots, probably for some million-dollar project. "I wasn't staying. I just had to bring something back."

"You didn't interrupt anything. Come in. I insist."

Only James with his perfect hair and perfect suit and perfect English accent could make those words sound like they were a request. Alexis glances at James, probably wondering why the heck he'd do something like that. She wants me here as much as I want to be here.

She rests a manicured hand on his arm. I'd say she's about to let him down gently, telling him exactly what she thinks of that suggestion. "That's a good idea. I'll grab something to drink."

What? A good idea? And did she just say something to drink?

James leans toward her a little as Alexis brushes past him. "Not my first, my dear."

I don't see how Alexis responds to that because she's gone, apparently to get some refreshments. James stands there, holding the door open, a polite, expectant smile on his face.

Good manners have me walking in, realizing this guy would be a formidable force in the marketing industry. How do you say no to such cultured, seemingly genuine politeness?

At least we won't be alone. The rest of the people involved in this manipulative industry are obviously in the lounge room.

But as I walk into the familiar but never welcoming cottage, I see that there's no one else here. Just me, Alexis and James. I stop, the dining table to my left littered with papers, Alexis and James to my right.

That was Alexis laughing? I don't think I've ever heard my mother laugh. I lift a hand to my forehead. My poor brain isn't coping with these revelations, and they are making the world spin again. Now is not the time for the world to start shifting again.

"Are you okay, my dear?" James is stepping forward, concern crinkling his face. "Maybe you'd like to take a seat?"

I straighten. This is not a place I can show weakness. "I'm fine, thank you. I...just haven't been here for a while."

"All the more reason to take a seat."

James pulls out one of the dining chairs and I take a seat even though I know how uncomfortable they are. These straight-backed pieces of art were made for aesthetics rather than comfort.

I glance at the papers spread across the dining table, realizing a couple of them are maps. The one in the center is the biggest, the tightly spaced topographical lines outlining a mountain range to the north, a slow, sensuous river to the south, and dense forest covering most of it like a blanket.

James notices me looking. "Our upcoming project."

Our? Alexis is collaborating with someone?

The clacking of heels on the wood floor announces my mother is back. She carefully places a tray with a carafe and some glasses—I didn't even know we had a carafe—on the end of the table. "A set of luxury eco cabins. We're going to tap into the ecotourism market."

My mother is going ecologically sustainable? I seem to have lost my voice, most likely because my brain is too busy processing all of this. I look up from the map, noting the proximity Alexis and James are standing in.

James steps forwards. "We thought you'd like to see, since you have such a strong conservation focus yourself."

I glance at Alexis. I can't imagine she's been talking too much about me. She stands there, stiff and silent, and as always, I have no idea what she's thinking.

I look back down at the map, and when my gaze processes

what's actually on it, it doesn't move. In fact, it freezes, my eyes widening as I take in what I'm seeing.

I stand, my chair scraping back on the timber floor. "You can't build here."

Clack, clack, Alexis moves to the table. "We've analyzed the data. This is an ideal place for this sort of venture."

Alarm spikes through my veins. Surely this can't be what I think it is. "No, I mean this land, it's not yours to build on."

James looks like he is tensing, but then he smiles again. "That is only a matter of time."

"What?" My voice is sharp and high, reflecting how my heart-beat is feeling.

Alexis crosses her arms. James may be slow on the uptake, but she's picked up on my rising panic. "We intend on purchasing it."

My hands bunch tight and hard. "That land is not for sale."

Alexis tilts her chin. "How do you know?"

I glance back down at the map. Those lines are so familiar because I've walked them with Orin, I've flown over them on the back of a white wolf as he carried me through the trees.

My Bonding was amongst those sweetly curving lines.

I point to the angry red shape that has captured a chunk of the reserve, a slice of Mother Nature that holds the Glade. "Because this is state land. No one can purchase it."

Not even hungry tourism moguls looking to exploit it.

James glances from Alexis to me. "It was passed in Congress. Dozens of bills have allowed federal government to turn over acres of public land to the state. It's about maximizing private profits through resource extension."

Sounds like loss of protection for acres of land to me.

"No." The single word whooshes out as I collapse onto the chair.

"We thought this would be something you'd be happy about."

I see James stepping toward my mother, but my mind is too full to process what his words, his spending time in Alexis' personal space, means. The Glade, the sacred space of Weres, is up for sale.

And my mother is trying to buy it.

I shoot up again. "You can't do this."

James tucks in his chin. "But why not, my dear?"

Man, he's lucky he's English, because those last two words are starting to wear thin. "Because that land is virgin forest. You can't develop it."

Alexis' arms tighten until they look like a pretzel. I doubt James notices that her eyes narrow just a little. "It's up for sale no matter what. That's why we elected an eco-village. If we buy it, the land use is sustainable and as minimally destructive as possible."

"Exactly." James is nodding. "We can use it to educate tourists about this unique area. It will have a strong conservation focus."

No, no, no. "You can't buy it."

I don't know whether I should aim this appeal at James or Alexis. James seems to have a heart, but we barely know each other. He's unlikely to take my wishes into account. But although Alexis should be able to see how important this is to me, the likelihood of her stopping this because I've asked her to is...

I turn back to James. "You can't."

James glances at my mother, clearly confused. "I don't understand, Alexis. This was going to be—"

My hands are fists at my sides, and my head feels like a pressure cooker. "I don't care what you thought. This is wrong."

Alexis drops her arms, taking in a breath. "We already have investors. It's too late."

The pressure explodes, creating a maelstrom in my head. The room spins, Alexis and James moving in a way that makes me fell nauseous.

Good grief, not again.

CHAPTER SIX

"I'M WATCHING HER REPEAT MY MISTAKES, JAMES."

"You don't know that's what this means. Let's not jump to conclusions."

"It's exactly what happened to me. I'm telling you, she's—"

I sit up, hand to my forehead, acknowledging I just fainted again. An image of Dr. Martinez telling me she needed to see me floats through the swirling fog in my mind. Maybe I do need to get this checked out.

"Are you okay, my dear?"

James is crouching beside me, and I discover I'm lying on the leather couch. He must've caught me and carried me over. "Thank you, but I'm fine."

I push myself up, annoyed that the image of my mother is still moving, until I realize she's pacing. She pauses but doesn't come any closer. "What did the doctor say?"

"That I'm fine. I've had two big shocks in as many days. This isn't that big a deal."

Alexis steps forward, stops, then steps back. "You need to get this checked out."

Her words slide through my memory. *It's exactly what*

happened to me. Surprise has me straightening. "Why? What do you know?"

Alexis snaps back like I just slapped her. "That you're repeating my mistakes."

Even James sucks in his breath at that one, but those words don't sting anymore. I wonder what image Alexis has painted of herself that this man has considered going into business with her. When he moves to stand beside her, placing a hand on her arm, I finally acknowledge that their relationship is probably more than just business.

Not that I care. Right now these two are the greatest threats to the Glade we could have imagined.

"You can't buy that land."

Alexis' face is unmoving. "It's for sale. If we don't, someone will."

James smiles. "And we'll be protecting it whilst allowing people to enjoy it. It's the best possible outcome for all."

It's the worst possible outcome.

I look from one to the other. "You're not going to change your mind, are you?"

I must be seeing things, because Alexis' shoulders seem to sag. "We've been working on this a long time. Why can't you see this for what it is?"

"You," I point an accusing finger at her, "destroying the area I love?"

I seem to have pushed a button, because Alexis inflates. "I thought ecologically sustainable would be something you'd want!"

I pull back. Something I'd want? She was thinking of what I'd want?

I stand up, glad the room stays still, and head for the door. I've had enough of revelations. I'm barely processing the ones I've already been dished up.

"That would have been convenient, wouldn't it, Alexis? That this was something I wanted."

I turn away, glad that the room stays where it's supposed to be. I'd like to walk out of here with some sort of dignity.

I'm out the door before there's a response, nor do I bother to see what she thought of those words. I need to get out of here and talk to my pack. We're up against more than we realized.

No words follow me as I head down the front path, glad an escape is in sight. I'm at the gate before I hear the door open and shut behind me.

"Eden."

I turn, even without hearing James' cultured English tones I would have known it was him. He's the only one who would use my name.

Hand on the gate, I can't help the defiant look I throw him. "How did you know my name, James?"

He stops, frowning.

"What?"

"Can you tell me how you discovered my name?"

He stares as he searches his memory. "Of course Alexis would have—"

"Did she? Can you remember the moment she said it?"

James' mouth opens then shuts. "I'm sure she would have..."

"Well then, at least you've heard my mother say it."

I'm out the gate without waiting for a reply. Let James chew on that knowledge for a while and then let's see if he thinks that Alexis and I can have a relationship. I power forward, stretching my legs to take the biggest steps I can so I can get away as quick as I can, ignoring the twinge of the cut the bear left me with. I'll text Tara when I get to the main building, there's no way I'm waiting around here.

A couple of cars drive past, but I don't pay attention. How do we deal with this and Kurt? But when one toots its horn, I turn around. Seth is hanging out of the cab of his truck, dark brown hair whipping in the breeze as he waves.

I step into the parking lot on my right and he follows, not sure how I feel about having someone to talk to right now.

Pulling into a bay, he walks over and wraps me in a hug. Seth and I have had an unusual bond since he lost the Were part of him and became human. The day he saved my life as Dana was about to attack me showed he'd finally realized the mistake he'd made aligning with Kurt. But it also meant he collided with Noah. All it took was one scratch to draw blood, and now we're both misfits in the land of Were, wondering exactly where we slot in.

"Hey, Eden. Didn't expect to see you here."

I pull back, taking in his smiling face. "I was returning something. What are you doing here?"

Seth's hand comes up to rub the back of his head. "Dropping off a patient for Emily."

Ah. My smile becomes knowing. "Looks like she found a new helper, huh?"

I'm not sure, but I think Seth blushes. "Some rich lady's poodle had a toothache. She was more than willing to include pick-up and drop-off in the dental treatment."

It's heart-warming to see the positive that can come of everything that's happening. "So things are going well?"

"It's early days, we're trying to take it slow. I have a whole history that she can never know about, and I'm still figuring out...well, me."

It's hard not being able to tell Seth that I understand some of what he's going through. I'm a leader of a network of supernatural beings that many believe I don't belong to. But at least I don't have to hide it from Noah.

"She wants this too, Seth."

The few times I've been at Shoshoni Vet Centre there's been

an extra bounce in Emily's ponytail, a sparkle amongst her freckles. Reuniting with Seth has changed her world.

"She's said that." There's both heaviness and hope in Seth's tone.

I nudge him with my shoulder. "Not to mention she's the best vet in the state."

Seth shrugs. "There's no way I could have stayed away." He pulls up a wry grin. "I'm only human, after all."

It's not the first time I've heard him say that over the past few weeks. It's like he's testing out his new self, one that has meant he can be with Emily, but one that meant he's lost a big part of his identity.

I reach out to grasp his arm. "I'm pretty sure Emily loves you irrespective of who you were or who you'll be. Believe me, you have no idea where that can take you."

The smile that my words spark is the broadest I've seen. "I can see why Emily hired you on the spot. You've got a way with people, you know that?"

I look away, and the movement sparks another wave of dizziness. I stare straight ahead, knowing I need to get this checked out, but knowing there are bigger things on our horizon.

Seth peers a little closer. "You don't look so good. Everything okay?"

I chew on my lip as I glance around. This Glade decision will affect him too. The parking lot is empty, but I still take a few steps toward the trees. Seth follows, his smile fading.

When we're at the edge of the forest, the trees at our back and the Inn before us, I sigh. "I just found out the Glade is for sale."

Seth's intake of breath is sharp and hard. "Oh god. It's happening again."

"What? What do you mean—again?"

Seth is looking at his hand which is flexing by his side. "My mother." He stares as he loosens it. "She died the last time the land was for sale."

"Oh yes. Seth, I'm so sorry."

He turns to me. "Weres were pretty divided about how to handle it."

And the implications just levelled-up. Kurt and his determined greed. How will this tie into whatever his master plan is?

Seth cocks his head. "So, what are you going to do about it?"

Is this what leadership feels like? The expectation that you have the answers? Or maybe it's about giving the sense that you know what to do next. I straighten. "Noah and I are leaving tomorrow to talk to the Weres around the state. It looks like we're going to have something to discuss." My eyes widen as an idea strikes me. "Maybe we buy it ourselves."

Seth glances back at the Inn. A couple is walking out, holding hands, probably heading to the parking lot. I'd say our conversation is about to be over.

He nods slowly. "That's a truck load of money to raise." As the couple nears he takes a step forward. "But you and Noah are definitely something else. If anyone can do it, it's you two."

Well, I'm something else, that's for sure. I shove my hand in my pocket, reaching for my cell. "Crap sticks."

Seth arches a brow. "You've spent too much time with Tara."

I pull out the keys to the silver truck from my pocket. In all the drama I forgot to hand them back. "I still have the keys to the top of the range truck my mother gave me for my birthday."

"And?"

"I was there to give it back."

Seth shakes his head. "I'd take the car."

"What?"

He looks at me like I'm not as smart as he originally thought I was. "It looks like you're going to need it."

"I refuse to take anything from her."

"You're letting your pride get in the way."

I don't bother to hide my frown. "We have a perfectly good truck."

"Ah, you're about to trek around the state for who knows how long, for who knows how many miles."

I cross my arms.

"You're going to need something reliable."

I clench my jaw. "I'm not that desperate." Seth doesn't realize I'd cycle around the wilds of Wyoming before I take that thing.

Seth's grin is cocky and he nudges me with his shoulder just like I had earlier. "Plus you could sell it."

I look at him in surprise.

"Wouldn't it be the ultimate irony that some of the money you use to buy the Glade from under her nose came from the pimped-up truck?"

I look at the keys in my hand. There's a part of me that likes that idea. There's another part that knows we're going to have to raise a lot of money.

Seth steps toward his vehicle. "Emily and I have another delivery to make. That eagle I brought in is going to a sanctuary. But we're going to make a stop along the way at the lands office. We need to see what sort of timeframe we have."

"Great idea. Call me when you find out."

"We need to fix this, Eden." Seth pulls open his car door but then stops. His gaze is somber as he looks at me across the space between us. "I believe my mother died for a reason."

With that, he pulls out and drives away. I stand there, feeling the weight of a whole lot of lives resting on my shoulders. Would they accept my suggestion as easily as Seth has?

This time I do pull out my cell, but it's not Tara whom I'm texting. *What time are you planning on getting home?*

Missing me?

I miss you like I miss cheesecake.

Whoa, that's a lot! Heading back shortly. Gotta pick up the pickles.

Considering they have to get Mama Pecorino's special pickles from the little deli on the other side of town, he'll be a little while yet. My fingers hover, but then I quickly type. *Ok. See you then.*

Everything okay?

At this distance I doubt Noah can sense my agitation. But he picked it up in our few short words. My heart swells and I calm a little. It seems the last Precept was right—it's together that we develop our strength, because we certainly just conquered some of the awful emotions that burst through when I saw that map. I wrap my hand around the pendant resting on my chest.

It will be. I love you.

I'm not sure if I like reading or hearing those words more...

We'll test it out when you get back.

Can't wait. I love you too.

As I head back to my birthday gift truck, I realize I have some time before Noah is back. I glance at my watch. It gives me enough time to pop in and see Dr. Martinez.

PART II
NOAH

CHAPTER SEVEN

"EXACTLY HOW LONG ARE YOU GOING FOR?"

Mitch is eyeing off the food and supplies stacked in the back of the truck. The four-person tent was a splurge; there've got to be some bonuses to doing what is essentially a Prime Alpha campaign tour.

"This way we can go into the remote areas and know we have everything we need."

Mitch shrugs as he climbs into the driver's seat. Great. It's his turn to pick the music. "Not sure you needed that many cans of vegetable soup is all I'm saying."

I jump into the passenger side. "Coming from the guy who is about to drive over to Mama Pecorino's for a jar of pickles."

That has Mitch's lips pursing. I can't help the chuckle as I settle back. I should be home in about an hour or so. Eden and I have practically been inseparable since our Bonding. Being apart for even a short period has my hands twitching to touch her again.

Mama Pecorino's little delicatessen sits at the edge of town. Most places would go out of business so far from the main shopping area, but not Mama Pecorino's. Connoisseurs of fine food are willing to travel for her home-grown delicacies. Oh, and pregnant Weres.

We're almost there when a flash of red hair has me turning in my seat. "Did you see that?"

Mitch slows, glancing over his shoulder. "See what?"

"I think Tara decided she couldn't wait."

Mitch frowns. "She didn't mention anything."

I crane my neck, but the body which was carrying the distinctive Channon trademark red hair has turned down a side street. "I'm pretty sure that was her."

"Maybe it was one of her sisters?" Despite the doubt in Mitch's tone, he checks his rear vision mirror then executes a U turn. Tara's mother and her siblings have been laying low since Kurt was banished.

"I know she's short, but there's still a height difference between ten-year old Christa and Tara."

Mitch grunts as we come up to the place I saw her. We climb out, but the alleyway is empty.

"She must have gone down there." I point to the path at the end of the side street. I breathe in the air then glance at Mitch. He's registered it too. A Were has been here recently.

We follow the faint scent and it heads straight past the building. At the edge of the store the path continues down the back. Tara, or whoever it was, has gone down there.

I can sense Mitch's unease, and I don't blame him. This is odd. Really odd.

We keep walking, the Were scent a string our noses are following. Behind the shopfront are Mama Pecorino's gardens. This is where her famous pickling cucumbers are grown. The fields lie fallow as winter is approaching, a broad expanse of open land. The forest which surrounds any town in this area is not far behind.

It's at the edge of the trees that we both see it. A head turning, red hair catching in the breeze, before she slips between the trees.

Mitch growls. "That's not Tara."

I have to resist the drive to shift. Which means it can only be one person. One person who isn't welcome in the Phelan-Channon territory.

We're both striding forward, boots sinking into the soft swales of soil waiting for spring to let something grow and live again.

My fists clench. "What is she doing here?"

"We're about to find out."

We don't pause at the edge of the trees; her scent is stronger now. Dana isn't far away.

In fact, we find her several feet in. Dana is standing in the center of a small clearing; big enough that she's open and obvious, small enough that the trees around still keep it shaded and secluded.

She's either stupid or desperate to meet us here. I doubt there are two Weres that want her gone more in this world.

We step to the edge of the trees and fury rips through my muscles. The Alpha in me strains to mete out some justice.

"I wouldn't come any closer."

Mitch is a live wire of anger beside me. This is the girl who betrayed his mate. "You don't get a choice."

We fan out a little, keeping our forward momentum. Dana glances between us. "I've come here to talk."

The need to shift ripples over my skin. "We're not interested in anything you have to say."

This is the girl who almost got Eden killed.

Dana steps back, flicking her Channon hair over her shoulder. She probably means for it to be a gesture of arrogance, but my Were sight picks up the tremble in her hands. Good. She should be nervous.

"I have a message."

"You can tell it to the packs."

The metallic scent that heralds a shift tingles in the air. Either

Mitch is ready to pounce, or Dana is thinking of running. Dana's eyes flash wide and she steps back. In either scenario she'll end up our prisoner.

Dana must read our intent because her hands come up, palms out asking us to stop. "If I don't go back, there will be a war."

We pause, glancing at each other.

Dana steps forward, reclaiming the small distance she'd lost. "You saw what happened when Dad lost Tara. What do you think will happen if I don't come back and he loses me too?"

Mitch and I stare at each other. Thank god we're twins, because we silently agree to see what she has to say…before deciding whether we take her down or not.

I straighten as I turn, reminding Dana exactly who she's dealing with. "You've got two minutes."

"Stay where you are."

I don't know why Dana would think the length of this clearing is enough to keep her safe now that she's foolishly decided to return, but I'm happy to give her the false sense of security. We hold ourselves where we are, several feet apart, tense and focused.

Mitch's dark brows are low. "You're running out of time."

"Dad knows."

This is what she's here to tell us? "Everyone knows about the last Precept."

Dana rolls her eyes, seeming to gain some confidence. "That Precept only reinforced what we already had planned."

"Spit it out, Dana."

"Do you know what it means?"

United we conquer. It seems pretty self-explanatory, but uneasiness is starting to creep over my skin. Kurt's views have managed to skew things with some pretty bloody dangerous consequences. I wait for the rhetorical question to be answered.

"There's far more to conquer than we realized, isn't there, Noah?"

My breath in is slow and measured. This feels like it's going somewhere I can't predict.

"Dana, I'm not the Prime Alpha." Mitch has stepped forward. "No one will be surprised that I attacked you, and I have less people to answer to for the outcome."

But Dana is obviously feeling cocky, because she barely glances at Mitch. The hazel eyes that are so warm and lively on Tara are cold angry on her younger sister. "He knows."

I'm trying to piece together the cryptic clues Dana has given me so far. Kurt knows of the last Precept. Kurt, the one who believes Weres should use their strength for power.

I uncross my arms as realization fills my chest. "He's always wanted to dominate."

To rule.

A smile sparks at the edge of Dana's tense lips. "And the last law confirmed what he already knew."

"You're wrong." I'm so angry, I have to consciously unclench my jaw. "He's wrong. That's not what the Prime Prophecy is about. We are not here to conquer anyone."

"Then what exactly are we uniting for, Noah?"

Mitch's hand slices through the air. "I'd hurry up and get to the point if I were you, Dana."

Mitch is starting to lose the fight for control. Dana's questioning, the one vulnerable point no one has voiced, hits a nerve. We've never articulated exactly what we're uniting Weres for.

As I watch Dana stand there, solid in her convictions, steeped in hate and anger, I start to realize exactly what the Prime Alpha is going to have to conquer.

She flicks her hair again, this time jutting her chin up a notch. "We unite to conquer them all." She stares me straight in the eye as she delivers her next words. "The weak and the fearful, human...and Fae alike."

It takes all my Alpha training not to let the sucker punch

those words deal show. My stomach clenches and my breath vaporizes. What did she just say?

Dana tilts her head. "I told you he knew."

Oh god. Kurt knows about the Fae. Pride takes second place as I realize I have to ask. "How?"

Dana's slow smile slices over her face. She knows she has the upper hand right now. "We've been watching. Only to discover we weren't the only ones."

From the corner of my eye I see Mitch's fists unclench. He's realizing we need to hear this.

Dana doesn't notice, she's looking nowhere but me. "There was someone else fluttering in the shadows, a moth to Eden's flame."

Hearing my mate's name on Dana's lips has anger shooting down my nerves, but I ignore it. It's obvious Dana has a story to tell, and she's enjoying being center stage.

"It was a man. We figured he was some creep or something because he seemed to know her movements well. He seemed to know her well. But we got close one day, and saw that he looked just like her."

I should get a bloody acting award for the amount of times I've had to contain my surprise. Instead, I let the anger show. "What do you know, Dana?"

"We've been following him for a while." She shrugs. "Including the times he left, which is when we discovered who he was."

Mitch's voice is a low growl. "I wouldn't be jumping to any conclusions if I were you."

Dana smiles a little. "We didn't need to." She looks back at me. "I should've known she was more than human. But the daughter of a king? Did not see that one coming."

I don't reply. Anyone who didn't realize Eden was more than average is an idiot.

"But then again, we didn't know the Fae existed."

But now they do. That knowledge starts to spark its implications. All of a sudden, we're dealing with far more than we realized.

I stare at her hard. "You need to stop whatever you have planned, Dana."

"It's too late."

When she moves, I go on high alert, particularly when she delves into the bag on her shoulder and pulls something out. I realize it's a camera a second before she uses her Were strength to throw it across the small clearing. I catch it, knowing whatever is on it, isn't good.

"Turn it on and watch."

I look up at Mitch, who nods. He'll keep an eye on this traitor while I check out whatever message Kurt has sent us.

I press the power button and the digital screen flickers to life. An image of a bird fills the screen and I realize it's a video of some sort. I press the triangle on the screen, determination outweighing the dread at what I'm going to find.

The ruby colored bird flits from one branch to another and the image blurs a little as it loses focus then sharpens again. The bird now dominates the screen, its head sharply turning one way then the other.

"I can't believe it." A male voice, infused with wonder, whispers through the speakers.

The bird seems to startle, wings fluttering, darting further into the canopy. Before the camera can focus again it flits off.

"Damn." The man sounds disappointed, and I'm not sure why I'm watching some bird watcher's diary.

Until I hear it. The man must too, because the camera swings around, trying to locate the direction the growling is coming from. My instincts, sharpened by years of tracking and honed by my Were senses, tell me the camera just has to move a little more to the left and we'll see what neither of us is probably ready to take in.

When the camera finds the bear, monopolizing the screen as it rears on its hind legs and roars, I tense. Whoever that guy is, he would have been in serious danger.

He must realize it because two words filter through the speakers. "Oh god."

When a second round of roaring reaches the speakers my heart sinks. I know exactly what is going to happen. A russet colored wolf barrels at it, teeth bared, his massive body like a battering ram. He collides with the bear, teeth sinking into its furry hide. The bear's roar is a mixture of fury and pain as it swipes at the wolf.

But Kurt yanks his wolf body away, the bear's dagger sized claws slashing at nothing but air. Over and over again Kurt attacks, ripping into wherever he hits—chest, vulnerable stomach, exposed wounds. Blood becomes a gory suit for both of them.

The man sucks in a sharp breath and the camera drops. All that fills the screen is spiked grass, but the speakers are full of the fight and pain happening not far away. Roars and growls and violence are the background of what was supposed to be a bird watcher's scenic home video.

The man groans, gasps, and goes silent.

I press stop, knowing I don't need to see anymore. Kurt would have known that a human was watching. And recording.

Anger is once again boiling like a cauldron, its tendrils skipping over my skin. It knows what will give it voice, and right now, I'm not sure why I'm not unleashing it.

Mitch glances at me, his eyes asking what I just watched. "Kurt attacked a bear, knowing full well it was being recorded."

Dana cocks her head. "He didn't kill it." She studies me for long seconds. "You guys did."

As the pieces fall into place, the fury unleashes. The injured bear that was at the house. The one Eden tried to help. The one she couldn't calm—because it was set on revenge against the ones who wounded it so badly.

The one who landed her in hospital, unconscious and injured.

Mitch must realize that I've just passed snapping point, because he's at my side in a split second. His arm slams across my chest, but he's too late. They need to know the consequences of their actions.

"This is what they want, Noah. She needs to go back a Were."

Bloody twins. They know exactly what to say to deflate you. All it would take is to break her skin and she would no longer call herself one of us. Although the tension ebbs, I still push against his arm. "I wasn't planning on turning her."

Mitch's arm tightens over my chest, but he knows this is just for show. "Dana's right. You do that and you'll just give Kurt the green light to start this thing."

Dana steps back, her hands coming to grip her bag. What she doesn't realize is that Kurt was probably willing to sacrifice her to see if I'd snap. He would be more than willing for her to be a lamb for his cause.

The disgust is what ultimately calms me. Kurt won't get to say how this goes.

By the look of Dana, she knows exactly how close she just came to some serious Prime Alpha action. Even from this distance I can see the effort she makes to swallow.

Mitch's arm drops and I straighten. "You need to stop this, Dana. You've seen this is bigger than just Weres."

"Actually, it just shows you this is what we're destined to do. With Fae we didn't even know about slinking around doing who knows what, we need to show who is ruler. It's what the world needs."

I bet she's just about quoting Kurt word for word.

"Kurt will never rule Weres, let alone anyone else."

Dana's eyes flare as her chest inflates. "We will lead Weres as the ruling species." She flicks her hair. "And that camera was to let you know it has begun."

I cross my arms. "The Prime Prophecy began centuries ago and it was never for that."

Dana is stepping back, deciding her message has been relayed from the looks of things. "Fools. You have no vision, no concept of what we can be."

I don't say anything. Dana is starting to sound like a fanatic, which is just what Kurt is looking for. And then I get an idea. "Tara doesn't agree."

That stops Dana in her tracks.

Mitch narrows his eyes beside me. "She would have liked you to meet our child in a few months."

Dana's shoulders tense like an arrow just pierced her between her shoulder blades.

I can't help myself, I send the final barb. "We'll tell her you stopped by."

Dana starts striding away, glancing over her shoulder, her cold and calculated facade finally cracked. The look she shoots us is full of anger and something I can't define.

In a flash, she shifts, and a red wolf is looking at us. My hands are balled into fists again as she watches us. Civilization is on the other side of the nearby garden. She's making a statement by pulling such a risky move. Anyone could come along and see us facing off against a mammoth wolf.

With that, she's gone, agilely leaping into the forest.

Mitch steps forward, determination carved into his features, but it's my turn to put up an arm.

"Let her go."

Mitch raises his brow. "Let her go?"

I wait and watch as Dana disappears into the trees.

"She's going to take us right to him."

CHAPTER EIGHT

MITCH LOOKS BACK TO THE GAP DANA JUST DISAPPEARED THROUGH. "We're going to follow her?"

"Yep, although we won't catch her on foot."

"And she'll smell us as Weres."

I look at my twin, knowing the penny is about to drop. "But she went north."

Mitch's eyes glow as realization dawns. "And there isn't much up north…"

"Nothing but a highway that leads to the next town."

We turn and stride toward the truck. Our best bet is that Dana has headed to Bowerman or beyond. I doubt she'll risk remaining Were for long. Kurt's plans will be bigger than that. Which means she'll have to shift back to human, and slink on home.

And we'll be there to see exactly where that is.

As we jump into the truck, I know Mitch is doing exactly what I am; trying to get his head around the implications of what Dana just told us. There's nothing but the rumble of the engine as I pull out of the parking lot and onto the highway. Nothing but the rumble of the engine as the realizations slam into me one after the other.

"Kurt's been following and watching Eden the whole time."

Mitch is staring out the windshield just like I am. "Yeah."

"Kurt knows Eden is the Changeling daughter of the Fae King."

"Yep."

My hands tighten around the steering wheel. "The target on her just grew."

"Yes, yes it did."

I glance at my twin. "Feel free to disagree whenever you want."

Mitch puts his hands up in a show of reconciliation. "Hey, when the Prime Alpha is right, the Prime Alpha is right."

"Thanks," I mutter, turning back to the road.

It looks like the Prime Prophecy just got real.

Mitch pulls out his cell and starts texting. "I'll let Tara know we're going to be late."

"Good idea."

The first thing Tara will do is let Eden know. And then the rest of our family.

The road slices through pine forest for miles. We don't see a trace of Dana, but neither of us expect to. She'll run as a wolf for as long as she can, deep in the woods, but eventually she's gonna hit civilization, and then she'll become human again.

All we have to do is find her and she'll take us straight to her traitorous father.

The one who has a score to settle with Eden.

My fingers tighten on the steering wheel, and I kind of like the way my knuckles go white. They speak of the strength I'm going to need to do what needs to be done.

A gas station comes into view in the distance. I glance at the needle, and figure we'd better pull in. When we set out this morning, the plan hadn't included heading out of town.

Pulling in, I notice that the owner seems to have a thing for potted plants. Big ones, little ones, even a couple of massive ones, are stacked around the main building, particularly around the front entry. They obviously had an eye for it because it gives the feeling you're in a little slice of nature rather than a gas station.

I glance at Mitch and he shrugs. "Trying to cancel out their carbon footprint?"

I shrug too as I head around the back, knowing that's usually where the fast-flowing pumps for the big rigs are. May as well stay out of sight.

Mitch jumps out as I start pumping the gas. Even if we weren't twins I reckon I'd pick up on the tension pulsing through his body. He can't keep still. It's the same unease tangling every one of my muscles.

We're heading around the building when he stops. "You've got to be kidding me."

I look up to see what has caught Mitch's attention, and stop. Dana is crossing the road, as casual as can be, and heading into the building.

All that tension morphs into simmering anger. "Bingo."

Mitch crosses his arms, his gaze focused on the door Dana just went through. "So we wait?"

I pull us back around the corner. All the vegetation at the front of the building is actually hiding us from view. "Yep. My guess is that's her car over there." I jerk my chin toward the battered hatchback on the other side of the petrol station. "Then we follow at a distance. We only need an address and we turn around. We'll face them as a pack."

Mitch nods, face stony. He has his own reasons to hate the father of his mate.

We step back, moving further into the shadows of the building. Dana shouldn't take long. She probably needed a drink after her little run.

We stare at the door like we're willing her to come back out.

"What's taking her so long?"

I stretch my shoulders. "I don't know, maybe she had to go the bathroom."

"Do you want me to go check?"

I stare at the door as I consider this. It hasn't moved since Dana went through. "No. If we give away that we're here, we lose our lead on Kurt."

Long minutes pass. Our shoes scrape over gravel as we shift and wait. This is taking too long.

We both step forward at the same time. Something is wrong.

Passing through the jungle-like entry, we enter. The place is small, only two short aisles of groceries and cans and a counter to the left. Apart from a girl behind the cash register, the place is empty.

The girl, blonde and spectacled, smiles at us. "Hi, was it just the gas today?"

I look around again. She couldn't have just disappeared. "There was a girl in here."

"Dana?"

That has me spinning around. "You know her name?"

"Yeah, sure. She comes here all the time."

I blink. Dana has been here before?

The girl smiles, the act pushing her glasses up as her cheeks dimple. "Although she usually comes with Kurt and the others."

Mitch's eyes fly to mine, surprise making them round. "The others?"

The girl's mouth snaps shut. She looks from me to Mitch and back again, obviously wondering what the heck's going on. I pull in a breath, checking to see if Dana is still here. She was, but the scent is getting weaker by the moment. Bloody hell, there must be a side door or something.

I look at Mitch. She must've known we were here. I want to slap myself. How could we have been so stupid?

The girl shifts back a little. The irony that she's feeling unsafe with us when Kurt and Dana are regulars here isn't lost on me.

I yank up a smile. "Sorry." I pause, the false explanation of why we're acting so weird dissolving on my lips. Now that I'm a little closer to her, I notice the girl's eyes behind her glasses. There's something oddly familiar about them. "Have we met?"

The girl shifts back almost imperceptibly, her brows moving further down. "I don't think so. Was it just the gas?"

I make a concerted effort not to clench my fists. Now that Dana has managed some sort of vanishing act, I can't afford for this girl to shut down.

Mitch nudges me with his shoulder. "Man, you can't try that line on her."

I turn to him, confused. "What?"

"Yep, and there you go with your 'I have no idea what you're talking about' act. This routine is getting boring, bro." Mitch turns to the girl. "He tries the 'have me met' line with every cute girl he meets."

You've got to be kidding me. But the girl blushes, eyes dropping as her mouth tips up a little. That sense of familiarity hits me again, but I can't figure out why. She's obviously not Were, and I'd swear I haven't seen her around Jacksonville.

Mitch shakes his head with a grin. "You'd totally have a boyfriend."

The girl pushes up her glasses, the blush now a flame on her cheeks. "I'm too busy for a boyfriend."

I throw Mitch a warning glance, we're about as far from two single human guys as you can get. He winks, obviously enjoying my discomfort.

He takes a step forward, his friendly smile stuck on his face. "You said you know Dana?"

His forward trajectory stops and his Sir Charm-a-lot smile drops when a screech pierces the room and two great, big wings fan out behind the girl. An owl, a darned big owl, leaps from the shadows behind her and lands on her shoulder.

The girl turns her head as she lifts her hand to stroke its chest. "Sh, Shamus, these guys are just paying for their gas."

As we watch, the bird, his saucer sized eyes staring at us, ruffles and seems to relax. His body drops, like he's snuggling into her shoulder. One of his eyes blinks, then the other, before both lids droop.

"You have a pet owl?"

The girl rubs her forehead on the bird. "Yeah, my stepdad hit him with the car one night when I was a kid." She turns to me, a contented glow softening her features. "Long story short, he kinda adopted me and refused to leave."

As the bond between girl and bird becomes obvious I suck in a breath. I look at her eyes again, and it all falls into place. Behind those glasses, they ever so gently tip up at the edges. Add that to her affinity for the bird, and I'm pretty sure I'm looking at a Changeling. I glance at Mitch, wishing I could tell him.

I turn back, wanting to do some investigating. "How did your dad feel about that?"

"My stepdad was pretty used to me bringing in strays." She giggles and the owl ruffles himself. "Although I don't think he expected this one to stay."

That's the second time she's made the distinction that she has a stepfather. When the girl looks up at the bird again I mouth one word to Mitch. "Changeling."

Mitch's face has 'no way' stamped all over it, but he quickly recovers. Mitch will only need three seconds to take in the eyes which are so much like Eden's, heck, even some of the manner-isms the minute an animal is in the picture, and see that I'm right. I turn back, knowing we now have far more questions than we have time to ask.

And unfortunately, the missing Dana is our first priority. "We were hoping to catch up with Dana."

"You know her?"

Mitch's smile is back. "We grew up together."

Which is technically correct. She was practically family until she was brainwashed and tried to get Eden killed.

The girl looks at the two of us. "Well, Shamus has never screeched at anyone else but you guys and them, so it must be some Jacksonville gene or something. And there's one thing I know, animals don't lie."

There was a time Eden put more faith in animals than humans, too. I wonder how growing up with a father who didn't hang around has affected this girl?

"Yeah, their business brings them through here quite often."

I bet it does. "I'm disappointed we missed her."

Mitch doesn't have to fake his disappointment. "Yeah, me too."

"They'll be back at some stage. They're always keeping an eye out for land since that new law was passed in Congress."

Huh? I suppose greed is Kurt's middle name. "I didn't know Kurt got into real estate."

The girl's smile grows wider. "They buy blocks of land before they can be developed and turn them into sanctuaries and reserves." She glances up at the owl. "Places where animals like Shamus can live."

Mitch coughs beside me. He'd be thinking the same thing I am. That's the weirdest alibi we've ever heard. I rub my lip. It makes sense though. What better way to endear

himself to anyone than look like an environmental evangelist? I glance at the girl. If Kurt knows of Avery and the Fae, did he realize this girl is probably a Changeling too?

"Where are our manners? My name's Noah, and this is my brother, Mitch."

"Hi, I'm Willow, and you've already met Shamus."

I grab my wallet and pull out some cash, passing it to Willow. "Do you know when they'll be back?"

"They've been coming more often, but there's never any regularity." Her smile is apologetic. "I couldn't tell you when they'll be back."

"Thanks anyway." I step away, realizing that all this little trip has generated is more questions. At least we'll be back at home before it's dark. As we pass through the doorway I'm hit by the smell of foliage and green.

I turn to find Willow watching us. "You created this, didn't you?"

She pushes up her glasses as the owl ruffles himself. "Yeah."

I smile, realizing that in some ways, the Fae are getting it right. "Nice sanctuary."

If I didn't have heightened Were sight, I wouldn't see the blush that rises up Willow's cheeks. "Thanks."

I turn to join Mitch outside—it's time to go home.

"Noah?"

Willow moves a little behind the cash register, likes she's shuffling from side to side. "You know when you can sense stuff about people?"

A Changeling would. I nod, like this stuff happens to people all the time. "Sure."

"I think you need to talk to Dana. Kurt's always seemed… driven." She pauses, looking to gauge my reaction.

So Kurt has given some story about being a philanthropist. But her spidey senses are saying something else. I figure it's time to be honest. "Kurt has a lot of anger in him."

Willow sags. "Yes, he does. But this time, when they were heading back to Hazel's Inn, he was more intense than usual. I think Dana should be careful."

I nod. Between the greenery and this girl's warm heart, I have a suspicion I know why Dana knew there was a side door she could use. "She likes coming here, doesn't she?"

There's that blush again. "Yeah, she does."

I turn back to the door, Willow just gave us a lead, but then I turn back one more time. "You should take the time to find a boyfriend."

Her blushing couldn't be missed now, not even by a human. Willow's quiet, reflective voice follows me out the door "Thanks Noah."

As I stand amongst the greenery I look at Mitch. "Did you hear that?"

Mitch holds up his cell. "Hazel's Inn is in Bowerman."

Which is about another hour north. We're back at the car when Mitch asks the obvious.

"So, what now?"

"Well, we have two choices. We either head home and talk to the others."

He nods his head to the left. "And lose the trail even more."

"Or we keep going for a little longer and see if we can find it again."

And then a nod to the right. "On our own."

I wish Eden were here. I always seem to think more clearly, feel that bit more confident, when she's beside me. There's so much I need to tell her—she wouldn't be surprised to hear that Kurt's obsession with her hasn't diminished. But Kurt knows of the Fae, which is next level stuff. Actually, his discovery has probably fueled it.

What would she think of that? Eden always introduces an angle I haven't considered. And when we reach a decision, there's that sense of assurance that we're on the right track.

But Eden's injured, just out of hospital. I know she's tried to hide it, but that bump to her head has affected her. And Kurt has been following her for months. She's actually safer right now with her pack, rather than trekking up into the boondocks on a wild goose chase.

I look at Mitch, who's been waiting patiently for me to reach a conclusion. "I doubt it will take long."

His blue eyes light up, telling me that's exactly what he wanted to hear. "All going well, we'd be home by dinner."

"I say we go further north and see what we can find. We'll either bring home an address—"

Mitch slaps me on the shoulder as he opens the driver's side door. "Or we'll get to see how many more Changelings we can find."

CHAPTER NINE

WHEN EDEN'S CELL GOES STRAIGHT TO MESSAGE BANK, I FROWN. She's either forgotten to charge it, which wouldn't be the first time, or she's somewhere without any service, like the Glade. I don't bother leaving a 'call me' message. Depending on when she rings back, I may not be able to answer.

Plus, in an hour or two, I could have some really good news.

I start dialing again. "I'm going to ring Dad."

Mitch nods. "Good idea. Tell him he may want to go and get some pickles himself."

Dad picks up after the first ring. "Hey, son."

"Hey, Dad. We've taken a detour, so letting you know we won't be home for a few hours."

"A few hours? That's one heck of a detour."

I pause, not sure where to start. My hand tightens around the phone. If Kurt knows of the Fae, then where does that leave every other Were, including my Dad? Who knows, but it's not a conversation I can have over the phone.

I hear Dad shuffle. "Something's happened."

"Yeah, the short version is that Dana stopped by and we're following up on a lead on Kurt."

There's a pause and I can almost hear the gears shifting in Dad's head. "What's the plan?"

My tension eases a little. I'm not sure if Dad has gone into cop mode or Alpha mode, but his calm what's-next attitude is just what I need. "We're checking out the lead before we come home. It seems he's been hanging around."

There's another pause as Dad processes that. "How much?"

I glance out the window as I feel my whole body frown. "He's been watching for quite a while."

"I see."

I hope he does. "Is Eden around?"

"I thought she was with you?"

There's genuine surprise in Dad's voice so I know he's not kidding, which just winds the tension another notch tighter. "No, she wanted to get rid of the truck. I would have thought she'd be home by now."

"I haven't seen her, but then again, I've been in the garage cleaning up after Mitch."

I glance at my twin, and when Mitch rolls his eyes I know he heard. "Could you keep an eye out for her then? Kurt...seems to have a personal vendetta."

Dad grunts. "We suspected as much. She'll be safe with her pack, son."

I allow myself an extra-long blink. That's exactly what I needed to hear, and exactly why I'm glad Eden isn't with us now. Bringing her closer to Kurt when we don't know what we're dealing with is just plain stupid. "Thanks. We'll be home by nightfall."

"I hope so. I'm pretty sure your mother is baking stuffed peppers again."

I groan. "Not the slow cooked ones."

Mitch seems to still beside me.

"Afraid so."

Now it's Mitch's turn to groan. For some reason Mom hasn't

realized that slow cooked recipes call for a lower temperature so you don't create dried-out oven crispies.

Mitch's eyes widen. "And we didn't get the pickles."

I can just tell that Dad's frown matches ours. Hungry Tara isn't something anyone of us feels capable tackling.

"We'll pick up something for dessert."

"Good idea, Noah. Stay safe."

I can't help but grin. Dad is the one who's home with Tara-of-the-cravings. "You too."

I hang up. Slow cooked peppers or not, at home with our pack is the safest place for Eden right now.

Bowerman appears on the horizon, and I focus on the growing skyline. I shouldn't be surprised that Kurt set up camp in the largest city this far north. It's a smart home base; not too far from Jacksonville, but also within a day's drive of most packs in the area.

I type the name of the Inn into my cell, and Mitch and I are silent as the polite, disembodied voice instructs on how to get there.

The Inn, which is a fancy term for a motel, is an old one in what looks like a run-down suburb. Grey rooms march along in a row, single windows a Cyclops in each one. My eyes scan the parking lot, which is pretty empty. I'm not surprised Kurt has chosen somewhere dingy and small like this one. If you're wanting to stay off the radar whilst you stalk and scheme, this is the place to do it.

The absence of Dana's car is a disappointment. The only vehicle here is a rust-spotted convertible—not something a Were is likely to drive, especially one trying to lay low.

Mitch pulls in, parking outside reception. "May as well have a look around while we're here?"

I arch a brow at him. "See what we can sniff out?"

Mitch rolls his eyes as he climbs out. "Prime Alpha jokes are so lame."

A quick glance through the glass front door shows us that reception is unattended. I'd imagine security and scrutiny isn't a priority here. We head around the back to the rooms, knowing we're not likely to find much.

I scan the ground, my tracking instincts kicking in, but the gravel doesn't give me a thing. Plus, even if there were boot marks or footprints, they could be anyone's. Mitch surreptitiously fills his lungs, but I'm gonna bet all he'll scent is the stale cigarette smell from reception and the sickly tang of air freshener trying to cover it all up. Just like me, he won't find a trace of Were or Channon.

It looks like we've hit a dead end.

We prowl down to the end of the units, knowing we won't find anything, but needing to work off some frustration before we get back in the truck.

I give Mitch a shove. "On the upside, we'll probably be back in time to get the pickles."

Mitch shakes his head as he smiles. "That's true. No point all of us being disappointed and grumpy."

I'm about to say something about Tara's fragile relationship with grumpy when the door on the unit in front of us swings open. We both pull back as a trolley stacked with cleaning products barrels out.

"Oh gosh." A woman, thin and bedraggled, pulls up short, one hand grabbing the trolley, the other flying to her chest. "I'm so sorry."

I smile, it looks like this woman has enough stress going on right now. "No harm done."

The woman pushes a limp strand of hair off her face. "I usually check, it's just that..." She straightens, not bothering to finish the sentence.

Mitch smiles too. "We just figured the trolley knew we needed some freshening up."

The woman doesn't smile, not that I blame her. And he says

my jokes are lame.

I step around, thinking we should probably move on before this gets any more awkward. We're almost at the next unit when I stop, an idea sparking.

I turn, pulling my smile back up, and walk back. The woman is still standing in the doorway as she organizes her trolley.

"I don't suppose you've seen Dana or Kurt Channon? They stay here sometimes."

The woman straightens but remains in the doorway. "They're not here."

Excitement surges through my body—she obviously knows who I'm talking about. "We figured that." I glance at Mitch. "I can't believe we missed them."

Mitch's hand whacks my upper arm. "I told you she said Tuesday."

My glare is pretty genuine. Why do these acts always involve me getting walloped? "Sorry, I should have listened."

Mitch shrugs daintily, which is an achievement for a Were. "I'm not the type to say I told you so."

I have to hold my eyes still, no matter how much they want to roll. A giggle has me turning back to discover a girl, maybe eight years old, slipping from behind the woman.

If I thought the woman looked washed out and unwell, this little girl looks even paler and skinnier. Her chestnut hair hangs like seaweed around her head, and her bird-like shoulders seem to jut out from her blue dress. I'm taking a guess that this little girl isn't at school for health reasons, possibly serious ones.

Despite all that, she's smiling and still giggling. I wink at her, at least someone thinks Mitch is funny.

The woman steps to the side, her voice a hush. "Quiet Hazel. These gentlemen were just leaving." She looks up. "I'm the owner of this Inn. I'm sorry, I can't give out the information you're looking for."

I nod, seeing the determination in her tired eyes. Maybe knowing they were here will be enough for us to go on.

But Hazel steps further out. "Dana and Kurt left yesterday."

I throw Mitch a triumphant look, even his guess was wrong. I wrinkle my nose at Hazel. "Don't get either of us to plan your birthday party."

Hazel giggles again and her mother's face softens. She reaches out and strokes back the hair that had fallen across Hazel's face. The gulp of air that I suck in I can't help, but I manage to keep my eyes from turning into saucers.

Her eyes! Just like Eden's, and just like Willow's at the truck stop, they angle up ever so slightly at the corners. Green and smiling, they study me.

It can't be...

I shove my hands in my pockets and grin down at her. All of a sudden, I'm doing a different type of digging. "Is your dad as bad at remembering stuff?"

Hazel's smile slips but doesn't completely disappear. "I don't know. Mom says he's a drop kick, so it's possible."

Hazel's mother chokes and blushes, but she doesn't tell her daughter to hush again. She's watching her daughter like she's watching a flower bloom.

I chuckle along with Mitch next to me. I know that we're here to find Kurt, but I can't help but ask the next question. "Do you have a pet?"

The girl's fragile shoulders droop a little. "I tried to hatch an egg once, but it didn't work."

A Changeling without an animal to connect with is like a Were without a pack. A shaft of anger slices through me, all these Fae guys leaving behind children to try and thrive when they never have a sense of who they are. Look at what it did to Eden. I glance at Hazel's mother. Look at what it did to Alexis.

I look from Hazel, to her mother, and back again. I step forward and squat down, making a point of talking in a pseudo-whisper. "I say start small, ask for a hamster maybe. Sometimes adults don't realize how much we need a furry friend in our life."

I glance up and Hazel's mother is biting her lip. "She doesn't normally talk to strangers."

I wish I could explain that Changelings and Weres seem to have an affinity, but I can't, so I just shrug. "But she's just drawn to some people?"

The woman's eyes widen. "Yes."

"I know another girl like that."

Mitch takes a step to stand beside me. "In fact, she knows Dana too."

I stand slowly, knowing Mitch is reminding me of why we're here. "I don't suppose they were heading back to Jacksonville?"

The mother shakes her head. "I can't answer that question."

I shrug like it doesn't really matter. Even though it really, really matters. I glance at Mitch. "We'll have to give them a call."

The woman smiles. "That would be best."

I respect her for maintaining her professionalism. She's obviously tired, this place needs money and maintenance, and her daughter is sick. Despite this, she's not giving away her client's personal information.

I respect it, but the frustration flares anyway. We were so close.

"They were going to Safe Aviary." Hazel's face has lit up. "Mommy, maybe we could go to Safe Aviary?"

Jackpot! I channel my excitement into my smile. "That sounds like a cool place."

"It's this wildlife sanctuary for raptors like eagles and falcons, and they just got in a pair of golden eagles."

Heaven for a Changeling. "I bet that's one of your favorite places to visit."

Hazel's smile lights up her whole pale race. "It really is."

I wonder if Hazel has color in her cheeks when she's there, whether Changelings are that closely linked to the earth. If that's the case, it must've killed Eden to grow up moving from one congested man-made city to another.

Hazel's mother is stroking her hair again. "Maybe we'll go there this weekend."

"Could we? I love you, Mommy!"

The mother smiles as she shakes her head. "But first I need to get these rooms done."

Hazel grabs the handles on the trolley. "I was helping, remember?"

The woman glances at us, apology and thanks blended across her tired features. My guess is that Hazel's 'helping' is what had that trolley almost take us out.

I wave at Hazel as we leave and her returning wave is enthusiastic until she breaks into a fit of coughs. I turn away before I allow myself to frown. How could this child's father be okay with her growing up like this?

Mitch slaps and grabs my shoulder. "Looks like we'll be visiting Safe Aviary ourselves."

I nod, wondering how the heck all this Fae-Changeling info fits in. Our paths are now irretrievably woven, but I have no idea what it means. "Let's see where it is, but with the trail gone cold, we might as well head home."

Mitch pulls out his cell and focuses on the screen. I stare out the window as he types. It can't be a coincidence that the two places we've found a link to Kurt have both had Changelings. What am I missing here?

"That's odd."

I lean over to peer at his screen. "What?"

"There's no place called Safe Aviary around here."

"Are you sure? That's definitely what Hazel called it."

Mitch shoots me an unimpressed look. "My hearing is just as good as yours, you know."

"Well, it's not Prime Alpha level, but I'm sure it's pretty good."

My joke hits his unimpressed face and falls flat. I sigh. "Maybe google raptor sanctuary."

Mitch's fingers work quickly over his little keyboard. "You've got to be kidding me."

I lean over further. "Now what?"

Mitch holds up his cell and I read the script across the screen. Shock has me pulling back, but my Were eyesight can still make out the words. "No way…"

Mitch turns the phone to him as if to check. "It seems so. It's a bit of drive, maybe three hours away. East this time."

I pull the keys out of the ignition. "It doesn't look like we're going home yet."

Settling into Hazel Inn wasn't what I was expecting to do, but I know it's necessary. As I press the speed dial number again, I find myself desperately wishing Eden picks up.

She does after the first ring. "Hey."

"Hey." I absorb the sound of her voice. The warmth and yearning I hear in that one word settles me like nothing else can. "Sorry, I can't talk for long, my phone's almost flat."

Just like not knowing we'd need gas, I hadn't planned on needing my cell charger.

"Where are you?"

"We came across a lead on Kurt so we followed it north."

"Are you okay?"

"We're fine. We did learn some stuff though." I pause, knowing this isn't a conversation to have over the phone. Eden is far less safe than we thought. And far less alone. "I have a lot to tell you."

"Me too." She pauses and I wish I was there to sense how she's feeling. "You sound tired."

I sigh. I'm not tired, I'm disappointed. "It doesn't look like we're coming home tonight."

"Oh."

"And I wish I could explain, but I can't. Not like this."

"I understand." Somehow, there seems to be a smile in Eden's voice. I love how she just gets it. "I'll be cold tonight."

Another reason to hate Kurt. "I'll be sharing a room with Mitch."

"Neither of us will be comfortable by the looks of things."

My smile is welcome as I press the cell a little closer. I wish we could talk for longer. It makes the distance seem less isolating. "How are you feeling?"

"Well, there's no Were healing going on, but my leg doesn't hurt anymore."

I let another knot of tension unravel. Having Eden safe and well is essential to my equilibrium. "Good. Stay with the pack, okay?"

"Are you going all protective on me?"

"Kinda." My smile grows then dims. The image of the bear ploughing past Eden seems to be branded into my mind. I suck in a breath. No wonder he was so enraged—he'd smelled the same animal who had injured him so cruelly. I doubt the king of the Fae could have gotten through that furious burn for revenge.

"Noah?"

But I push it all away. I won't let the knowledge that Kurt has been hanging around spoil the moments I have with my girl. She's safe with our family, plus I'll be home tomorrow. "Sorry, I was just thinking. I know you can take care of yourself."

"Well, I've learned I'm stronger than I realize, that's for sure."

I know Eden is saying that in a good way, her warm tone tells me as much, but a little part of me has always worried that one day she'll decide this is far more than she ever signed up for. I know it's irrational, but love can lack rationality sometimes. I try for a touch of my own heat. "I'm looking forward to the reunion."

"Just remember that I love you, okay?"

"That's one thing I can't forget. I love you too, Eden."

"See you soon."

She hangs up, and I can't help but stare at the phone. Man, we're acting like lovesick teens. It's another day apart, not some extended separation.

Impulsively, I send her a text.

Mitch is looking at me as I look up. "She okay?"

I glare at my cell, like it's its fault I can't be with my mate. "I hate that I couldn't tell her why we're not coming home."

Mitch picks up the remote, even though neither of us ever have time to watch TV. "I'd be worried too."

I tilt my head, not sure where that statement came from. "I'm not worried."

"Ah, except that the last two times you weren't completely upfront, Eden jumped to some pretty interesting conclusions."

I frown and turn away. I'm going to put that comment down to first-time-father jitters. Now is not the time to bring up that both times something like this happened, Eden assumed she wasn't enough. And ran. "We've come a long way from that, and you know it."

Mitch sits, more like flops, onto the edge of the bed. "Sorry, man. You're right." He wipes his hands down his face. "I think I'm just getting testy cause this was supposed to be a drive to get some supplies and it's turned out…"

I flick on the TV, realizing Eden was right. I am tired. Nor does Mitch need to voice what we've both thinking.

That Kurt is planning everything we were afraid he would be, but far closer to home than we ever realized.

And that he knew about others like Eden before we did.

CHAPTER TEN

THE LETTERS STAMPED ACROSS THE ENTRY ARE INDISPUTABLE. IT seems Hazel had pronounced it correctly, but we'd spelled it incorrectly. Safe Avery is a raptor sanctuary all right.

And it also bears the name of Eden's father, the King of the Fae. With all the convenient coincidences yesterday, this was one we had to look into.

The parking lot is empty this early in the morning, which is what we wanted. What's more, with heavy clouds steadily rolling in, I doubt there will be a lot of visitors today. We stand beside the truck, taking it in. The place is big, and relatively new looking. Tall, chain-link fences angle out from the brick entry. Netting soars high up into the sky behind it like a circus tent.

I look at the closed sign on the entry door. "I don't think that should stop us from a little sightseeing."

Mitch flexes his shoulders. "They probably don't realize that this sort of fencing won't keep Weres out."

I flash Mitch a grin. "They know there's no reason to keep us out."

All we want to do is find out if this is somehow linked to Kurt...or Eden. Then we head home.

We strike left, following the towering black wire fence. Behind the building is an open courtyard with paths branching out. This is where visitors would stand, poring over brightly colored maps as they decide whether they want to see the savannah enclosure or bird feeding show first.

We just want to see who runs the place.

We keep walking down, but the place seems empty. Well, empty of humans. Once we've moved past the bird aviaries, the sanctuary opens out. The fence disappears down amongst some trees. "More of a safari experience down here," Mitch muses.

"Hazel said there were elk, so that makes sense."

"Gotta feed the raptors something, I suppose."

I give him a shove. "Somehow, I doubt they're here to demonstrate the circle of life."

A movement catches my eye and I pause, squinting through the fence. For long moments I don't see anything else, and I'm just about to turn away, when the light catches again. I lean in closer. There is definitely someone down there, but the distance and the long grass obscures them. In fact, there are two people talking.

As my Were eyesight hones in, I yank in a breath. It can't be…

Mitch has seen them too, because his fingers link through the chain as he peers closer. "Now what's the chance of that?"

I glance up at the top of the eight-foot fencing. It angles in at the top, more focused on keeping the wild animals in than intruders out. "I think we might need to investigate."

Mitch steps back, curiosity and a hint of determination glinting in his blue eyes. "Prime Alphas first."

I leap and grab, fingers spearing through the wire holes. With one great pull and push, I clear the top and land on the other side in a crouch. Mitch is beside me a second later.

One of the men look up, and I'm not surprised that he heard us land even though they're quite a distance away. His hand comes up to shield his eyes and I make a point of waving.

The blond man's hand raises slowly in acknowledgement then drops down. I'm not sure whether Orin is happy to see us or not.

Although he smiles as we approach, I get the sense that his equanimity has been ruffled. If he was a calm pool of water, something definitely just caused some ripples, and it's interesting that that's us.

"Hey, Orin."

Orin reaches out a hand and we shake. "Noah. Mitch. What a wonderful surprise."

I turn to the older man standing beside him, stomach tense. If we're about to meet another Changeling I'm going to have to do some serious rethinking. Surely, there can't be that many around here.

But although the man's brown eyes are narrowed, they're certainly not tilted. There's a good chance this guy grew up with his father.

"Noah, Mitch, this is Harold. Safe Avery's caretaker."

I reach out to shake his hand too, and I make sure I return his strong, sure grip. This guy is more ruffled than Orin is to see us. "How did you guys get in here?"

I glance at Mitch. It's time to beat him at his own game. I whack his shoulder. "I told you it wasn't open yet."

Mitch blinks but recovers quickly. "Then how come that door wasn't locked?"

I turn back, pulling up a broad smile for Harold and Orin. "We've heard so much about this place, we thought maybe there was an early morning tour or something."

Orin is shaking his head, a smile thinking of tipping up his lips. "Harold, these two men are my family. They've obviously stopped off for a visit."

My smile stays where it is. It seems we have.

Orin's eyes zero in on me. "How did you find me?"

I stare right back. I'm not making any more assumptions

about who knows what or who's been doing what. "We came across Dana, and she seemed to know where to find you."

Orin straightens as he sucks in a breath. "I see."

I wait, hoping for a sign to tell me what that means, but Orin does his statue impersonation.

"That's unusual." Harold breaks the staring-standoff, and we all turn to find him squatting on the ground. His fingers brush the matted grass at his feet. I hunch down beside him, curious as to what he's looking at.

The golden grass is crushed and bruised, which isn't surprising considering there are now four people standing here. But then I see what he sees. Beside the prints of boots are what looks like indentations in the soil. Indentations what could only be made by claws.

"What animals do you have here?"

Harold frowns. "We have elk and the odd white-tailed deer in here, the savannah plains enclosure, but no predators."

"No dogs?"

Harold shakes his head as he pushes upright.

I glance at Mitch as I stand, and we glance around. There aren't any more animal prints, but ahead is a trail where someone has walked into the open grassland before us. I've either read the tracks wrong, or...

I turn to Orin. "It would be great to have a bit of a tour."

Orin is studying me again, and I wonder if he's anything like Eden who can read me like a book. I'm happy for her to do it, but my mysterious mate-in-law? That, I'm less comfortable with.

He nods. "We were doing our morning rounds before we open. It would be wonderful if you could join us."

Harold grunts. "We check out the elk first before feeding the birds."

Mitch opens his arms. "Lead the way, Harold."

A dirt track spears ahead and into the grassland and we follow it, Harold and Orin in the lead, Mitch and I behind.

Mitch's arm brushes mine and without looking I nod once. He just asked if something is up.

I take in the morning sun brushing its light over the sea of grass, knowing there are animals peacefully grazing not far away. I can imagine this place is popular, it's beautiful and there's something quite centering about it. "I spoke to a little girl who loves this place yesterday."

Harold glances over his shoulder, his cranky wrinkles the most relaxed I've seen them. "We provide a very unique experience."

I breathe in the smell of golden grass and blue skies. "I can understand why. This place looks relatively new."

Harold slows his step so that we come up beside him. Orin continues walking ahead, seeming to be focused on his surroundings. "The owner built it just over two years ago."

Mitch tilts his head. "Avery?"

Harold's eyes seem to light up at the mention of that name. "Yes. What an inspiring man."

I look at Orin's back, wondering how okay he is with this information being shared. It seems Avery hasn't been that far away either, and I'm not sure what that means.

Harold has inflated like a proud parent. "He bought the land and built this sanctuary."

"Wow." Mitch's voice is genuinely impressed.

"Being the caretaker is a privilege and an honor."

I rub my lip, watching Orin as I say my next words. "He must be loaded."

"This is what Avery does." Orin doesn't turn as he speaks. "He invests in reserves by finding those that realize their importance."

My gaze doesn't leave his back. "And then what?"

Is it just me, or did Orin just tense a little? "He moves onto the next. His work is vitally important."

Mitch's arm brushes mine again. I wonder if he realizes that we're just as much talking about the Fae as we are Avery. The buying of land and establishing sanctuaries also sounds like the lines Kurt fed Willow, which means once again, he's one step ahead of us.

"It sounds like important work."

"Yes. It is."

I tilt my head even though Orin can't see me. "What do his children think of that?"

Harold perks up at that. "Avery has more kids?"

Orin turns, his gaze on me and unwavering. "This is bigger than that."

My hands fist and I consciously relax them. Sick Hazel living in the city that is probably choking her, Willow and her pointedly named step-father, Eden carrying the pain of a wound she had no part in.

I can see what they're trying to do, but I'm not convinced their system is working.

I frown, a thought hitting me in the solar plexus. Eden and I have proven one thing over and over. I wonder if it will have the same impact on Orin. "What could be more important than the power of connection?"

It's the foundation of uniting.

The satisfaction at seeing Orin's calm facade fracture is sweet. His jaw relaxes as his mouth pops open, and his eye widen. He quickly recovers, but it's too late. His brief lapse just showed me that he's either thought of this himself, or he didn't expect me to think of it myself.

The feeling is short lived when Harold's voice slices through my inner victory dance. "God no."

We rush forward, turning the bend Harold just disappeared around. He's kneeling beside an elk, its grass-colored body lying prostate on the ground. Harold raises his hands as he looks up and they're smeared in coagulated red.

We're around him in a flash, seeing what brought him to his knees. The elk is dead, and it wasn't a quick or painless loss of life. Its hind legs bear tears and cuts, but it's the ragged flesh at its throat that's been torn and mangled. The animal's neck is stretched, its lifeless eyes wide with terror, its tongue distended and protruding like it was bellowing exactly how much death hurts.

Harold sags as Orin turns his head away.

Mitch and I step closer, taking in the carnage. I point to the soil not far away, and I can tell Mitch sees it too. Boots lead up to the animal, but something else shredded it.

My head snaps up. "Is this the only one?"

Orin's eyes widen in alarm before he turns and strides down the track. "Harold, wait here while I make sure this is an isolated incident."

Harold pushes up, looking like he might disagree. But Orin already has an arm on his shoulder. "You need to look after your health."

Harold blinks, one hand coming to his chest. He kneels back down and begins to stroke the animal, probably knowing the comfort is too late, but I get the helplessness which drives him to do it anyway.

It's only a few yards down that we find the next one. Orin kneels slowly as he reaches out his hand. He closes his eyes as he stays there for long moments, silent and grieving.

This time I brush my hand over the coarse fur. The body is still warm. I look up at Mitch. "This was done last night."

Mitch is already scanning the horizon, thinking. "Do you think he did it, or got one of his power greedy followers to do it for him?"

Tension has my muscles wound up as I clench my hands. "I'm not sure."

Orin stands, his calm features now grim. "The path doesn't go much further."

There's a sharp left, and I hold my breath in anticipation of what we're going to see. Around this corner are three elk, alive but skittish. They flinch when we round the bend. Orin walks slowly but surely toward them and the magic I've seen Eden weave so many times soothes them. Their heads drop, their taut bodies relax.

I look around, but there are no more dead bodies for our brains to process. Maybe it was just two?

The path looks like it loops back, once again heading in the direction of the main buildings. We move forward, hopeful that the carnage is over.

But over the next rise is the final gory declaration. We move forward in a state of shock, and I try to understand why. This time five elk have been lined up, throats shredded, bodies bloodied. Orin collapses, his knees sinking into the crimson soil. My hand grasps his shoulder, this would be a personal loss to a Fae, not just the violent death of an innocent animal.

I see Mitch scanning the soil and do the same. There are a few paw prints around, and although they're big, they're too trampled to provide much information. Any prints deep enough have filled with pools of blood. Just like the last one, there's nothing but boot marks leading up to the animal. Whoever did this was wanting to confuse, to raise questions.

I look back at the way we just came, then back toward the bird area. The killing seems sporadic, we find elk grazing like nothing has happened, then we find more butchered carcasses. Something strikes me. "They're looking for something."

"And leaving a deliberate trail of blood." Mitch mutters.

I look around. What were they looking for?

Orin shoots upright. "We need to check the bird enclosures."

Mitch and I follow his frantic footsteps. This time I brush my arm with his, growling under my breath. "We need to stop this."

Mitch nods, that short, sharp movement saying 'damn straight.'

Orin heads straight to some of the larger enclosures. A quick scan shows they are intact. It seems whoever did this was looking for the impact of larger animals. Orin looks at us, his tilted green eyes grieving but determined. "There's one more cage, but this one isn't for the public."

He heads south again, passing through a gate marked 'Staff Only'. Orin isn't looking for the signs we are, so I catch Mitch's eye when I notice the booted prints in the soil. They could be Harold's, but then again... Mitch's lips thin as he acknowledges the possibilities. The gate is also intact, which is a good sign.

Tucked behind a brick building is one last aviary, this one a little larger than the others.

Orin's fingers grasp the wire. "Oh no."

I quickly join him and brace myself for more blood. But inside there's nothing but a golden eagle, alive and alert, watching us. "It looks fine, Orin."

Orin is already shaking his head. "She does." He turns to me. "But her mate is gone."

I'm scanning the cage like a second golden eagle is something that would be easy to miss. But the perches are empty, except for the hunkered down bird sitting on the highest one.

Mitch frowns. "There are meant to be two?"

Orin's arms sag at his side. "Yes, the female was only brought in recently. She had been separated from her mate when he was captured by poachers. He's been here, healing. They were only just reunited."

"Avery has been looking after them?"

Orin nods. "Some animals tend to become quite bonded to certain Fae."

Like Eden and Caesar. Like Willow and her owl, Shamus.

"My father has spent quite a bit of time with these two. The male wasn't healing, and the female was failing to thrive, until we reunited them that is."

Mitch narrows his eyes at the big bird that is sitting there, looking at us. "So it's not okay that one of them is gone."

"No. They're a mated pair, the symbol of the unbreakable bond of love."

I don't snort, even though I want to. Fae are far more love 'em and leave 'em types.

"They are as deeply connected with each other as they are with him. One would never stay behind if the other had gone."

I rub my bottom lip. "Why are they not with Avery?"

Orin looks away, staring once again at the lonely, majestic bird. "Avery has been spending too much time in cities recently. He is unwell. He needed time to heal."

Just like Willow…although no one has told her mother how to help her get better. Her mother is tied up trying to earn a living seeing as the father of her child skipped town. But now isn't the time to have that conversation.

"Orin!" Harold's voice is pitched and panicked. "There's more."

Orin is already at the gate. "Harold had a health scare recently. I need to see to him."

I nod. "We'll be here."

With Orin gone, I point to the metal door of the aviary, which is very much shut. "Someone let him out."

Mitch crosses his arms. "Yes, someone did."

And we both have a pretty good idea of who that someone is.

I make a split second decision. "We need to do the same thing Kurt has."

"Ah, venison isn't my thing."

"Hilarious. I'm going to head back to the car, you let our friend here out and I'll follow it. Kurt is banking on her taking him straight to Avery. This guy will take me straight to Kurt."

Mitch's dark brows power down. "That's not something you should do on your own."

I sigh. He's probably right. "I'll wait in the parking lot. We'll go together."

Mitch relaxes a little. "Okay."

Orin is back, and the missing eagle looks like it may be down the bottom of his to-do list. "I'm going to have to deal with this before the sanctuary opens."

I grab his shoulder and squeeze before heading past him to the gate. "We won't get in your way. I'm just going to call Dad and let him know what's happened."

Orin nods, distracted. The guy has got a tough day ahead of him. "Tell Eden I said hello."

I'd like to say hello, except my stupid phone is flat as a tack. "Sure. I'm looking forward to getting home tonight."

Which is an understatement. The longing to be back beside my mate is overwhelming.

As I head to the exit, I pull my car keys out of my pocket.

Kurt's bloody threats are about to stop.

CHAPTER ELEVEN

THE ENGINE IS IDLING AS I WAIT FOR MITCH. IF AVERY HAS STAYED in the area, we'll need to follow as much as we can in the truck. If he's headed to the forest, then we'll get to shift.

I hear the cry of the eagle, its call of freedom, before I see it. High up in the sky, its massive wingspan circles the sanctuary, and I can relate to its sense of anticipation.

You want to find your mate. Believe me, I know the feeling.

It soars up, finding the warm updrafts, and flies east. I drop the truck into gear and start driving toward the entry. Mitch, where are you?

Now that the eagle has set his course, he angles like an arrow. I accelerate, but Mitch isn't even in my rear vision mirror. I power out the gates, I can't wait. This is too important.

The bird seems to be on a mission, because it flies due east, straight into the sun if it wasn't so grey. I squint up at the low lying mass. It's going to be harder to see him in these conditions, but I'm determined. I'm not going to lose him.

I accelerate again, glad to see the eagle is heading away from suburbia. It would suck to be stuck at a red light like the law-abiding future cop I want to be and have to watch our one lead disappear into the grey horizon.

The road starts to wind north, so I find the next right—some unnamed track—and turn. The eagle coasts high above me, probably loving the feeling of slicing through the wind.

Suddenly, he banks, subtly but definitely taking a southerly shift. I watch, our trajectories no longer parallel, as his new direction starts to move away. Pine trees line the road, which turns out to be a lazy, winding strip through the forest. There's no way to tell which way it's ultimately going.

The eagle's wings twitch again, and it definitely takes a south-easterly course. I lean forward over the steering wheel. Damn it. I'm at risk of losing it.

Making the call, I pull the truck over. Jamming my phone in my pocket, I jump out. The eagle is reaching the horizon where evergreen tops meet charcoal sky. He's not waiting for anyone.

With a quick glance over my shoulder, I shift. I can't afford to lose him. I need to know where he's heading.

The moment I'm in wolf form, I connect with how the eagle must be feeling. Wind whips at me, carrying the promise of what's to come. I breathe in the scents; freedom, wilderness, possibilities. Just like the eagle, the barriers between me and what I want have just been shattered by the potential of Mother Nature.

Powering through the trees, I watch the bird overhead. It cries out once, then twice, and I wonder what it's trying to communicate. Maybe we're getting close, it would be logical for Avery to have one of his bases nearby.

Maybe he's calling out to his other half, knowing she's not far away.

Thirty minutes later, I've decided the eagle's call was a heads up that this would take a while. The forest grows denser and wilder, the ground touched by nothing but the paws of the scampering animals I hear.

Just the way I like it.

Without warning, the eagle banks again, then swoops down and lands amongst the branches of a towering pine. From his perch, he angles his head, looking down and around.

I slow, then halt. Is this some kind of pit stop? Did he need to catch his breath?

He launches up into the air and I get ready to sprint again, but a moment later I see why. A matching eagle, deep brown and crowned in gold, meets him mid-air. They swoop and swirl amongst the grey sky, the heavy clouds seeming to come down and meet them so they can be part of the joy.

I feel my smile curve my lips. Now that's an impressive reunion.

I look back down, scanning among the trunks standing guard. Which means one of my targets is nearby. Either Avery or Kurt must be in the area.

I move forward cautiously, paws softly crushing the damp pine needles, breath shallow and quiet. The trees open out to a grassy area, a squat, haphazard mountain of rocks on the other side. Squinting, I see what could possibly make this hill special. A crack, created by drunken rocks, stares at me several feet away.

I wait, but the cave remains a silent, black opening. Is Avery actually here, or are his eagles waiting for him?

I sniff the air, but the breeze coming from behind me gives me nothing but resinous pine, rich earth, and the promise of rain. I sniff again. And those waterworks will be soon.

Investigating the cave is the next logical step, but I hesitate. Usually, holes in a hill only have one way in and one way out. If I go in there I'll effectively trap myself.

I circle around, keeping to the edge of the trees. The first drops of rain start, dragging the air temperature down with them as a mist draws in. If Avery is here, surely he would have come out by now. I hear a cry high above and glance up. The eagles have lifted into the air and angled south. Great, this was just a pit stop.

The rumbling growl is so low it takes a few precious seconds to register. But the baritone snarl reaches me with its hate and message—I'm about to start...and this won't be ending without bloodshed.

I turn, and Kurt is on the other side of the clearing; a ragged, russet wolf. His fur is a little longer, his eyes a whole lot more hateful since last time I saw him.

When his throat was between my jaws.

I don't growl, but I sure as heck ain't smiling as I straighten. I stare, and stare hard, communicating my own message—you aren't walking away without justice being served.

Kurt steps right, circling the clearing. I mirror him, happy for him to dance with his inevitability. Another few steps as we continue the waltz and Kurt moves closer to the hill. When I see something move in the darkness of the cave, I pause.

Avery.

The eagle brought me straight to him, but they also brought Kurt. I watch Kurt step sideways again, now standing outside the mouth of the cave.

He grins in a godawful, glowering kind of way. I keep my eyes zeroed on him. Does he know Kurt is there? But he steps sideways again, relinquishing the place as guardian of the cave.

This time, I make my own sharp movement to the right. Kurt instantly mirrors it, all growls and threats, but obviously maintaining his distance. Good. He knows I'm no longer the inexperienced Were he challenged to a Claiming. With Eden, because of Eden, I'm now the Prime Alpha.

Eden. The one Kurt blames for all this.

Anger, cold and determined, has my head dropping. I make another sharp movement, this time forward, but Kurt doesn't come to meet me. His muzzle serrates, his teeth baring, as he takes another step to the right.

Satisfaction adds to my steely resolve. He knows he has one shot, and if he misses, he's either human or lacking a pulse.

The rain picks up in intensity, but I don't care. This is my opportunity to end this. Another step to the right and I'm almost outside the cave entrance myself. Once I'm between Kurt and Avery, then I'll attack.

Two more steps and the rocks of the hill come into my peripheral vision. The ground squelches beneath my feet, its fullness telling me it probably rained not long ago. This place is about to turn into one giant puddle. Two more steps and I can feel the solidness of the rocks behind me. The mouth of the cave isn't far away.

Without warning, Kurt leaps, and I cover the last few feet. I'm now the force Kurt will have to go through if he's realized Avery is in there. I straighten. The anger and the determination pour out of me in one mighty roar.

My head drops as the sound dies, eyes lazering in on the Were who stands for everything we are not. I growl, low and hard.

Bring. It. On.

It's all the invite Kurt needs, because triumph sparks in his hazel eyes as he surges forward. Water splashes out as his paws power into the ground, the mud splattering his russet fur.

My heart rate quickens as time slows. Kurt's wild eyes, angry and hate-filled, tell me how he wants this to end as he comes closer and closer. I don't move. He's about to find out who decides what tomorrow looks like.

The light that sparks his eyes, unholy and manic, almost makes me smile. Kurt is celebrating too early. He leaps, and I rear up to meet him, mouth open, ready to show him what the Prime Alpha can do.

But Kurt arcs high, higher than I expected, and my jaws clamp hard on air. He sails over and behind me, landing on the rocks above. I turn, facing the mouth of cave, rain obscuring what I'm seeing.

What the hell is Kurt doing?

This time, the rumble that starts doesn't stop. It starts above me, then comes from beneath me. I watch as a brown wall of sludge starts to shift, its intent to crush the distance between us. There's a shaking of the air, a muted roar, the knowledge that thousands of pounds of weight are about to pay homage to gravity.

As the avalanche of soil and rocks comes at me, I have no choice. I leap forward and the blackness of the cave swallows me.

CHAPTER TWELVE

I'M ROARING LONG AFTER THE MUD HAS STOPPED LAYING A MASSIVE wall of earth and rocks across the entry.

I did not just get trapped! Kurt is not still out there!

As my lungs roar my fury, my heart screams one word. Eden.

I'm ripping at the soil, massive paws not big enough as I tear at the dislocated earth. Beneath the veneer of sludge, I start to get a sense of the size of the boulders that have come crashing down. But I can't afford to stop. Every moment is another one that brings Kurt closer to Eden.

I jam my shoulder into the rock before me and push. The cold, wet surface is determined to remain where it just landed, but I'm determined too. Nothing will keep me from Eden.

"I doubt even the Prime Alpha can move those monoliths."

A muted glow fills the room and I turn, squinting in the gloom, surprised but not shocked when I see the figure of a man shrouded in the blackness. Avery, King of the Fae. Eden's father is sitting at the back of the cave, only a few feet away.

But I don't have time to bond with my father-in-law. Kurt is out there. And so is Eden.

I turn back to the mountain I now have to move, shifting back to human. I need to get my bearings, come up with a plan. I'm scratching at the mud and sludge, not caring as the sticks and gravel tear at my nails. "We have to get out of here."

"Yes. We do."

Frustration is firing through my body so I use it as fuel. I step one way then the other, hands feeling the wall of earth that is keeping me here. I just need to find a weak spot, one I can exploit. Then Kurt is going to pay.

"But it won't be today."

I spin, frustration bursting into anger. "I can't afford to sit around and wait."

Yanking my phone out of my pocket, I hold down the power button. All I need is one phone call. I'm not some passive Fae who's going to sit around hoping this will turn out okay. It's a relief to see that I have reception down in this rock hole, but Eden's number goes straight to message bank. Helplessness starts to swallow the anger, and it's not a sensation I enjoy.

"Do you not trust your pack?"

That has me pausing. The fact that I trust those I love to keep Eden safe meant I followed Dana in the first place. "They will protect her with their lives."

Avery nods in the gloom, his dark hair pulled back the way Eden's used to be. "Then we wait."

I let the anger take over, blazing and violent, as my fist powers into the stone next to me. "I don't leave the ones I love!"

Pain shoots up my hand, a lightning shaft spearing through my bones and exploding along my nerve endings. Damn it!

"I never left."

Cupping my bruised hand, I slide to the floor, the stone scraping my back. I welcome that pain like I do the agony in my throbbing knuckles. "Bull crap. I've seen what you left behind."

I look up, now that my eyes have adjusted to this tomb, and notice that Avery is not only sitting, but half-lying back in some sort of knobbly, wooden recliner. As silence finally settles, I notice his short, raspy breathing. Orin's words come back to me. "You're sick."

"Only as sick as the earth. I come here to heal and rejuvenate when I can."

I listen to the labored breathing for a few seconds, take in the paler than pale skin. I don't point out that it doesn't look like it's working. I frown. It seems the Fae really are closely connected to the earth.

I look around, thinking maybe there's some miraculous back door. But the cave is small and compact. Someone has chiseled out a couple of shelves above Avery's head, where two jars sit along with a container of water.

I squint, after growing up with Mitch and his woodworking passion, I can recognize hand hewed furniture anywhere. "This place is pretty well set up."

"It is not mine."

My eyebrows shoot up. "Someone else lives here?"

Avery inclines his head. "At times. A man named Reed comes here often."

I wait, wondering if catching his breath is the only reason Avery is hesitating.

"He is a Changeling who needs a break from the man-made world sometimes."

I look around at the rough home Reed has built. "So he's a bit of a hermit."

"Yes."

"Who can't cope with the real world."

Avery sweeps an arm to encompass everything around and above us before dropping it back in his lap. "This is more real than the world you speak of."

"But he struggles to survive in the world you dumped him in."

There's silence in the cave. I snort, muttering my next words knowing full well they can't be escaped in this small space. "Because he doesn't know where he belongs."

There's a raspy intake of breath a few feet away from me. It may be the alarming situation I find myself in, or maybe it's all the fallout I've seen of the Fae's choices, because I don't feel remorse. Avery needs to know what his actions have meant for those he says he loves.

"It wasn't always like this. Alexis felt like she belonged, and she knew where she was going."

So we're justifying, are we? "She certainly does."

Avery shakes his head. "The woman I fell in love with isn't the one you see now."

"A woman with a rock for a heart?"

"Alexis was the warmest, most loving soul I'd ever met. There was no one else I wanted more to have a child with."

Man, he does sound like he had it bad. Or still does... "You said you never left."

"I had to leave. But I couldn't stay away. The irony that she remained in cities has meant that my ailing health has been my penance."

I think of Eden and our connection. How would I be if she upped and left with no explanation? "Well, what you did changed her. Maybe she felt like she belonged when she was with you."

And once that link was severed, she found the next lifeline she could grasp. The safety of mergers and ledgers.

Avery is silent. Even his rattly breathing is muted. I don't bother wasting time trying to see what effect my words have. The Fae can be pretty unreadable when they want to be. Not to mention now isn't the time to delve into family wounds. That trajectory was set the minute Avery left, and my loyalty is to the girl who ended up being his collateral damage.

Tension winds tightly through my muscles as I realize something. "Mitch doesn't know where I am."

"Orin has not been to this place."

I have to consciously unclench my hand from around my phone. "Freaking great."

"We have friends who can get us out."

"I'm the strongest Were there is, if I can't move these rocks, then whoever or whatever you call, isn't going to shift them either."

"Ah, but there's one of you. Strength comes in many forms."

I squint, taking in this man who looks so weak and speaks with such strength. "What do you mean?"

"Well, you've pointed out yourself. Working as a silo hasn't worked…"

Avery raises his hand, and my Were sight sees the tiny insect crawling on his palm. He lifts it to the wall behind him, and the ant scampers onto the granite. I watch as it taps and tests with its antennae, then stops when it finds dirt. "First, we'll need oxygen. Then, as my strength regains, we can call the others we will need to help."

I swallow, not sure I like that this is the best we've got. Ants are going to dig us out? Maybe some squirrels when Avery musters up some energy? "How long will this take?"

"A day."

My teeth clench. "We don't have that sort of time."

"Maybe two."

I shoot up, and dislodged dirt splats and splodges behind me. "Kurt is out there, Avery! And so is your daughter!"

The one he's said he loves so much.

Avery closes his eyes for a moment before opening them again. "She is well protected."

I yank my phone up once more, glaring at the man. There's calm and then there's freaky serene level placid. Has this guy been hanging out with Yoda?

I press the speed dial button again, but Eden's phone goes straight to message bank. I stare at the screen, not sure this cave is going to be able to contain my frustration. The battery icon has nothing but a fine line at its base. One percent left.

I speed dial again, this time calling Dad.

"Noah! Where are you? I've been trying to call for the last two hours."

"Sorry. I had a lead." Dad starts to talk but I cut him off. "I don't have much battery left. Is Eden with you?"

"That's why I rang."

There's a pause, and it's not a silence I like. "And?"

"Eden is M.I.A."

I shoot upright. "What?" My voice ricochets between the stone walls.

"She didn't come home last night, said she was staying late at Seth and Emily's."

I want to pace, but can't. "You have to find her, Dad."

"I know. Everyone is out looking. She's not answering her cell. When are you back, son?"

Dammit. Fear is hammering in my chest, the phone slippery in my palm. "I'm trapped in a—"

The phone cuts out and the screen goes black.

I look up at Avery, who is sitting up with alarm. "Eden is missing."

PART III
EDEN

CHAPTER THIRTEEN

"You said the last place would be the final one." Seth's voice, although not whiney, is certainly frustrated, maybe bordering on surly.

I sigh, fingers tensing around the steering wheel. "I know."

"How much longer?"

Who knew bringing Seth would be an exercise in Fae patience. "I told you. Until I know it's time to go back."

"I was kinda under the impression that would be after a day or two."

So was I. But I haven't heard from Noah. I pull my phone from my back pocket, glancing at the screen. Its rectangular digital screen is blank.

"What happened to your phone?"

"I dropped it." After I was given the news at the hospital. It had slipped out of my hand as I'd considered the words I was going to have to say. I'd gasped in dismay as I watched it crash to the floor and the screen crack down the side.

But in the end, it was a blessing. I'd texted Tara to let her know my cell was playing up and I'd be late. But then I'd got the phone call from Seth telling us we only had a couple of weeks until the sale, and I'd headed to his place, glad for the excuse not to go home.

And then Noah had told me he's not coming home.

I keep my hand on the steering wheel, although there's somewhere else I'd like to hold. I know Weres tend to do things quicker than humans, but it's becoming apparent in only a few short days that I won't be able to hide my secret for long.

Seth glances at his own screen, shoulders sagging. "Although reception out here is pretty crappy."

I pause. "Have you heard from Emily?"

Seth's hand tightens around the one link he has to the girl he loves. "Not much."

"I'm sorry." It was Seth's decision to come with me that has caused strain on their fledgling relationship. Those two have been through so much, and only recently reunited. "Why don't you go back? You've already done far more than you needed to."

Seth's shoulders straighten as he tucks his phone in his back pocket. "I chose to come, remember? No matter how much you argued against it."

"Does Emily know how stubborn you are?"

Seth grins. "She says it's one of her favorite things about me."

I arch a brow. "Really?"

Seth's grin grows, his brown eyes sparkling. "Mostly when I say I'm stubbornly in love with her."

I roll my eyes. Seth and Emily have survived greater things than a few days of forced separation.

I slow as we come to an intersection. "Which way?"

Seth's eyes narrow as he scratches his chin. "Right?"

"Being a little more sure would be helpful."

"Hey, every mile we've headed further north we've driven further into the wilds. It's been a while since I've visited the Langs."

I indicate and turn right. The first few families we visited were scattered in small towns. Finding them hadn't been hard seeing as Weres always seem to have some leadership role in the town. Everyone knew where the Bardolfs or the Lyalls lived.

But now that our campaign has gone longer than expected, our feelers are reaching out wider. Who knows if the Langs are going to welcome us the same way the others did?

The dirt road becomes a little bumpier and narrower as we continue. So far, reaching out to Weres to raise money for the Glade has been a success. Although there's still more to raise, we have two more weeks and it's been a promising start. The Glade is the holiest site for Weres, irrespective of their origin, and the threat of its purchase has mobilized them in a way I doubt Noah and I could have. They are uniting against a threat to what they hold most dear.

It feels good to be part of that.

"Left here."

Seth points to an even narrower track up ahead, and as I turn, I discover it's also bumpier. "Are you sure we're going the right way? It doesn't look like anyone's driven down here in a while."

Seth grins. "Not particularly, but hey, who knows where we could end up?"

I shake my head. Seth's happy resilience is great company, but also mildly frustrating.

I keep going, figuring he's found all the other packs. The pine trees crowd in and brush the side of the truck. I hope it's not getting scratched, I'd hate for it to lose value for when I sell it. The track takes one or two sharp turns, almost feeling like we're doubling back on ourselves. Seth had better not be getting us lost...

But over the next rise it opens out, and the scene before me could aptly be described as Little House on the Prairie. A heavy-set log cabin hunkers down in a clearing, roughhewn timber fences surrounding it. One massive lodge pole pine tree has been left to stand guard over it.

"Yep, this is the Langs." Seth has already opened the door

before I've stopped the car. All the other times he's waited for me to approach first, affording me deference as the Prime Alpha mate. But this time he's bounded out and waiting at the gate like some excited puppy.

It seems the Langs are special people.

I join him, the usual nervousness starting to build. All the meetings have been positive so far, but the reality is, to them I am human. And I don't have Noah with me.

Behind me, Seth says what he's said each time. "You're gonna win her over because you're you."

And every time he says it, I wish I could hug him.

Seth opens the gate and I walk through. A single person steps out of the door of the cabin to greet us—a woman. It's the smallest reception I've had, and I'm not sure if that's a good thing. In my mind, I revise my carefully considered spiel, pulling in a calming breath.

"Hello." I'm keep my voice is light and warm. "I hope this is a good time."

The woman nods her dark head once.

"I've come with news of the Glade. We need your help."

The woman steps forward. "You are his mate."

I nod slowly. "Yes, I am. My name is Eden."

Her smile is slow but sure. "Then the Lang Pack welcomes you."

She steps to the side, a smile spreading over her features, and the tension tugging at my jaw lessens.

The woman indicates for us to enter and we step through. The cabin is simple, a nuanced mix of the simplicity of the East and the stark roughness of these parts. I can't help my next thought; I don't think this pack has much money. I glance around. I think this pack is a pack of one.

"Thank you for allowing me into your home, Mrs. Lang."

"Please, call me Nian."

My smile holds a hint of relief. This woman seems so calm

and welcoming. Even if she doesn't have much to contribute, I think I'm going to enjoy this visit.

"Thank you. I'm sure you've heard of the last Precept's arrival."

Nian's nod is sharp and resolute. "It is what needs to be done."

Seth leans forward. "And Noah and Eden are the ones to do it."

I don't swallow, although I want to. Pressure, much?

Nian crosses her hands on the timber table. "I came here, to America, to be close to the Glade, the oldest place of its kind." Her gaze is steady as she looks between Seth and me. "Of our kind. It is the soul of so much."

I nod, knowing she speaks the truth. "So you know it's in danger?"

"It is a reflection of the divide and disconnect that is happening everywhere."

I lean forward too. "Of Weres?"

Nian looks at me for the longest moment. "Of many things."

I sit back a little. I have no idea what that means. I open my mouth to ask, but Seth jumps in first. "We've seen that. What do you know, Nian?

"The division is not new."

I exhale, that's what I was afraid of. The greed for power was planted in Kurt long before Noah and I met.

"But the discontent is hidden."

Seth leans back, his arms crossing. "Less and less so, in fact."

Nian angles her head, looking directly at me. "Let me ask you some questions."

I have to make a concerted effort not to pull back, not sure how I feel about that. Instead I smile, waiting.

Nian's features mirror mine, her dark eyes crinkling as her lips tip up. I don't think much gets by this wise old Were. "Who are you uniting?"

"Ah, Weres."

Nian's smile dips a little. "And what for?"

I blink. "To conquer..."

The smile is gone now, and I want to squirm in my seat. I know I'm failing some sort of test. Her face is serious as she asks the next question. "Conquer what?"

I open my mouth, then close it. Looking away, I stare out the small square window. It frames the forest that is so omnipresent. "To be honest, I don't want to conquer anyone."

The smile bursts back, and I'm not sure why. I just told her that I don't want to do what the last Precept is calling for, haven't I?

Nian tilts her smiling face. "Nor are the Prime Alpha pair very united right now."

Okay, now she's getting pushy. I tilt my own, unsmiling face right back. "We're never apart."

My hand brushes over the pedant hidden beneath my shirt. Noah and I are connected in a way that means distance, even one so great that we can't feel each other, can't undermine it. That's what faith is all about.

To my surprise, Nian leans back and lets out a bark of laughter, and with such gusto that she slaps the table as she comes back. I glance to Seth, not sure what that's supposed to mean. Seth shrugs, but he's smiling.

Still chuckling, Nian rises. "I thank you for taking the time to visit a lone Alpha. It's been a pleasure."

We both stand, because although she's done nothing but raise questions, Nian seems to have her answers.

I reach out a hand to shake hers. "Thank you, Nian. You've been truly gracious with your wisdom."

Nian grasps it with both of hers. "My pack will help anyway we can."

I glance back at the roughhewn cabin, inhabited by this one woman. My guess is she makes enough to survive in this wild part of the world and not much more. "You've already given enough."

We're out the door and back in the truck before Seth speaks. "You know she's loaded, right?"

I turn, keys poised to go in the ignition. "What?"

Seth grins. "Yeah, Nian is descendant from one of the great Chinese dynasties."

"Oh."

His grin grows. "I'd say your Glade fund is about to get a healthy top up."

I look back at the simple log cabin. If that's the case, I've come away with far more than money. Nian's questions have got me thinking that I don't have as many answers as I thought.

We drive back out down the narrow, rutted track. My guess is this awful road is a deterrent for anyone thinking of heading down here. Seth checks his phone, and I look at him askance.

He shakes his head. "No reception."

I sigh. The separation from Noah is almost a physical pain. Deep in my chest, my heart knows that something is missing.

As we reach the main road again, Seth's phone dings. Then dings again and again and again. His grin is one I only see when one person is on his mind. It looks like Emily is missing him just as much.

Pulling over, I grab my own phone. I turned it onto silent long ago thanks to Tara's own campaign. There is a text or a call on the hour, every hour, and they are almost descending into some pretty raw language. Even Adam has stopped, figuring that the one Were barrage Tara is coordinating would have to wear me down.

But she wouldn't understand. I can't go back. Not yet. At the rate I'm going, why I'm staying away is going to be noticeable even before Weres will be able to scent it.

Scrolling through the veiled threats, I find the one text I was looking for. Is he home yet? Is he calling me back to his side?

Except there's nothing but the one I received yesterday. Noah's gently glowing words make my eyes sting, but they aren't about coming home. *I love you. Looking forward to uniting xoxo*

"So where to next, Alpha?"

Tucking my phone back into the console, I pull out. "You know I hate that title."

"Which is pretty much why I use it."

I look at the road stretching out before us. I want to go home, but I can't yet. "Who else have we got to see?"

"There's only one more pack in the area…"

Why does Seth have that cautious, warning note to his voice? "And?"

"Well, it's the Tates."

It takes a few moments for the name to trigger a response, but when I remember who the Tates are, I suck in an involuntary breath.

Daniel Tate was the Were who was banished after almost exposing the existence of Weres. Noah told me of Daniel's treason, his blatant desire for Weres to show their power.

Maybe it is time to go back. We've raised a significant amount of cash, a good start that will hopefully be enough to bid Alexis out of the Glade.

And Seth wants to go home. He's testing his new relationship with Emily when it's the last thing they need.

I pause at the intersection, knowing turning right would have me in the direction of home.

Where the Phelans are. Possibly without Noah.

And where the Glade is.

My heart feels like it just capsized. I grew up with Alexis. I know the tax brackets she plays in. I've seen the wealth which her deals can generate. She won't be coming to that auction with tight purse strings.

Every dollar counts.

I turn the indicator onto left. "Let's squeeze one more in."

Seth's brown brows spike up. "Just head down the highway. You can't miss the Tate Ranch."

As I accelerate, Seth begins to text. He's probably apologizing to Emily about not coming home tonight. I wish I could speak to Noah, even though I know I can't.

Nian's questions have managed to stick in my head. They whisper of the fact we're stumbling in the dark as we follow this Prophecy. There's so much that is still unclear. But ultimately, there's one question that I've been ignoring. Avoiding because I don't know the answer.

Noah has never considered it. Nian never mentioned it.

But it's one that has grown roots in my mind

How do I unite them when I'm not one of them?

CHAPTER FOURTEEN

SETH WAS RIGHT. YOU COULDN'T MISS THE TATE RANCH. EVEN from a distance you can see the multiple green roofed buildings, proudly announcing their importance through their size. The main homestead looks like a small motel, whilst the barn is big enough to house a plane. To top it all off, a pool glistens out the back.

I tell myself I'm not intimidated by money. I grew up with an abundance of it and have seen firsthand what it does to people. The addiction to the power they believe it carries is one of the reasons I'm here. My mother's never-ending thirst has meant she isn't willing to let it go, even for her own daughter.

Still, I'm conscious enough of the status money brings, making me doubly aware I'm approaching the ranch in a top of the range brand spanking new truck. The thought has me frowning, it suggests there's more of my mother in me than I'd like to acknowledge.

We move slowly down the circular drive, taking in the white timber fence with a rose planted at every post.

My fingers are tense around the steering wheel as I glance at Seth. "You've been here before?"

Seth's jaw works like he's gritting his teeth. "Yeah. I met with Daniel once."

Being reminded of Seth's history, and the time he aligned himself with Kurt, has me slowing even more. Maybe this wasn't a good idea.

If there's anywhere we're going to find the division that Nian spoke of, it's here.

If there's anywhere that Seth isn't going to be welcome, it's here.

The driveway becomes paved as I approach the main homestead. A large porch surrounds it, extending forward into an undercover area. You can park outside the front of this house and leave your car and never get wet.

As I step out of the truck I notice the grey clouds look like they've sunk. I'd say that in a few hours you'll be able to see why this setup is so useful.

Seth is beside me faster than any other place we've visited. I glance up at his grim face. "We'll keep this one quick?"

His nod is short and sharp. "Yep."

The couple who come out are middle-aged. The man is tall like most Weres but rounded in the middle in a way I haven't seen in any other Alpha. The woman is wide and soft looking. Both have a broad smile on their face.

I step forward, pretty lamplights glowing in what would otherwise be a gloomy front entrance. "Hello, I'm—"

"Eden." The woman steps forward, arms extended. She engulfs me a hug, every part of the body that touches me warm and soft. "We're honored to have you here."

A little surprised, a lot relieved, I smile as I pull back. "Thank you, it's wonderful to meet you."

The woman steps back and she looks over my shoulder. Her smile does the impossible and grows even wider. "Seth, how wonderful to see you again."

Seth steps forward into his own hug, his own face relaxing. "Maria. It's been too long."

Maria pulls back, her hand coming up to cup Seth's face as she studies him. "How are you?"

I can tell Seth's smile is genuine because it holds the touch of sadness that defines his loss of Were status. "Bittersweet I believe is the term. I lost something important, but also gained something I've wanted for a long time."

Emily.

The man steps forward. "Welcome to Tate Ranch. My name is John, I'm the Alpha of our pack."

I smile as I extend my hand, ignoring that my stomach has just twisted into a clove hitch. "Thank you, John. Your ranch is gorgeous."

Maria beams, hands tangling in her skirt. "We'd love to show you around."

We collectively look at the sky beyond and the clouds that seem to be getting darker and lower. I even notice John scenting the air surreptitiously. His Were senses are reading how far away the rain is.

"Maybe another time."

Maria's laugh is delighted. She looks back up to her husband. "Did you hear that? They're coming back."

John grunts, shaking his head a little. "Come in, we know you're here to talk."

The inside of the house is just as grand as the outside. There's lots of polished timber and big, chunky furniture. But despite the obvious money, this place says home. The couches look used enough to be comfortable, and the rugs have tracks worn into them from the countless feet that have spent time in here. I grew up with money, but our homes never looked like this.

John and Maria take us to a sunken lounge and gesture for us to take a seat. We both decline the offer of a hot drink. I can feel Seth's tension despite the warm welcome.

I perch on the edge of the sofa, not sure if it's the importance of what I'm asking for, or whether it's because I'm here with the Tate pack. "I'm sure you've heard of the threat to the Glade."

John nods sagely. "Yes. Word has got around."

Maria shifts forward, her round face stamped with sincerity. "We want to help."

I hear some movement behind me and turn to find four people walking in. Some young, some older, they all smile and move to stand behind the Tate Alphas. I glance at John and Maria, but they simply smile at the new additions and turn back to me.

It seems we'll have an audience. I take in a fortifying breath. I'm going to have to get used to talking to more than two people. "Thank you."

John leans forward. "What do you need?"

Three more people filter in, spreading out like a fan on the opposite side of the lounge room.

My hands, clasped in my lap, tense around each other. "Money at this stage. The plan is to win the land at auction."

John absorbs the information for a moment. "And if we win, who will own it?"

He's not the first Alpha to ask this question, and I know I can't afford to pause. "The Prime Alpha pair will."

John thinks even longer on this one. Five more people slide into the room, as quietly and as unobtrusively as you can, considering this is a two-person act playing out in a lounge. "So the Phelans will own it."

"The Prime Alpha represents all Weres."

Maria reaches across and grasps John's hand. I'm not sure what she's trying to communicate, but I hope it helps.

I hear more people at the doorway to the lounge, but they must stop there and wait. They can feel the room is holding its breath. This is obviously a large and a wealthy pack. A pack that had seeds of discontent bloom before their eyes...and those of all

Weres.

John sucks his chin in, which seems to emphasize his pot belly. "I have seen Noah's strength."

I nod. You'd be blind not to. But I also notice the absence of me in that Prime Alpha equation. The human.

"And I respect your courage."

I nod again, wanting to give a sigh of relief, but knowing that wouldn't be smart. Courageous people don't flop back, their breath whooshing out. They just stare solemnly at the Alpha across from them, taking the compliment like it's warranted.

Maria's hand is looking like it's strangling John's. The Weres behind them haven't moved.

John takes a deep breath, his gaze never breaking mine. "The time for Weres is changing. We need uniting. And the Prime Prophecy will do that."

I wonder whether those words were for himself or the pack assembled behind him.

I don't let my held breath out, wanting to grip my pendant, but I don't. "Saving the Glade has united us already. It is showing us what we can achieve when we work together."

John smiles, the big craggy, smile of a happy Alpha. "I look forward to being part of it."

Maria's breath whooshes out like someone just released a valve. The crowd, it looks like twelve people could be standing there, all move as they relax. Their smiles match those of their Alphas'.

Maria stands, looking like her excitement has her needing to move. "I'm going to get us some tea and cakes." And she's gone, despite our earlier polite 'no thanks.'

John watches his wife leave. "You'll have to excuse my mate. Her heart is as big as this ranch."

Seth's smile is gentle. "There's nothing to apologize for. Maria is known for her generosity and love to nurture."

John looks at us, green gaze steady. He opens his mouth, then closes it again. I wait, hoping the desire to say what he's considering wins out. "What happened..."

Without conscious thought, I send out calming vibes. It's obvious this is difficult for him.

"When we discovered it was Daniel who had betrayed Weres, and then when he said everything he did at Council, it broke Maria's heart."

My heart clenches. "She was close to him?"

"She's close to everyone in our pack, it's in her nature. But Daniel was raised on the ranch, his mother was a good friend of Maria's before she passed away when Daniel was a teenager."

The Weres around us shift, one or two murmuring agreement.

"It must have been difficult for her to have him banished."

John's look of assent is grave. "The humiliation merely compounded the loss."

I nod. Words would only diminish that sort of pain.

"The fractures that have been forming amongst Weres first showed in our pack. That is not a badge of honor."

This time there are nods from the pack behind him, some louder murmurs of agreement.

Maria bustles back in, carrying a tray with mugs and little cupcakes. She sits it on the coffee table between us, and Seth doesn't waste any time in reaching for an iced morsel. "Maria is known for her cooking."

She grins. "Beth and I took cooking classes together."

That has me smiling too. It doesn't surprise me that Beth's cooking is legendary. "Well then, let's see if you've picked up any of her skills."

The cupcake is light and sweet and not nearly burnt enough. I smile at Maria. "A little undercooked."

Maria laughs her sweet laugh, looking pleased. "We can't all reach Beth's heights of culinary skill."

With the tension crushed by cupcakes, the rest of the pack

starts to mill around, chatting. Feeling a little like I'm at one of my mother's old cocktail parties, I talk to several Weres. But as I chat, I discover this is nothing like those forced, impersonal gatherings. These are warm, friendly people who are curious about what I stand for.

And I'm happy to stand for the Prime Prophecy.

Seth hasn't been far from my side since we arrived. It makes me wonder what has his radar on alert. The Tates are obviously looking to move forward. As John and Maria approach us, he steps aside, asking them to join him.

I pretend to sip my tea, knowing I'm eavesdropping, but telling myself I need to get a sense of any undertones in this pack.

Seth clears his throat. "John. Maria. I just wanted to say that I'm sorry."

Oh gosh. He's talking about the betrayal with Daniel. Seth knew what Daniel was up to, he was complicit with the desire to expose Weres.

Maria is teary as she grasps Seth's hand. "In the end you made a different choice. That gives me hope." She squeezes it before releasing it. "And you've done your penance."

I swallow. Seth will never again be a Were.

I decide it's time to leave. Everything that needed to be said has been said, and Seth doesn't need to be reminded of this past any longer.

I step in, placing a hand on Seth's arm. "I'm thinking we may want to get moving. It'll probably be slow going with the rain coming in." I turn to John and Maria. "Thank you for your hospitality and support. Your lovely pack has been very welcoming, which is saying something considering how many there are."

John chuckles as Maria beams. "And they're not all here, either. Some of them are out tending fences, including our son, Jared." He glances to the window. "My guess is that they would've worked as quickly as they could to try and beat this weather. They'll be back tonight or tomorrow morning, I'd say."

I'm already heading to the door. "Then I'm sorry I missed them." I smile. "Maybe next time."

Maria's smile amps up to blazing. I think having even the human half of the Prime Alpha give them the tick of approval has meant some sort of redemption.

Out at the truck, Maria and John stand with their pack behind them. The rain which I'd used as an excuse has made sure I'm not a liar. It's a steady downpour around us.

Maria pulls me in for one last hug. I squeeze her back, saying a silent thank you. We've all seen today what unity can mean. I pause when I hear her gasp, quiet but inescapable, beside my ear.

Maria pulls back and I look into her shocked face. Her eyes do the impossible and widen some more.

Oh no. She's scented it.

Frantic, I glance past her to Seth and John, but they didn't hear her sound of shock. Looking back, I know I have to choose my words carefully. "Maria—"

Realization dawns across her rounded face. "Ah, I see."

I hope so, but I can't afford for this to be said out loud. "I haven't…"

Maria smiles as she releases me and steps back. "Then I won't say anything either. But I'm looking forward to when we both do."

I try not to sag with relief, but my shoulders still drop a good inch. "Thanks, Maria."

"Next time."

Actually, I think I'll like coming here with Noah.

The rain is coming down with force, the sound a steady drumroll on the roof above us, as we climb into the car.

Seth mutters beside me. "You doing all the driving isn't good for my image."

I pop the keys into the ignition. "It frees you up to do the royal wave as we leave."

Seth smiles as he waves to the people standing outside. "This is what I've been reduced to."

I'm smiling too as I turn the keys…except nothing happens. There's a click and little else.

I frown and try again. But there's no engine roaring to life. I look at Seth, 'uh oh' stamped all over my face.

Seth glances at the dash. "Did you leave the lights on or something?"

I roll my eyes. "It was daytime when we arrived. We didn't need headlights." But I check anyway when I turn the ignition over a third time and nothing happens. "How are you with cars?"

Seth's look is dry. "I spent my childhood trekking the state with my hippy mother. Anything with four wheels was nothing but a necessary evil."

I stare at the dash like it can give me some answers. Why does this have to happen now?

Maria and John look at me in puzzlement as I climb back out. The only thing genuine about my smile is the embarrassment that powers it. "It won't start."

Seth is already opening the hood and we collectively stare at the shiny metal hulk that sits in there.

John scratches his head. "I'm not so familiar with the newer ones. Give me a John Deere and this would be a different scenario."

Maria shrugs beside him. "If you could bake a soufflé in there maybe I could help."

My stomach sinks incrementally as each potential hero is struck off the list. A small part of me is angry with Alexis for managing to do this to me, even though she's halfway across the state.

I jump in the driver's seat again, knowing it's useless but trying anyway. There's the click of the turning key and nothing else.

I climb out, unsure of what happens next.

"Stay," Maria says. "Our son, Jared, will be back from inspecting the fences tonight, tomorrow morning at the latest. He has a way with cars." She gestures to the multiple buildings behind her. "You can even stay in the guest bungalow if you like. It will give you a little privacy."

I look from the car to the solid wall of rain that isn't far away. This was our last stop, and I hadn't thought of where to go next. Another night in a hotel somewhere from the looks of things. The call of home tugs somewhere deep inside me, but I'm not sure that it's time to go back yet. Maria's reaction as we hugged has shown that my secret isn't going to stay one for much longer.

John nods, agreeing with his wife. "We would be honored for you to spend time with our pack, and Jared will have you on your way first thing in the morning."

To be honest, I don't think we have a lot of options. "That would be wonderful, thank you."

Maria claps with delight. "Yay!" With that, she rushes inside. I suspect more cupcakes are on the menu.

I head to the back door and Seth follows me. His brows are low as he looks at me. His voice is whisper quiet so John can't overhear. "Are you sure this is a good idea?"

I shrug, because I don't have an answer for that one. "What choice do we have?" I whisper back, leaning in to get my bag.

If I can't trust my fellow Weres, who can I trust?

CHAPTER FIFTEEN

THE FIRST THING I NOTICE WHEN I WAKE UP THE NEXT MORNING IS how quiet the Tate ranch is. I've never stayed at one before, but I would have thought that given its size, there would be engines rumbling or cows bellowing or people talking.

But there's nothing.

I roll over in bed, one hand tucked under my cheek, the other wrapped around my middle as I use the brief moment of quiet to calm myself. There's been no word from Noah, and that's starting to make me nervous. We've never been apart like this, so I have no baseline, but I know we'd be talking more often than this. I know my reception has been patchy, and it may have been for him too, but it's still unusual.

Maria's shocked face as we hugged floats in my mind. When one Were knows something it's only a matter of time before many Weres know something. Word of mouth is the communication which keeps the packs connected over such great distances but still keeps their existence secret.

It looks like it's time to go home.

I curl around myself more tightly, happiness starting to sing in my veins. Staying away has been harder than I thought, but

Weres have come together to raise a lot of money for the Glade. It feels good knowing I'm going home with some good news.

And surely Noah is home by now. I wrap my hand around the wolf pendant, gripping it tightly. I'll get to share the words I've been carrying for so long.

I push up and stretch. I can just imagine the happy dance when I tell Seth it's time to go home. His reunion with Emily is going to be a beautiful one.

I dress quickly, noticing that the dizziness has barely been present the past couple of days. Dr. Martinez said that would probably happen, and I'm glad she's right. Fainting in front of any of the Weres we've seen doesn't exactly say Prime Alpha. Especially when they believe you're a run-of-the mill human. It's also meant I can focus on what I need to do…not what I have no idea what to do with.

Next thing I notice is that I'm hungry. I grab a piece of fruit from the bowl that was placed in the room. This ranch says money as much as the places I grew up in. Who has a fruit bowl in their guest bungalow? Heck, who has a guest bungalow?

Seth is coming out of the adjoining room as I head out, dressed and ready like I am. I'm glad he's an early riser like me. Each motel we've stayed at he's been waiting at the truck when I come out.

I pull up a chair in the little kitchenette, wondering when the Tate ranch will start to wake up. Seth rummages around in the cupboards and pulls out a pretty jar crammed full of muesli.

I roll my eyes, smiling. "Of course."

Seth grins as he finds himself a bowl. "I'm pretty sure she makes her own."

Excitement bubbles in my belly. "I have good news."

Seth looks up from the milk he was pouring, looking like I might be Santa and about to make all his wishes come true.

"Yeah?"

But it's a voice from outside who speaks next. "I have a gift for the Prime Alpha."

Seth shoots upright, his eyes wide. Their shocked brown depths come to rest on me. "Don't go out there."

Alarm has the apple feeling like acid in my stomach. "Why?"

Seth looks up at the door, then back at me. "I knew we should have left."

"Why, Seth?" I'm standing now, the anxiety hardening my voice.

"That's Daniel."

What? Shock roots me to the spot. "As in banished Daniel?"

Seth strides to the door but then stops and whirls to face me. "This isn't good, Eden. He's not supposed to be here."

And yet he's openly calling me out. Daniel is looking to start something.

The need to have Noah by my side skyrockets, and the hand that comes to my belly is involuntary. What have I done?

Seth's face hardens. "I'll go out there and see what the bastard wants. You wait here."

Those words have me moving. I stride up to Seth and then straight past him to the door. "We'll both go out there, Seth. It's the Prime Alpha he wants, it's the Prime Alpha he'll get."

I open the door, driven by a courage that I don't feel. I have no idea what I'm about to face.

What I see is certainly not what I expected.

A young male, strong and built like a Were is standing on the paved area before us, legs spread, arms crossed. His face is defined by the grim smile it holds. "Hello...Eden." He holds up a small piece of something then drops it to the ground.

My guess is that's part of my truck's engine.

But it's the small, confused woman next to him who captures my attention. "Emily?"

When Seth repeats her name behind me, it has the same level of surprise, but a strong note of dread. As much as Seth loves

Emily, as much as he's pined to see her, this is not somewhere he'd want her to be.

Emily's eyes widen, her eyes frantically scanning for the one who just said her name. "Seth!"

Seth is around me and rushing toward her before I can draw a breath. They meet halfway across the paved area, bodies instantly melding and arms holding tight. They stay there for long seconds, and you get the sense that something was just righted in their world.

Seth pulls back, hand cupping Emily's face as his thumb strokes her cheek. "What are you doing here?"

Emily's freckled face is soft with adoration. "I missed you." She straightens, like she's just snapped out of a dream. "Oh, and Daniel said you needed my help. Something about a serious injury?"

Daniel huffs a snort of laughter. "That's the plan."

His words send ice down my spine.

Like that was their cue, people start to seep in from around the buildings. They're all Weres, all young and strong, all hostile looking.

Seth pushes Emily behind him, eyes hard as he watches our audience assemble.

"What's going on, Seth?" Emily's voice is full of confusion, underscored by concern.

I step forward. There's no room for fear here. "That's enough, Daniel."

Daniel snorts as he crosses his arms. "You hold no authority here."

One more person joins our tense assembly. Dana comes forward to join Daniel, a smug smile plastered across her face. "Hey, Eden."

My hands clench. "Dana."

"Dad's on his way. He had to look after something, but he's looking forward to saying hi to you too."

I know Dana wants me to bite, to ask what she means by that. But Noah is stronger and faster and smarter than Kurt. I won't buy into her empty threats.

Although I haven't heard from him…

My hands clench and harden, feeling like rocks. I won't let them undermine my faith in Noah. "This is not what Weres are about."

Daniel puffs up, his face contorting. "This is exactly what our strength and power is destined to do."

Seth is moving back, slowly and steadily, ushering Emily with him. Although Daniel and Dana watch, they don't say anything. Tension rises through my chest, clamping around my heart. I don't know what Kurt's band of Weres want, but it's not good.

I look to Dana, although she's Kurt's daughter, my sense is that she's the one I could gain some traction with. "Noah wouldn't want this, Dana."

Dana's eyes flicker but she crosses her arms. "Noah isn't here." Her arms tighten some more, an angry but defensive motion. "And Noah is as weak as his mate. You two don't deserve Prime Alpha."

"Is that what your father said?"

Dana opens her mouth and I know she's going to deny it, but I don't care. Discussing this is better than whatever actions these angry Weres have in mind.

"Enough!" Daniel steps forward, his roar making Dana jump. "Kurt knows exactly what the Prime Prophecy is asking for." There's a murmur of assent from the Weres fanned out behind him. "The last Precept says it all. United is exactly how we're going to conquer those weak, selfish humans."

"No, it's not." I keep my voice level, but loud and strong. "And you're not uniting anyone, Daniel. You're dividing Weres in a way that will only destroy us."

"You don't get to say that. You're one of them."

My hands ball once again. He assumes that means human, but

even though that's not true, it's a secret I cannot share. "And yet I was chosen, what does that tell you, Daniel?" I turn to the red-haired girl beside him. "Dana? What does that say about what the Prime Prophecy is really about?"

There's a rumble amongst the Weres as Dana glances at Daniel.

"Eden!"

Oh god no.

"I've made croissants, with my own butter no less!"

There's a clang as Maria drops the silver tray she was carrying, said croissants falling, hitting the ground and crashing in a spray of pastry.

"Maria, I need you to—"

"What's going on?" She sucks in a sharp breath, shock widening her eyes and slackening her mouth. "Daniel?"

Maria coats that name with everything this pack has been through. Disbelief. Betrayal. Grief.

And something I hadn't considered. Hope.

I want to shut my eyes, hoping that when I open them I won't see what I see next. But I can't afford to, the Weres that want something different are starting to fan out. They have to, because more Weres have just joined them.

It seems Maria brought some of her pack to have a morning chat over her handmade-down-to-the-butter croissants. They form a line behind Daniel and his supporters.

Daniel moves further into the center of the paved area; Seth, Emily, and I in front of him, Maria and her pack members behind him. This is probably how he looked at Council, a strapping young male glorying in taking center stage.

"Hello, Maria." Daniel's voice hasn't changed at seeing his surrogate mother and pack leader, he barely glances at her as he talks. "You've arrived just in time for me to tell Eden what's happening next."

Maria's hand comes up to her throat. "What's going on,

Daniel? You shouldn't be here."

"I follow the true leader, Maria. And he knows that we have the right to move wherever we want. No longer will any Were be banished to obscurity."

Maria swallows, eyes wide and frightened. "Daniel, no..."

But Daniel's already turned away. "So, we came here for more than just a chat." His friends, his pack of mutineers, start to move a little. "And we don't want to disappoint Emily after coming all this way."

Seth seems to inflate beside me as he tucks Emily further behind him. I shift a little closer, knowing I have no powers of strength or speed. I'm a poor protector of the two I have depending on me.

Seth's frown is ferocious as he stares at Daniel. "You won't touch her, you traitorous bastard."

Daniel smiles. "Or what, Seth? You'll beat at me with your fists? Maybe get a kick or two in?"

The derision dripping from Daniel's words show exactly how much of a threat he thinks that is.

"Daniel!" John, although pot-bellied, is tall and gnarly enough to pull off angry Alpha. He strides forward to stand beside Maria, who now has a tear staining her cheek. "You are to leave this ranch at once. Traitors are not welcome here."

The remaining members of the Tate pack flock around their Alpha. Their angry gaze amplifies the words that John just slammed across the space.

Daniel turns and takes in his old Alpha. The man who guided him and led him for most of his life. "I will." He glances back at me, then Seth, then stares straight through him to Emily. "Once I've finished what I've come here to do."

"No," John roars, the confidence and power of an Alpha magnifying the denial. "Whatever you think you're here to do, it's the bidding of greed and selfishness. That makes you no better than humans."

Daniel rears back like he's been punched in the chest. He stares at John for a moment, before turning back to me. "This is what's going to happen."

I take in all the stakeholders who now fill this courtyard. Seth trying to desperately protect frightened Emily. Maria, her heart breaking all over again. John and the Tates. Daniel, determined to see this through. Dana, watching like this is getting bigger than even she predicted. The area around me is shrinking, the stakes raising with each minute.

I shove the fear and the doubts aside, cramming them into a corner of my mind. If Noah were here he would be saying exactly the same thing.

They just wouldn't see him as a vulnerable target. Noah is the Prime Alpha, none of these Weres would consider attacking him. If one drop of their blood were to be shed, they'd turn into what Seth has become—the human they believe I am.

"First, you all," Daniel looks at his old pack, "need to understand something—the Glade that you're all fighting for. Did you know it's Eden's mother that we are protecting it from?"

There's a gasp from the Tates, the other Weres nod in satisfaction, several of them crossing their arms. They all look to me, half waiting for me to deny it, the other half waiting to see me squirm.

I'd step forward if I could, but I refuse to leave Emily, the one who is the most vulnerable in this awful mess. Instead I stand there, pretending my heart isn't hammering with the force of a jackhammer. "It's true." I ignore the startled gasps from the Tates. "But Alexis is one of many who will not succeed because of what Weres have united to achieve. That is how we will win the right to own the place most sacred to us."

Daniel narrows his eyes at me. Take that, you self-serving shifter.

"Us?" Daniel asks. "Us? The Glade is the sacred place of Weres —not humans."

I clench my teeth as Daniel drops his gavel on the clincher of me being chosen to be Prime Alpha. How do I tell these people I'm their leader when I'm not even one of them? "The Prime Prophecy—"

But Daniel has stepped forward. "But you're not just human, are you?"

I snap my mouth shut. Where is he going with this?

Daniel turns to the Tates. "She never mentioned it's her own mother who is attacking our sacred place. But she's also never mentioned who her father is, has she?"

Seth jumps in, saving me in my muted shock. "That's enough, Daniel. Have you ever considered that maybe Weres need to discover their humanity, not shun it?"

The glare Daniel throws at Seth is dark and full of promises. It tells the crowd who he'll be coming after next once he's finished with me.

"The one piece of yourself that you couldn't bring to share with your new pack, Eden. The one truth that your kind has kept a secret from all, is that you are part Fae. In fact, you're the bastard daughter of Avery, King of the Fae."

Shock wipes my mind clear. I stare at this Were, unable to process how he knows this.

The Tates are staring at me in horror. Daniel's Weres are staring at me in disgust and contempt. I don't have the luxury to see how Seth is taking the news, which is probably a good thing. Any sense of betrayal he'd be feeling would stab like a knife.

"It seems the Fae have hidden even deeper than we have. It's what gives her the power to subdue us. She believes she's more powerful than us, than Weres. How could she want what is best for us?"

I look around again, not knowing if I need to defend this or honor what it means. The Fae have so much they could contribute to Weres and humans.

Dana steps forward, her face finally finding an emotion to

settle on. Triumph raises her brows high and tips up her lips. "You've never been one of us and you never will be."

Daniel turns to stare at me, shoulders straight and determined. "This is how it's going to go. We are going to show what the strength of Weres can do. But we won't be shifting until the last moment. Your Fae powers won't save you or your friends."

It's no longer tension banding around my chest. Now fear at the very real threat that Daniel is promising has my chest so tight it hurts. How do I tell him that I never wanted to conquer them? "No, Daniel. This is wrong."

"What are you going to do, Prime Alpha?" He sneers the last two words. "You have no power over us."

Dana tilts her head. "She won't die. We'll make sure she lives to tell the tale."

Not enough air is getting to my lungs. So that the truth of Weres' existence can be leaked. From the lips of a broken, bloodied human.

"The freak on the other hand…"

"Enough!" It's John's voice that slices through the promises of pain that Daniel has thrown down. "You will not spill blood on Tate land, Daniel. This ends now—or do you wish to face your own pack in your aim of hurting innocents?"

In a flash, the Tates shift. Twelve massive wolves, grey and brown and shades of everything in between, line up. Maria, now a dove grey wolf, is no longer the teary wife watching one of her pack turn against her. Like the others, she's a growling mass of animal, ready to stand for what she believes in.

Daniel turns to me and I hold my breath. This is his opportunity to stop this, to avoid the blood that is going to be spilled.

Slowly and deliberately, Daniel smiles. The light in his eyes simultaneously darkens with determination and glows with hunger.

Oh no.

CHAPTER SIXTEEN

DANIEL, DANA AND THEIR CREW REMAIN FACING US, DESPITE THE threat that just exploded behind them. Most of them look unperturbed by the turn of events. One or two look worried, at least one's features match Daniel's—welcoming what is about to come.

The Tates form a semicircle behind and around John. Their growls are low rumbling threats of what will happen if Daniel makes a move.

Seth's emotions are the strongest. His fear is tightly contained in a cage of determination. He's human, but he'll do anything to protect Emily. Emily whimpers, but I don't have the luxury of turning to see what she thinks of everything that's unfolding before her. At least when I saw a Werewolf for the first time, he was there to save me.

Not threatening to kill me.

Daniel stretches his neck and rolls his shoulders like he's about to step into a boxing ring. One move from him and the domino effect will begin. He'll run forward, looking to shift at the last moment, giving me no time to stop him.

But the Tates are only feet behind, waiting, ready to pounce.

Their reflexes are just as sharp, their commitment just as solid. They'll attack a split second after Daniel and his Weres.

But Seth's tight tension and Emily's growing fear are a testament to our odds. If Daniel or the others don't get to us on the first wave, then they will once the bloody battle breaks out. The truth is, Daniel is the closest and the Tates have to get through him to protect us.

And I hate that I need protecting. This is not what the Prime Alpha should need.

Seth moves forward, and I move with him, my hand coming up to rest on his arm. I want to help in the small way I can, in calming the tension that has him in its grips, enabling him to think clearly. I feel his anger, his sense of helplessness, his powerful desire to protect what is important to him. I channel everything I can into our one point of contact, unsure whether he can feel it like Noah does. We're going to need all the courage we can muster.

My whole chest aches with the inevitability of what is about to happen.

Daniel stills, the absence of movement telling me this is about to start. The Tates tense as a pack, a coordinated weapon, waiting for the first move.

Without warning, Seth turns his face to me, eyes wide with a commotion of feeling. I take in his slack jaw and raised brows, confused. Is he unsure of what's about to happen? Is he scared of how this is going to turn out?

He stumbles forward, and my hand tightens on his arm but he slips through as it looks like his body is crumbling.

"Seth!" Emily moves forward, her own safety no longer a concern.

Oh no, he's fainting?

Daniel shifts, like this was the green flag he was waiting for—for someone to collapse under the tension that was at crushing point. John Tate's head lowers, waiting for a crime to be committed so that he can punish it.

But Seth never hits the ground. I'm delivered the final unbelievable surprise when a chocolate-brown wolf explodes onto the pavement.

There's a collective gasp, the motion making everyone pull back a heartbeat. This isn't supposed to be possible!

Seth seems to hold himself there a moment, possibly the most disbelieving of all. His massive broad head looks down at his massive broad feet then back at his massive broad body. His eyes come up to meet mine.

Those canine depths are full of astonishment and wonder.

"Seth?" It's Emily's voice that is full of bewilderment and confusion.

My head is full of all four. I changed Seth back?

Seth looks back at Emily, but it's the next gasp that grabs our attention.

Dana has stepped forward, eyes wide with horror. She looks from the brown wolf who straightens, owning the pride that is swelling through him, to me. Her mouth works but no words come out.

I fill my own chest with a breath of my own, there'll be time to process this later. Now that I have a Were protector, the balance of probabilities just shifted.

"Daniel. This is bigger than you bargained for. End it now."

But it's not my words that have those around Daniel moving a little, their tight little circle of determination loosening. They are all looking at Seth, varying shades of shock shifting across their faces. The Tates straighten, their own wolf eyes wide.

What the Prime Alpha can do was known, it was prophesied. If a drop of blood is spilled, then the Were becomes nothing but human.

But no one knew that the other half of the Prime Alpha could turn them back. We have the power to take but also return.

The Weres around Daniel take another step out and two lift their hands in surrender. Dana watches them do it, her face is a mask of indecision.

I step up beside Seth. "We never considered that uniting Were and Fae is what the Prophecy requires. But this," I rest my hand on his deep-brown fur, "is the power of unity."

Just when I thought Seth couldn't get any taller, he grows another couple of inches beneath my hand. Emily comes to stand on his other side, her body trembling, but there nonetheless.

I look directly at Daniel. "You want a cause? Well, you just got one."

The two with their hands raised step back, moving closer to the Tates. Three others turn to watch them retreat, then join them. Moments pass before the last ones move to stand beside them, now a disjointed group, no longer sure where they fit.

Daniel shifts back to human, and he and Dana stand alone, facing what they were the catalyst for, the Tates still wolves behind them. They've recovered from the shock far quicker than the others and are now waiting to see what Daniel is going to do. I know I need to think quickly before these two predators become the prey.

"Let this go. Go back to Kurt and tell him it's over."

Dana's eyes are shimmering, and despite everything she's put me through, my heart goes out to her. We're all a product of our parents' legacy in some ways. Kurt has sold her nothing but hate, and now she's seeing the power of connection. I'd be confused too.

I'm looking at her when I say my next words. "Tell him you've seen what we can achieve together."

Dana turns, looking at the fragments around her—the Tate wolves, the supporters who have now defected, Seth and his human supporter...Daniel and the stubborn set of his jaw. With her hand over her mouth, she spots a gap amongst the medley and flees as fast as her human legs can take her. Like she's either lost something and is desperate to find it, or hurting that what she thought was real is actually a lie.

I hope it's the latter, because then there will be some hope that this has ended.

Now there's just Daniel left.

His eyes narrow as he looks at me. "Do you think this changes anything?" His arms shoot out wide. "Do you really think that we're the only ones?"

Seth takes a step forward, a low growl rumbling through his body. My hand sinks into his fur and I can feel his need for retribution underlying the anger at Daniel's total lack of remorse. I clench my fingers a little, letting him know we've got this.

"What about when word of this spreads, Daniel? The Prime Alpha pair can take away what makes you Were, but can also give it back. We're not conquerors, but ones who unite."

Daniel's lip curls in disgust. "I will never accept you as our leader. You will never be one of us."

This time, those words don't sting. I don't need to be one of them to show what the Prime Prophecy is about. "No, I'm not. And what you don't understand is that this is a strength." I glance behind him, where John Tate has just shifted to human. "Plus you don't need to be beholden to me. You have an Alpha who you answer to."

I look at the big, burly man who stands there, his chest pumping in and out. Maria shifts next, her eyes sorrowful as she moves close to her mate. The one place this can go wrong now is if John rejects what I've just said. If he has an ounce of belief in what Kurt is peddling, then I am once again alone, a Changeling floundering as she tries to find her place.

John's chin drops to his chest, his eyes dark and grave. "Daniel. You have shamed us twice now. The next full moon will decide your fate. Until then, you will not be leaving Tate Ranch." He glances at the supporters who had followed him. "You will have the opportunity to see the truth, or you will face the same fate."

He indicates for Daniel to walk ahead. His foolish followers join him and they head for the main building. Considering how quickly they abandoned him, I'm hoping they'll see what power should really be about.

Maria glances at me and I nod. She needs to be with her pack.

Seth shifts back to human. He stands there, staring at his hands as he turns them one way then the other. My eyes sting as I take in the wonder that colors his face. This was something he never even wished for because he never thought it was possible.

His head shoots up as someone moves beside him. Emily has taken a step back, her mouth open and slack, her eyes trying to take in Seth and everything that just happened. Seth turns, his face morphing from wonder to worry. He raises his hand, palm open and trembling a little, reaching out to her. Emily looks down at the outstretched offer but doesn't move.

I bite my lip. He's probably scared he's just had one gift given only to lose another.

Emily looks back up, her eyes moist as tears dart down amongst her freckles. "This is why you had to leave?"

Seth's hand remains mid-air as he nods. "It's a sacred secret. And we don't bond with humans."

Emily's gaze darts to me, a million more questions blooming in her confused eyes, before she looks back at Seth. "But…"

Seth swallows. "My ability to shift was taken from me. The moment I was nothing more than human I sought you out. I never wanted to leave."

Emily's lip trembles and the tears are free flowing now. "So what does this mean?"

"I don't know. What Eden just did, it isn't supposed to be possible."

My own eyes sting. I never thought Noah and I would be possible.

Emily is staring at Seth's hand, longing and indecision and swirling mix across her face. I watch as the woman who has been such a strong healer and role model looks like she's crumbling.

Seth's hand raises an inch. "Emily. If I hadn't fallen so hard and fast for you, I would have stopped this long ago. Way before I had to leave. But I did. And as much as losing being a Were hurt, it hurt to lose you more. Please don't let this mean I lose you again."

Emily's gaze slowly and tremulously raises to Seth's. "This is a lot to take in, Seth."

"I know."

"You've kept a lot of secrets from me."

Seth's hand stays where it is. "I know."

"And we don't know where this can go now."

Seth swallows a second time, and this time it looks like it hurts. "I know."

Almost as fast as a Were, Emily bypasses Seth's extended hand and wraps her arms around his shoulders. Seth takes a few seconds to realize he's holding everything he's ever dreamed of in his arms, before his own arms crush around her. He buries his face in her neck, his chest inflating as he draws in a breath.

Emily pulls back, her hands coming up to cup Seth's face. "I love you, Seth. Facing the unknown together is better than what I've already endured alone."

I look away as Seth's face lowers to Emily's. The emotion bursting from these two deserves some privacy.

I turn to find Maria standing beside me. I must've been so caught up in the emotion of Seth and Emily that I didn't even hear her approach.

Maria wipes at the corner of her eye before smiling up at me. "You're breaking down barriers, my dear."

"How is Daniel?"

"Angry." Maria sighs, staring off into the distance. "But he's with his pack now, this is his opportunity to understand what the Prime Prophecy is really about."

I think of Alexis. "Once they've hardened, it seems you can't always soften them again."

Which would mean Noah would have to take away Daniel's right to be a Were.

Maria inclines her head. "With all due respect, your highness, I'm hoping that's not true."

My mouth pops open. Your highness? "Ah, Maria—"

But Maria is already bustling away. "I'm going to pack you some treats for the road."

As Maria leaves, my hand finally comes to rest where it has wanted to from the moment Daniel appeared. It rests across my abdomen, cradling the gentle rise which I've managed to hide. Even after a couple of weeks, this secret is growing faster than I can hide it. It shouldn't be possible, but then again, neither were Noah and I.

I turn back to the bungalow. My truck can be fixed now seeing as it was tampered with to give Daniel and Dana time to arrive. Possibly for Kurt to come and wreak his evil. Well, Dana will find him and is about to show him exactly what he's up against.

At my next thought, my heart lifts. I hadn't been aware of how heavy it had become.

I want to go home.

CHAPTER SEVENTEEN

As I power down the highway, I'm glad Seth chose to drive back with Emily. I remember all the questions I had when the veil had been lifted from what I thought was reality—those two have a lot to talk about.

And I have a lot to think about.

Somehow Weres know of the Fae, and I'm not sure how I feel about that. The secrecy of my heritage had been an issue, that's for sure. But having it as public knowledge among Weres? How do the Fae feel about this?

And Dana would have returned to Kurt by now. Was seeing what both Noah and I are capable of enough to have him quit in his goal? No sense of confidence grows in my gut.

My palm comes to rest on my stomach. The greatest impossibility of all. How is it that I can feel the changes already? What is this going to mean?

When my phone rings I press the answer button before it's had a chance to finish the first trill. I'm desperate to hear Noah's voice.

"Where are you?"

My shoulders sag. "Alexis."

"Yes. It is. And when I have some of your newfound family asking me if I've seen you, then I know something is up. Where are you?"

My hands tense around the steering wheel. This isn't the person I want to be talking to. "Driving."

"They said they haven't heard from you."

I glance at the screen in the dash where Alexis' name glows across it, the one crack slicing through her name. Checking was something I should have done before pressing the little green phone. Was she worried or something? "Well, I'm fine. I'm on my way home now."

"Has there been any more fainting?"

I glance again. Is there a possibility that she knows? "No."

There's a pause, and I wonder if I have the bad manners to hang up.

"That's good news. Where have you been?"

I stare at the road for a few moments, wondering how to answer that, wondering why she's even asking. In fact, there've been only a handful of times my mother has even asked me that question. But there's enough dark matter between Alexis and me without adding lies to it. "Getting money together."

"For what?" Alexis' voice is slow and measured.

"To buy the land."

There's silence, and I'm glad I'm not there to see and feel the icy anger that Alexis is built of. I haven't always survived unscathed the times I've defied her, and this would have to be the biggest roadblock I've ever thrown her way.

"What?"

My foot relaxes on the pedal. Alexis sounds...betrayed. I push back down with determination. "I told you, you can't buy it."

"You'd do this to me?"

I frown. Why does she always make it about her? "I'm not doing anything to you."

"You hate me that much?"

My mouth slackens. "This isn't about you or me. It's bigger than that."

There's silence.

"And I've never said I hate you."

"I...I never saw this coming. After everything I've done for you."

That has the anger flashing up fast and hot. Alexis has never understood what she really gave me throughout those years of icy aloofness. I open my mouth, but her voice is coming through the speakers again.

"After everything I've given."

I try to ignore the lies she's feeding the both of us. "This is important to a lot of people, Alexis."

"Don't you see? No one should feel the way I did after he left. No one." What? I hold my breath, wondering where this is going. "You don't realize the higher it takes you, the further you have to fall."

I glance in the rear vision mirror, taking in the expanse of empty highway as I pull over. Alexis has never spoken of this. She almost sounds like she's talking to herself.

"And the fall is inevitable, I was just as confident that wouldn't be me. It didn't matter that I was young, or that a future was never discussed—he said he felt the same."

This time when my hands clench, so does my heart. "This is different, Alexis. Noah won't leave me. It's part of the reason we need to do what we're doing."

I straighten in my seat, staring out the windshield as a thought strikes me. Could doing this, trying to buy the land, be enough to show her how important this is to me? Would she back out of the bidding?

"Very well. I'll see you at the auction."

Those hard words, encased by ice, are the last ones I hear before the dial tone fills the cab of the truck.

My back gives out and I flop against the seat, my head coming back as I close my eyes. My teeth clench as I beat myself up for hoping. Again. How many times has this woman proven to me what comes first? For all her flashes of insight and vulnerability, whatever made Alexis the way she is, the damage is irreversible. Why can I not see that?

Putting the truck into gear, I pull back out onto the road. I'm heading home, and Noah and I are going to show her exactly what can be achieved when we're unified...not selfishly protecting ourselves.

Noah. My eyes sting and I swallow the longing that has lodged in my chest. I miss my mate.

I need him.

Scrolling through my phone, I find his number. Please, please, answer the phone.

But it goes straight to message bank, just like every other time over the past two days. I dial a new number, knowing it's time to get some answers.

"Eden?" Tara's voice is so full incredulity, I almost smile.

"Hey, bestie. Long time, huh?"

"Oh. My. Great. Galloping. Gobsmacking. Gallivanting. Gumdrops! I hope you're on your way home, girlfriend, because I'm planning on strangling you the minute you walk through that door."

This time I do smile. "I missed you too, and yes, I'm on my way home."

"Do you have any freaking idea what's been going on over here?"

"A bit, but you can fill me in later. I'm hoping to speak to Noah."

"Aren't we all? Don't you think there was a reason I was ringing you every hour, on the hour?"

I frown. "I figured you were trying to pressure me to come home."

"Well, that was it in the beginning."

Tension winds itself at the base of my skull. "What's going on, Tara?"

For the first time in this phone conversation, Tara pauses, and that scares me the most. "Tara?"

"Noah had a lead…"

"Yes, I know."

"Well—"

"Is that Eden?"

The faint note of Mitch's voice weaves from the speakers and spears straight to my heart. "Tara? Is that Mitch? Isn't he supposed to be with Noah?"

"Mitch came home two days ago, Eden. They thought they found Dad, but Mitch got tied up with some guy feeling like he was having a heart attack."

Tara stops and the truck loses momentum. My whole body feels like nothing more than air as I wait to hear what she has to say next.

Dana's words come back to me through the haze. *He had to look after something, but he's looking forward to saying hi to you too…*

"Noah was following him." You don't need Were hearing to hear the tremor in Tara's voice. "We haven't heard from him since yesterday."

PART IV
NOAH

CHAPTER EIGHTEEN

"You know, you're making the wolverine nervous."

I pause. It's darned hard to be full of anxious energy in a space that is only a few feet in diameter. "This is taking too long," I practically growl. Why did this cave have to be so far from civilization? The strongest animal Avery could call was a freaking wolverine!

"You could try moving the boulders again."

I throw Avery a caustic look. Spending the night with Eden's father has been, well, enlightening. I'd always imagined this man to be the love child of Yoda and Gandalf, and although he is definitely all 'wise, I am', I can also see where his daughter gets her spunky streak from.

I flex my shoulders, grateful for rapid Were healing. I've pushed, rammed, and pounded the boulders with every part of my body, both Were and human. All it got me was bruises and scratches and a desperate fear that I won't get there in time.

"You're right, you know." Avery hasn't really moved from the wooden dais in the depths of the cave. "She does need you."

I clench my teeth. *You're not helping, Avery.*

"But not to protect her. You just need to keep doing what you've been doing—believe in her."

I open my mouth to tell him I've already learned that lesson, but with love comes fear. Fear that you'll lose what keeps your heart beating and your chest breathing, but Avery hasn't finished.

"And yourself."

My mouth snaps shut.

"And the Prophecy."

I fall silent.

United we conquer.

I look at Avery across the lamp lit space. "It's bigger than we imagined, isn't it?"

"I suppose it's who you have to unite." He shrugs like it's no big deal. "And what you have to conquer."

I'm about to ask more when a thin shaft of light punctures the dimness we've been living in for twenty-four hours. I squint in disbelief. It worked? It's two steps and I'm at the little break in the wall of brown, confirming that what felt insurmountable has now, indeed, been breached. I reach in, ready to start tearing away at the soil myself when I jump back. A black, dirt-covered nose juts out, sniffing, then jerking back with alarm.

Avery stands, his eyes shut. His face is the exact opposite of how I feel—serene and smiling. "Your scent makes her nervous. It would be better if you stepped back."

You've got to be kidding me.

But I do as I'm told, hoping like hell that the faith I'm putting in this guy is well placed.

A paw, black claws looking disproportionately big, slashes at the soil and the hole steadily widens. More and more fractured light starts to filter in.

I look at Avery. "It's working!"

"Yes. Who would have thought?"

I ignore the sarcasm; the restless impatience is exploding into nervous excitement. I'm coming, Eden!

When the hole becomes big enough to see the whole wolverine, I wish I could hug it. It pokes its head in, gleaming black eyes alert and curious in its furred face.

Avery steps forward, nodding. The wolverine looks at him for several seconds and in the gloom it looks like it almost nods back before disappearing.

Eden's father turns to me. "Shall we go find her?"

I'm already at the hole before he's finished. Scrambling in, the space is just big enough for me to squeeze through, meaning Avery's lean form will be fine. The tunnel is short, only a few feet, but it makes a sharp turn as it navigates around one particularly large boulder. If I'd dug this, there's no way I would have been able to maneuver the obstacle course Mother Nature had created. Well, certainly not in one night.

The lungful of fresh air that I suck in when I reach the other side isn't because I've been cooped up underground for hours. My lungs suck in as much air as they can contain, drawing in the smells and possibilities carried on the wind.

I'm searching for Eden.

The wolverine has brought us out on the side of the hill, the entrance that Kurt caved in is several feet away. Two rocks provide steps and I'm back on solid ground, no chance of being trapped in a rock belly in sight.

There's rustling behind me and I turn to see Avery pulling himself out. But as my eyes adjust to broad daylight, it's not the wide-open space and trees and total lack of obstructions between me and where I want to be that has my focus, it's Avery that I really take in.

The shallow breathing, the skin tinged with grey, and the unmistakable strain that taking those eight steps have caused all tell me that Avery is far more unwell than I'd realized. He straightens and takes a step down to the first rock, only to have his leg give out. I leap up and grab him before he stumbles, then help him down to ground level.

The moment we're there, Avery straightens.

Giving him a moment, I take the time to dust off the dirt that hitched a ride as I pulled myself through the tunnel.

"Thank you."

I look up at him. "No. Thank you."

Chest still working overtime, he smiles. "Don't you have somewhere you need to get to?"

As my heart hungers to find its mate, I pause. I can't leave Avery here, not looking like that.

But Kurt has almost a day on me.

And no-one knows where Eden is.

And I'm the only one who can find her.

I look Avery up and down. He looks weak, but there's an inner strength about him that I recognize from his daughter. "Have you ever ridden a wolf?"

The surprise that bursts across Avery's face gifts me my own little flare of satisfaction. I bet not many people can say they've seen that expression on the King of the Fae's face.

I arch a brow. "Your daughter has developed quite a taste for it."

Avery looks at me, clearly weighing up his options. He's already seen how stubborn I am, and has realized there's nothing that will keep me from going to Eden. It's whether he's realized that I won't leave him behind that could waste precious seconds.

Avery shakes his head as he steps toward me. "Well, I imagine she didn't inherit that from her mother."

I shift and crouch down beside Avery. Slowly he climbs on, and I know I won't be able to run at my usual speed, but I'll take it. Any movement in the right direction is what my heart is crying out for. Avery settles on me and I notice that even though he'd be taller than Eden, he doesn't weigh much more.

As I angle for a gap in the trees, I wonder if the mental connection works with all Fae. *Ready?*

I'd like to see my daughter, thank you.

Apparently, it does.

As I run through the forest to the truck, I send my senses out wide. Eden and I have never had to test how far our personal radar can go, but I do know our connection has only become stronger since our Bonding. The only thing that has kept me sane is the knowledge that if something really serious had happened to Eden, I would know about it even if Kurt launched me to Mars.

I also start to wonder. Eden would have left for a reason, and not the one Mitch suggested. She's stronger than that, we're stronger than that. What has my hackles tingling and chest tightening, is that it would have to be a pretty good reason. Eden has loved the sense of belonging she's discovered with us.

I trust Eden to know it would have to be important, this isn't something she'd do lightly. It's the why that has eluded me.

And the insidious question which has wormed itself into my mind still doesn't have an answer.

Has Kurt figured it out before I have?

CHAPTER NINETEEN

WE'RE IN THE TRUCK WHEN I FIRST CATCH A TENDRIL. IT'S SO fragile, so insubstantial that my foot slackens off the gas. As the truck slows I concentrate.

It's there, faint but undeniable.

Eden.

I accelerate, relief powering everything in me, then anticipation levelling it up again. Beside me, I feel Avery relax, then from the corner of my eye, watch him sink back into the seat. His head leans back, eyes closing, as a small smile tips up the corner of his mouth.

I don't pay attention to where we're going. I don't really care. The location itself isn't important. It's the person who I've haven't seen in too long that is my sole focus.

We've been driving for over forty minutes before someone speaks again.

"Oh, yes." Avery's green eyes gleam.

I can't help the grin. "You feel her too?"

Avery's smile looks like it's inspired by the gorgeous glow of a new dawn. "Yes."

As the feeling gets progressively stronger, the band around

my chest begins to release its crushing hold. I have to make a conscious effort not to tell the speed limit to go to hell. My brain now knows that she's okay and that I'm on my way, but my heart thumps with impatience.

When I see the truck stop that Mitch and I originally pulled into, I turn in.

Avery glances at the dashboard. "We do not need gas."

I'm already pulling into a parking spot when I answer. "No. We don't."

Avery sits up straight, moving faster than should be possible considering his frail body. His eyes scan the empty area out the front of the building. There are no cars. No people. He'd probably look to me next, but I'm not there to know, or to tell him that there's a diesel pump around the back. I'm out of the truck and striding to the building, then when that's not fast enough, I break into a run.

The feeling of closeness, of deep connection, is so strong I can practically grab it like a rope and hand over hand, take myself to her.

I round the corner and my momentum comes crashing to a halt. A lean, lithe, auburn haired girl stops her own determined strides on the other side of the tarmac space. Her forest green eyes widen, then round, then glisten.

Eden.

My mate.

I breathe in as deep and as hard as I can. The scent of wildflowers, so faint but so powerful, threads its way into my heart.

We take each other in across the expanse. Which do I want to do more? Take her in with my eyes or take her into my arms?

My legs propel me forward because the answer is a no brainer. Every inch of my being has been craving the feel of her.

Eden seems to have lost the ability to move, because she's rooted to the spot. It doesn't matter, because I'm with her within a breath, holding her within a blink.

I crush all of her against all of me, hands sinking into her hair, face sinking into the curve of her neck. I worry for a second that I'm being too rough, but then I feel the hold she has on me and I know she's drowning in this moment just as much as I am.

"Noah."

That one word breathes life into my soul and I pull back, hands cupping her face. "God, I missed you."

My lips descend to hers before she can respond. The kiss we lose ourselves in is one of reaffirmation, reunion and reanimation. It tells me that although separation is going to be an inevitable part of life, I'm only a shadow of my soul when I'm not with Eden.

Her lips move beneath mine, reveling in the feeling, rejoicing in the sensation. Her arms wrap around my shoulders, impossibly pulling me closer.

It's that moment that I notice something is different. Her wildflower scent is different, earthier somehow, and then I notice the body that I've memorized is also different. It's subtle...but unmistakable to my Were senses.

I pull back, eyes wide.

Eden's arms stay where they are, her eyes studying my face. She's waiting to see what happens next.

I fall to my knees. My legs give out, literally losing the ability to keep me upright. My gaze settles on the subtle swell that confirms what my Were senses just registered.

I look up, so much emotion jammed into my chest is hurts. "You're...?"

Eden sucks in her lip, eyes moist. Slowly she sinks to her knees too, her beautiful, tentative face coming level with mine. "I'm pregnant, Noah."

I watch as I raise one trembling hand to rest on her stomach, then feel something clench deep inside me as Eden's hand comes to rest over mine. I know I need to talk, say something, but there's no air in my lungs. No words in my head.

Just shock.

No, amazement.

Actually, it's awe.

My gaze comes up to find Eden's, hoping she can sense all this. She has to—she's just prompted another one of the most intense moments of my life. Her tremulous smile, her green eyes pools of moisture and joy, feel like an echo of my own expression.

"We're going to have," I swallow, "a baby?"

Eden nods. "It's why I've been fainting."

"Fainting? As in plural?"

Eden rolls her eyes. "They've stopped now, just like Dr. Martinez said they would."

I glance back down to where my hand hasn't left her stomach. I caress it, reverence and trepidation tingling through my fingers. This is big. Really big. "But how? I thought you... We were using contraception."

Eden shrugs. "It seems the Prophecy had other ideas."

That snaps me back to reality. "That seems to be the theme of the past few days."

Eden's hand comes up to caress my cheek, leaving a trail of warmth across my skin. "I'm glad we're both back."

I grin, the happiness that just multiplied exponentially powering my smile. "I know that feeling."

"I have a lot to tell you." She glances down. "Apart from this."

"Me too." I wonder if her words are just as much an under-statement. "But first, I have someone for you to meet."

Puzzlement crinkles Eden's brow. She looks past me, beyond the bubble our reunion had created, glancing around. Grasping her hand, I pull her around the corner. I watch her face as her eyes settle on my truck, then zoom in through the windshield.

Her wide, forest green gaze flies back to mine. I watch and wait, allowing her time to process this.

"It's him?" she whispers.

I nod. "It's him."

Eden visibly swallows and her hand tightens around mine. I give it a squeeze and then wait. It's up to her how this goes. If she wants to turn around and drive off, I'd totally understand.

But Eden takes a step and then another. We walk side by side to my truck.

Avery is watching us intently as he climbs out, eyes looking like they're memorizing every inch of the girl approaching him. Eden stops a few feet away, studying him right back but giving nothing away.

"Hello, daughter."

"Ah...hi."

I suppose it's a start. I wonder if Avery, in all his watching and spying, noticed that the use of names in the family he created isn't something done lightly. Avery is going to have to earn the title of 'father.'

Avery's hand is gripping the open door and I narrow my eyes. Standing up for this long is hard work for him. "Eden..."

That has my mouth twitching. The great King of the Fae is at a loss for words.

Eden shifts her weight, a small frown twitches and then is gone. "Why now?"

I watch and wait, admiring my girl for her honesty and calling it what it is.

Avery seems to contemplate the question. He'd better give an honest answer, too. If he gives one of the cryptic remarks that Orin seems to favor, something like 'it was time,' my guess is Eden will turn around and walk away.

He sighs, glances at me, then back at his daughter. "I wish to do things differently."

Eden chews on her lip and I can sense the churn of emotion inside. This is the man who left her to be raised by an abandoned, bitter woman. This is her father. I feel her tense. This is the father who she just registered is sick.

She looks up at me, and I wait, letting her know that I'd understand whichever decision she makes. Her hand comes up to rest protectively on her stomach and I lose myself in her eyes for a second. This brave girl is carrying our future in more ways than one. This decision deserves some time.

She turns back to Avery. "It's together that we move forward."

Avery's smile is slow but sure. He nods, his forest green eyes full of pride.

I wrap my arm around Eden's shoulder. "That's something we talked about, wasn't it buddy?"

Eden looks up at me, brows tilted quizzically. "Did you just call him buddy?"

I grin and wink. "It gets his goat a bit, which is mostly why I do it."

She opens her mouth, but another voice cuts across. "Hey, are you gonna pay for your gas?"

We turn to find Willow standing in the doorway. Even across the lot her features are plain to see, including the tilted eyes that Eden always thought were hers alone.

I glance over at Avery, but he doesn't seem surprised to see this Changeling, which is what I would have guessed. The Fae probably secretly follow all of their offspring.

Eden is a different matter, though. She's staring at Willow and staring hard. I lean over and whisper, "We met another one in Bowerman."

Her startled gaze flies to mine. She looks like this is more of a shock than meeting her father, but then again, she knew he existed. "I suppose it makes sense that there are more of us." She turns to Avery. "Do you know her?"

"I have not met her directly, but I have been here before."

Oh yes, silently following his daughter and her mother.

Eden nods before turning to the building. Willow sees that we're coming and heads inside.

Eden brushes her fingers over the potted jungle that Willow has built around the entrance. I thought she'd appreciate it.

Inside, Willow's smile is apologetic. "Sorry, I didn't mean to interrupt anything."

Eden smiles back, not in the least bit surprised to see an owl hunkered down behind Willow. "I just met my dad for the first time."

Willow's jaw drops open. She glances past us to my truck outside. "Really?"

"Yeah. Really."

Willow leans back again, shaking her head. "I've never met my real dad. I mean, my step-dad's a great guy and everything, he recently lost his job so he's working for his brother as a second-hand car dealer just to make sure we're okay. But you always wonder, you know?"

Eden's smile softens. "I do. I know exactly what you mean."

I hand over the cash, and I sense Eden's gratitude. I'd be distracted too.

Willow pushes up her glasses. "How was it?"

Eden bites her lip. "Discombobulating."

I can't help a chuckle as Willow smiles. She hands me my change. "I hope it works out."

With a thanks, Eden and I head to the front door. At the last moment, she turns back. "Willow?"

Willow looks up, eyebrows raised in question.

Eden pauses, but must make a decision. "It wasn't about you. He left because he hadn't figured out what was really important."

Willow frowns and opens her mouth. But when she can't seem to find any words, she shuts it again. The owl stretches its wings and leaps onto her shoulder, nuzzling her cheek. Her smile is almost involuntary as she strokes him back.

Willow looks at us as we stand in the doorway. "That seems to take some people longer than others."

I glance at Eden as she nods. Wisdom seems to be part of Fae DNA.

We step outside and I pause, the first sense of disappointment since I arrived pricking at my chest. We now have to drive back in our separate cars.

Eden stops beside me. "Oh, I was looking forward to…"

Talking. Touching. Realizing that being apart was what needed to happen, but deciding we're never doing that again. I squeeze her hand. "Me too."

All of a sudden, her face lights up. "Wait here."

Eden spins around, her mahogany hair furling out like a sail as she heads back inside. My Were hearing picks up her next words.

"Willow, did you say that your step-dad is a second-hand car dealer?"

CHAPTER TWENTY

THE DRIVE HOME STARTS OFF SILENTLY. I THINK WE'RE BOTH conscious that Avery is sitting in the backseat after he insisted on it, and I sure as heck don't know what to say in this type of situation. So much has happened, but the dad who Eden has never met is in the car with us. There's so much to say, and no idea where to start.

But the awesome thing is that Eden and I don't need words. She tucks in close and curls around me as we settle for the drive, our connection doing all the talking. The love we've been carrying, held tight for when we're back together now flows freely, giving and receiving and recharging. This must be the plus side of being separated—the backlog of emotion that you get to revel in. Although it's not too long before I'm wishing we're anywhere but on a highway heading home to one mother of a talk. Looking and holding hands has never been enough when it comes to Eden.

Soon though, a sound fills the cab. Avery's rattly breathing rasps across the small space and we both turn back to look at him, only to find him asleep. Pale skin almost translucent as his head lolls to the side, the King of the Fae is looking less and less regal every day.

"He's pretty sick, isn't he?" Eden keeps her voice low as she turns back to me.

I sigh. "He hasn't said as much, but yeah, it looks like it."

"How did you find him?"

I rub my thumb over her palm as I watch the road. "Well, I was following Kurt, who it seems was following Avery."

Eden leans back into the seat a little. "That's how Daniel and Dana knew."

My eyes pop open. "Daniel and Dana?"

Eden smiles. "Who wants to start first?"

We spend the next forty minutes catching up on our little excursions. I'm not sure who has more to digest.

Kurt knows of the Fae.

The Glade is for sale.

Changelings are dotted around the country.

Eden turned Seth back to Were.

Avery has been following her all her life.

Eden is pregnant.

That final bombshell which still needs to be processed detonates just as we turn onto the drive. I slow as I approach the house. Avery has stayed asleep the whole trip home, only confirming how much everything is taking its toll on him. My family is inside waiting for us seeing as Eden texted Tara to let us know we're on our way.

But I want just a few minutes alone with my girl before the decisions we're going to face come at us.

As I stop the car in the driveway I turn to Eden. Nothing has changed and yet everything is moving, shifting, going who knows where.

Her eyes shine as that sweet smile of hers tips up. "Grandfather Douglas?"

I grin. Man, I love this girl.

We slip out of the truck, not bothering to shut the doors so we don't wake Avery. Sneaking out like two teens who don't have a Prophecy hanging over their heads, we head straight to the ancient pine that has born witness to so many of our moments.

Grandfather Douglas' branches wrap us up in shade as we find each other again. This time the kiss isn't about hello, it's about 'no matter what, we're in this together.' Pretty soon it's about 'we've been apart too long and man, this passion burns hot!'.

Mouths roam as hands seek, hearts reconnect as souls meld. The passion that we've barely had time to lose ourselves in explodes. Eden's hands are in my hair as my own skim down her back. I pull her in close, knowing how high this can go and getting ready to leap. But as all of her molds to all of me like two perfect halves, I feel the difference. My body and mind have memorized every inch of this girl, and they notice that there's something new. Eden's belly pushes gently into mine in a way it never has.

My heart soars as something even stronger than passion propels it. Eden is carrying my child.

I pull back and rest my forehead on hers. Our breathing matches the other, a little fast, a lot excited.

"Do you think it's a boy or a girl?"

Eden's eyes widen. "I don't know. I haven't let myself think about this, not until we've spoken. We never planned this, Noah." She glances down at her stomach, like it's hitting her for the first time too.

I arch a brow. "Story of our life, huh?"

Despite the curveballs that the Prophecy has thrown at us, Eden smiles. "It sure is."

"Well, we've spoken. Boy or a girl?"

Eden's hands come up to the gentle swell as she looks down. "Maybe a boy, blond and determined like his father?"

My hands cover hers. "Or a girl, green eyed and brave like her mother."

Eden twines her fingers through mine. "A child who will be loved and surrounded by family."

This kiss is gentle, two sets of lips full of promise. We pull back and simply hold each other, our excitement and wonder shifting beneath the canopy.

I know we're not supposed to feel like this. We're eighteen, for Pete's sake. We have years of college ahead of us and life's countless secrets and responsibilities.

But those numbers don't matter. Nothing like that has from the beginning.

From the moment we met in the hall and she ran. To the moment when she was almost attacked and I finally changed. To discovering she's the Changeling daughter of the King of the Fae. To discovering the Prophecy and the greed that wants it all. To our Bonding and now our child.

Our paths have been destined by a Prophecy that we keep thinking we understand, only to find out we really don't.

And as scary as that is, it's given me something that I never want to lose.

It's given me Eden.

She pulls back a little, placing a butterfly kiss on my chin. "Shall we go in?"

"I suppose so." I agree as I release her. There's a lot that needs to be discussed. "We have to introduce your dad to my dad."

Eden blinks. "This is going to be interesting."

We head back to the truck to find Avery awake and waiting. He's standing by the car, that serene Fae expression pasted on his face.

"That sleep looks like it did you well." Eden voices what I notice. Avery looks like he has more color to his face, maybe even standing a little straighter.

"Being here is healing."

Flashes of little Hazel fly through my mind. My theory that Fae need nature to be well is gaining more traction. "Good thing, because you're about to meet my family."

Avery nods, that serene look staying put. "I look forward to it."

Eden opens her mouth like she's going to say more, and I pause. She's barely spoken to her father, which I get. Where do you start? How will it end? But instead she turns and heads to the house. I glance at Avery before I follow. His serene face looks like it just got punched by the hand of regret.

The moment we open the door and step in, Typhoon Tara engulfs us. Although my hug is hard but short, there's enough time for me to register how much her belly has grown. It makes me realize that Eden will probably follow the same trajectory seeing as our child carries Were blood. My next thought surprises me as I realize how fast her body has changed in just a few days. Holy heck—or will it be quicker?

Tara moves onto Eden, squealing somewhere in the eardrum-bursting range. She pulls Eden in, jumping up and down, her bouncing belly looking just as jolly as her. But it all stops in a second as she gasps and pulls back, looking at Eden in shock. "Holy shit."

"Tara!" My mother's horrified voice is sucked in on her own gasp. She just realized why Tara probably used her first curse word ever.

Mom's hand flies to her mouth as her eyes well up. "You're...?"

Eden nods, smiling although I can feel her uncertainty. She's about to find out how many times my mother hinted to me at how ready she is to raise a house full of Weres again.

It's Mom's turn to squeal as she pulls Eden in for a hug, then pulls back, then brings her back in. "I'm going to be a double grandmother!"

Mitch's gaze grabs mine and I let him absorb how I feel about this. I remember his pride when we discovered Tara was pregnant. I'm pretty sure that same expression is now permanently stamped on my face. Mitch nods just once. Gotta love the twin bond.

Dad looks like he's going to burst a chest balloon or something. In that moment, I realize that Avery probably didn't know either. I turn to the man beside me to find his serene expression wiped off his face.

"My daughter is with child?"

My child. "Yes."

I could be wrong, but I'd swear that Avery's eyes fill with moisture. He swallows, those Fae eyes of his on no one other than his daughter. "This is a good thing, Noah."

I nod at the understatement. "It sure is."

As I watch the moving mass of love surrounding Eden, one that includes a German Shepherd and a Labrador bouncing like basketballs, I realize why she went away. We just saw what she would have known—you can't hide a pregnancy from Weres. But she also knew this changes everything, and with my impromptu solo trip, she decided to take this game-changer out of the equation. She knew I would have come rushing back.

My brave, self-sacrificing mate.

Mom seems to be having trouble letting Eden go. She keeps drawing her in for another tearful hug. I incline my head toward Avery. "She's well loved."

He glances at me, and yep, his eyes are definitely moist. "I can see that." He looks back as Tara turns to stand beside Eden, comparing the size of their bellies. "It warms my heart."

I nod again, no longer feeling the resentment I did at Avery leaving Eden. I'm not sure if it's because he's sick or because Eden now lives with more love than she knows what to do with. Maybe it's because Avery thought he was doing the right thing, and I'm starting to understand how easy that is to assume.

Mom smiles when she sees Avery standing beside me. "I see you've brought a—" Her mouth sags open, now too slack to form words. She looks from Avery to Eden and then back again, taking in the similarities. "Well then."

Dad is much quicker to recover. He steps forward, hand outstretched. "Welcome. My name is Adam Phelan. Any, ah, friend of Eden's is welcome here."

Avery smiles that Fae smile of his as he returns the handshake. "It is a pleasure and a privilege to meet the Phelan Alpha."

Dad's brows shoot up, but he takes it well. It's plausible that Eden has told Avery of the existence of Weres.

"I am Avery, King of the Fae. I thank you for your care of my daughter."

Dad's brows power back down. His frowning face seeks mine and I freeze. I've kept a secret from my father, from most of my pack. I wish I could tell him how much I wanted to share this revelation with him.

Dad's hand comes up to stroke his bottom lip. "It seems you've had to make some decisions as the Prime Alpha."

I arch a you-have-no-idea brow. "A guy told me once that a leader has to make some tough choices." I shrug a little. "I decided to listen seeing as he's my role model."

Dad grunts as he fights a smile. "You get your smarts from your mother's side."

I grin. "And my good looks."

Dad rolls his eyes before turning back to Avery. His face turns serious again. "I'm thinking we need to talk."

Avery nods. "I agree. Your son has made me realize the importance of your kind and mine working together."

Eden comes back to my side, the pride in her smile making my heart swell. At least she's almost as impressed with me as I am with her. I grasp her hand and I can't help myself, I drop a quick kiss on her lips.

I turn to the people around us. "I think we all need to do a little planning."

Mom claps her hands. "And I just baked some chocolate chip biscuits too."

We all look away except for Avery. "Sounds wonderful."

Poor dude. Oh well, partaking of my mother's cooking is kind of a rite of passage for anyone entering this house. "Let's move to the dining room."

We all move through and take a seat. I look around, liking how the space is filling and the number of people growing. Our pack is expanding in ways I could never have imagined.

Dad leans forward, his arms crossed on the table. "Although there's a lot going on right now, I think the Glade being sold is first in the order of proceedings."

Tara frowns. "The Prime Prophecy won't be anything if the Glade is lost."

Eden shifts forward in her seat. "Maybe fighting for the Glade is what the Prime Prophecy is all about."

I'm there beside her in a second, excited that we've barely spoken about this and yet we're on the same page. "Exactly. Maybe Were and Fae working together is what United We Conquer really means."

Dad is rubbing his lower lip again. "This is about more than just Weres."

Eden and I glance at each other before looking back at our families. "Yes," we say in unison.

Everyone digests this. Avery is the one who looks least surprised, but then again, he knew Weres existed. We never knew that Fae were around, let alone what their existence could mean.

Mitch nods like he's reached a conclusion. "So we need to win the Glade at auction."

Eden frowns. "Alexis knows that she has competition."

"The Fae will provide their support, financial and in any other way we can."

Eden looks at her father, startled. "Thank you."

Avery holds her gaze as he nods. It might be just me, but I think he's telling his daughter she has any support she needs.

Eden swallows and looks away. Tara looks at me, brow furrowed just enough to tell me she noticed it too. I try to send her 'patience, grasshopper' vibes. Eden will get there.

Mitch looks at us both. "How much have you raised?"

I look at Eden. Whilst I brought the Fae contingent to the table, this is what she's been busy with the past few days.

"Well, with the sale of the truck, we're at over seven hundred thousand dollars."

Mitch lets out a low whistle as Tara lets out a whoop and punches the air. "We're gonna own this thing." She grins at us all. "Quite literally."

I squeeze Eden's hand. "That's the plan."

Dad nods. "Okay. So with Were and Fae working together, we'll conquer the threat to the Glade."

Avery copies the action. "United in a way we have never been, we will create a strength we have never known."

I feel the hope pouring from Eden and realize that the feeling is even bigger than the two of us. It fills the room and lights up every face around us. For the first time since the final Precept arrived, I feel like we're getting a handle on what we need to do.

And that we're going to be able to achieve it.

Dad's phone rings and he glances at the screen, frowning. He's probably on call and not happy that our talk has to be cut short. He stands so he can take it in the lounge, turning to Avery in the doorway. "I'd love to sit down and learn more about the Fae."

Avery nods and smiles. "That's why I'm here."

Dad disappears into the next room and Avery's smile fades. His face tenses as a round of coughs shakes his body.

Eden stands. "First thing in the morning, I think."

Mom is up with her. "Good thing we always have the guest

room set up. You just never know when a friendly face is going to stop by."

Avery puts his hands up in objection. "No need, I have family in the area."

Oh yes, Orin. What is Mister Statue going to say about all of this? Is he even back?

But Mom is already bustling. "No problem at all. This way we can finish our plans in the morning. We have money to raise and supernatural beings to unite."

Mom disappears down the hall as Avery watches her, eyebrows raised. It seems Avery just learned not even a king can win against the force that is my mother.

Avery looks at Eden, obviously checking how the one person who has yet to welcome him feels about this.

Eden's hand tenses in mine and I wonder if I should offer to drive Avery to Orin's. I don't get a chance because Eden moves away from the table.

"I'll give Beth a hand."

My eye catches Tara's, telling her I-told-you-so across the table. She sits back, her hand rubbing her belly, satisfaction spreading across her face. I almost sag with relief. Tara-the-Meddler has been appeased.

Before Eden can leave, Dad is back, and he has his serious face on as he looks at us. "That was Joe from the land titles office. I asked him to keep me up to date about the land sale."

There's no way a phone call from Joe at this time of the afternoon can be a good thing. "And?"

"They're moving the auction forward."

Mitch's chair scrapes back as he shoots up. "What? They can't do that."

"From the sounds of things, it wasn't done above board. He wanted me to know but has sworn me to secrecy."

Eden gasps. "Alexis knows she has competition."

My mouth thins. She's also worked in this industry long

enough to know who she can persuade with her bucket of money.

Eden is very still beside me as I ask the question I don't really want to ask. "How long have we got?"

Dad's hand looks like it's about to crush his phone. "The auction is in three days time."

CHAPTER TWENTY-ONE

THREE DAYS WASN'T LONG ENOUGH TO CONTACT AS MANY WERES and Fae as we'd like. Our pot of money has grown, but that sense of confidence that we've got this evaporated the moment Dad told us of our new deadline.

We've all worked hard, everyone's phone dialing overtime. There isn't a Were pack who hasn't heard of what's happening, that hasn't been willing to help.

The Fae have done their bit, although it seems they generally don't have a lot of money. Like Avery, they spend all their resources on the planet they are so deeply connected to. It seems if there's a piece of land which can be used to connect people to Mother Earth, the Fae have been the ones to make it happen. Avery has his sanctuary, one guy has established a community garden, while another Fae woman has created an education center for recycling. They've contributed what they can, and although it isn't much, it means we've come to this auction with just over a million dollars.

In the dark space of my room, our hands and bodies entwined, Eden and I acknowledged that Alexis has the advantage. Her connections are all human, and humans have the power of numbers and influence. It's just that they are the least likely to care what this land could mean to someone else.

But time does what it always does, and seeing as it doesn't wait for man, it certainly hasn't waited for Were or Fae. As we arrive at the auction I see that Alexis' car is already here even though we're early.

We sit in our car—there seems to be an unspoken agreement that we don't need to rush out. We registered to bid two days ago, including providing proof that two young adults had the dough to be bidding on this land.

I stare out the windscreen, it doesn't look like many people are here, which is a good thing. "I can't believe how much you've done in just a few days. When we win this auction, it'll be because of the money you raised."

Eden's hand covers mine. "And yet it was you who found the other half of this puzzle. We wouldn't have the extra money we do without the Fae."

I can't help but smile. "It seems we make a good team."

"It appears so." The smile that graced Eden's face settles as she looks at me. "Thank you for bringing me my father."

"Did you speak this morning?"

Eden shakes her head. "He was already gone. He's looking stronger and stronger every day. Being here has been just what he needed."

"Or maybe it's being with his daughter."

Eden glances away and when she looks back her green eyes are a whirlpool of conflicted emotions. "He told me about Alexis, and how she used to be."

I nod. "She must've been a very different person."

"He also said he realizes the Fae have been doing things wrong. It's working together that brings change."

"United we conquer, huh?"

Eden smiles. "Pretty much."

Holding her hand, I sense her sadness. Is it grief at time lost with Avery, at the mother Alexis could have been, or at the fractures that no-one knows how to heal? "What are you going to do?"

"After everything that's happened, I'm mostly sad that he has regrets. I get why he did it." This time Eden's smile is tremulous. It makes my heart tremble in a way that almost hurts. "I'm looking forward to talking to him, to telling him it's okay."

I angle across and kiss this brave girl. As is her tendency, she's left me speechless again. When I lean back, I figure it's time to lighten the mood. The seriousness we've been carrying lately can't be healthy. "To be honest, when I went on my field trip, I was just looking to find out what Kurt's been up to."

Eden rolls her eyes. "Well, Dana would have told him what she saw."

Changing Seth back to Were. Another wonder of the world that makes Eden. "Well, he's found out that even when we're apart you don't mess with the Prime Alpha. This Prophecy is bigger than any of us imagined."

"Let's hope he's realized this is a fight he's not supposed to win."

I glance at my watch; it's time. I lean into Eden, keeping my voice low. "Ready to own the most sacred space to all Weres?"

Eden's smile is resolute. "We can't afford to lose, can we?"

We climb out and meet at the front of the truck, hands entwining and hearts thumping. Armed with the knowledge that we've raised a formidable amount of money, we move forward.

The auction is being held in the clearing where James tried to buy this all last time. The land has lain fallow since it all went pear shaped. The Glade is tucked not far away; a sacred haven the humans here know nothing about.

And yet are wanting to own.

When I see another car pull up, I'm glad we talked the others out of coming. The more this looks like a low-key auction the better. A bunch of tense Weres wouldn't help, no matter how much they want to be here. As two people climb out of the car I realize Seth obviously didn't get the memo. Or he ignored it.

He approaches us, face taut with the seriousness of what this auction means. The moment he reaches us he engulfs Eden in a hug. Eden holds him tight for a moment before releasing him. She knows just like I do that this is where his mother died last time we were protecting this land.

They pull back and Seth comes forward to shake my hand. "I had to come. I need to know that it wasn't for nothing."

I nod, there are so many reasons it's bloody important that we win this auction. "I understand."

Emily looks at us both. "I just wanted you to know, I won't ever speak a word to anyone."

Eden pulls her in for a hug too. "Thanks, Em. Believe me, I know it's a lot to take in."

Emily's look is wry. "It all kind of makes sense now. Including how good you were with all those cranky cats."

Which shows where we're at. Fae are no longer the world's best kept secret. I nod at Emily. And Weres are no longer unknown to humans. I have no idea what that could mean.

A movement catches my eye and I turn to see Alexis and James walking toward us. Grabbing Eden's hand we smile a goodbye to Seth and Emily. Securing the Glade is going to have to come first.

Alexis is dressed in some sort of power suit which seems to match James' outfit. It curls my stomach to see them coming at us all dressed to kill.

Alexis' eyes are steady as she takes us both in. "I didn't think you'd actually go through with this."

Eden's gaze narrows. "I told you this was important to us."

James pulls up a jovial smile, like we're at some cocktail party somewhere. "Are you sure you don't want to change your mind? We actually hoped this would be a peace offering of sorts."

I have to hold my eyebrows down. Alexis was trying to throw

out some sort of olive branch? "The best thing you could do is step down so this doesn't have to happen."

James is already shaking his head. "We have too much invested in this to do that." He looks at Eden. "This was Alexis' way of ensuring she didn't have to move again."

This time I have to hold my jaw up. Alexis was definitely looking to build some bridges.

But by being stubborn she could be doing the most damage she's ever done.

All of a sudden, an alien tinkling sound creeps in amongst the tension and James pulls his phone out. He looks at the screen and then at Alexis. "Our last minute investor." She nods and he takes a few steps to the side.

I can feel Eden's anger building, so it doesn't surprise me when her next words fly out. "I've met my father."

Alexis gasps, her whole body recoiling. "You're lying."

"You know I'm not. My guess is you knew he'd come back at some stage. He loved me too much."

Alexis looks like she's been slapped. I open my mouth, wondering if this is the time for all this history to spill out, but Alexis is recovering. Her face looks like a storm has just exploded across it.

"Yes, he did," she hisses. "And look where that got you." Her lip curls, the red lipstick now a twisted arc across her face. "And me."

Eden pulls back, and I feel her reign in the hurt and the anger. "Maybe the loss was worth the gain in the end."

"I couldn't understand why you can't let this go," Alexis seethes. "But now I do. You want to hurt me for what you think I've done."

James returns, holding out the phone to Alexis. "He wants to speak to you."

You can almost see the ice pouring down Alexis' body. She straightens, face composing as she turns and takes the cell phone.

Without looking at us she pushes it to her ear and walks away, her back straighter and more inflexible than ever.

I lift my hand to massage Eden's neck. Her frustration is palpable, and I try to work some of it out of her muscles. I never actually hoped that Alexis would back down, that would have been stupid—I just never considered she'd become even more determined. Not that it changes anything. We came here to buy the Glade, no matter how she feels about it.

Alexis speaks calmly into the phone, even smiling once or twice. Just like that, the ice queen is wheeling and dealing again. With a hard smile she hangs up, looking at James. She nods and he winks.

The auctioneer clears his throat and everyone stills. Everything feels tight in my chest. It's show time.

"We have a fabulous opportunity here, folks, just looking for the right developer."

My teeth ram down.

"Acres of pristine pine forest easily accessible to nearby towns. This land has the potential to be a central place for many a soul seeking what Mother Nature has to offer."

My jaw is starting to ache. I want to shout that it already is.

"Shall we start the bidding at four hundred thousand?"

The tightness loosens. That's lower than we were hoping. Eden and I stand still. We've discussed our tactic—wait and see what we're up against.

From what I can see there are about five interested parties. My guess is that along with the power to change the date of the auction, Alexis and James made sure this wasn't a widely publicized sale. That's fine by me, having less competition works in our favor too.

A middle-aged man raises his hand, nodding at the auctioneer.

"Wonderful. Do we have four-fifty? Anyone? Four-fifty?"

This time a red-haired woman raises her hand. An older

looking male behind her takes a step back. Probably some guy looking to see if he could grab a bargain. Well, he's underestimated what this lands means.

The auctioneer is warming up now. "Five hundred, folks. Who's willing to bid five hundred?"

The middle-aged man raises his hand again. The red-haired woman crosses her arms. I feel Eden shift beside me and I glance at her. Two down.

"Five-fifty."

This time Alexis raises her hand. Eden's eyes narrow. Her mother has jumped in the fray.

"Five-fifty to the lady that looks like she means business. Six hundred, do we have six hundred?"

The middle-aged man lifts his hand again, although this time he's not so quick or looking quite so sure.

"Six hundred thousand, thank you, sir." The auctioneer is sounding a little excited, which isn't a good thing.

Alexis raises her hand like some bored queen.

"And we're at six-fifty!" The auctioneer looks to the man, who wavers for a moment, then shakes his head.

I can feel Eden's hope rising. That's the only other serious bidder out.

"Six-fifty folks. A great price for a great piece of heaven. Surely we can do better."

Raising my hand like I know what I'm doing, I call out. "Seven hundred."

The auctioneer smiles. "Seven hundred from the young man with a mission. Do we have seven-fifty?"

Alexis has her I-sucked-a-lemon face on. "Seven-fifty."

The auctioneer turns straight back to me. Eden doesn't miss a beat. "Eight hundred thousand."

Alexis goes from sour to stormy. "Eight-fifty."

Tension twines between us. We're getting close to our maximum. "Nine hundred," I call.

Alexis pauses, and I hold my breath. James steps beside her. "Nine-fifty."

The tension dial turns up another notch. We can't let Alexis know this is our last bid, all we can do is hope that our last call is more than she's willing to pay.

"One million dollars." Eden's voice is sure, telling her mother we're not backing down.

Alexis' eyes narrow as she takes us in. She hadn't banked on our determination. She underestimated how far we'd go.

Without breaking the gaze she has locked on us, Alexis raises her hand. "One point two."

There's a gasp, maybe the red-headed lady, but I'm not sure. Eden's shock slams through me at the same time mine does.

"No," she breathes.

"One point two million, folks." The auctioneer is practically crowing. "And worth every penny too." He looks at us, two teens, clearly not expecting us to keep going. "Do we have one point three?"

My hands ball up. There's no way I'm letting Alexis win this.

I turn to Eden, knowing I don't have much time. "Dad said he'd put the house up for sale."

Her eyes widen. "What?"

"I know, it's a big ask. But this is important." Eden studies me for precious seconds. She knows we don't have a choice.

I raise my hand. "One point five."

The auctioneer looks like he's dancing the dance of the rich in his head. "One point five million," he practically shouts. He turns to Alexis, looking to see if that was the final nail in this godawful coffin.

Alexis glares at us as James leans in to say something in her ear. She doesn't acknowledge what he whispers, in fact, she seems determined to cut us down with her grey gaze. Eden's hand squeezes mine and the sensation of victory tingles between us. Alexis turns back to the auctioneer.

"Two million dollars." Alexis' voice is loud and hard, her words falling like a guillotine.

The auctioneer blinks, but being the professional he is, quickly recovers. "Two million dollars." He looks around. "Do we have anyone else?"

He knows his question is rhetorical. No one has the capacity to beat that.

Breathless, painful seconds pan out as the silence of defeat fills the air around us.

"Going once."

I draw in air through my tight throat.

"Going twice."

It catches, wanting to gain voice, but knowing it can't.

"Sold, to the lovely business woman who is now the proud owner of this parcel of potential."

The knowledge that we're out, that we've lost, hits me hard in the solar plexus. For seconds nothing moves. The breath that I just lost doesn't come back.

My shocked gaze finds Eden's. She looks like something has just died.

I open my mouth, trying to find air, maybe some words. But I can't.

Because something has died.

Hope.

CHAPTER TWENTY-TWO

As we run through the trees, Eden cradled low on my back, I can't see her tears, but I can feel them. Not in the drops of salt-water pain that the wind whisks across her face, but in the deep ache that has opened up in her chest. And there's nothing I can do because my own hollow wound is radiating through my body.

With the auction done, the land lost, we'd both known we needed to get out of there. I couldn't even face the call to my family before we'd disappeared into the trees. The moment I could, I'd shifted. Eden had pressed her forehead to mine, our connection communicating nothing but sorrow, before leaping on.

We'd powered through the trees, heading to the place which we no longer have a right to be at.

Flashes of what just happened hit me faster than the wind we're slicing through. Seth, standing ramrod straight, Emily holding his hand tightly at his side. James and Alexis hugging and smiling, the auctioneer pumping their hands in congratulations. Eden, face pale and eyes wounded.

We arrive at the Glade and Eden slips off. I shift back to

human, wanting to comfort her, needing the assurance of our connection. She sinks into my arms, the tears now gone.

We stand there for long minutes, lost and holding onto our anchors—each other. When Eden pulls back to look at me, her eyes mirror everything I'm feeling. Confusion blurs the green in her eyes as she looks up at me. "Noah, how do we…"

I close my eyes because her pain is compounding my own. "I don't know."

We were so sure we'd figured this out. But the reality is, neither of us knows how we fix this.

"Eden?"

A voice we hadn't expected to hear slices through our grief. We turn to find Avery standing beside the Precept Rock.

Eden straightens. "What are you doing here?"

"I've been coming here to heal. I thought it would be a good place to wait."

Which explains his rapid return to health. Except that, very soon, this place will no longer be around to heal.

Avery takes a step forward then pauses. "Something is wrong."

I stride forward, all of a sudden angry. Something is wrong all right. I head straight past him to the rock which stands behind him. The cryptic messenger has certainly grown since the last Precept arrived. It sits there, so proud, the words on it seeming so simple. Raw fury pumps through my veins, spurring an urge to turn this thing into rubble.

"Noah." Eden stands there, arms wrapped around her middle.

I look at her, torn between anger so raw it hurts and pain so hot it burns. "What else does it want from us?"

Her face is pinched and pained. "I don't know."

Avery comes to stand beside me. "We did not win the auction."

He says the words as a statement. They sound like a sentence, a sentence that just condemned Were and Fae.

I turn away, too much energy pulsing through my system.

Avery looks between us. "I didn't think Alexis would do this."

I practically growl. "Well, you underestimated her anger."

Avery seems to sag. "She was so full of light and love."

I bite my tongue, almost literally. Avery doesn't need to hear that she's now full of bitterness and hatred. The proof that the land we stand on is about to be desecrated is evidence enough.

When I hear the sound of something slicing air, I spin around, confused. There's no wind, barely a breeze.

The cry that follows answers my question.

Eden crumples, Avery catching her before she hits the ground, looking in horror at the straight shaft of an arrow protruding from her shoulder. Her face is pale, mouth open, as she looks down at the weapon impaled in her body.

"Eden!"

It takes me too long to get to her side, but the moment I'm there, I grab her hand. "Noah, it—" She looks past me and her eyes widen.

There's another zing of air and a second arrow lands beside me. My head shoots up to see what has Eden frozen.

Kurt, Dana beside him, is approaching steadily, a hunter's bow already notched with the next arrow. I jump upright, and the next arrow lodges between my feet. The voice that slices through the Glade turns my heated blood to frigid ice.

"The Precept Rock never lies, does it?" Kurt smiles, evil satisfaction twisting his features.

"Stop this, Kurt." I keep my voice low, although my heart is screaming for my injured mate.

"All Alexis needed was one last investor to bump up her portfolio." He tilts his head although the arrow never wavers from its target. "You'll be surprised how many Weres want this too."

The final investor on the phone! It never occurred to me that Weres would be the ones who made this happen. "This is wrong, Kurt."

"I don't think I've ever been more right, actually. When they saw it was the mother of the Prime Alpha mate trying to buy the Glade, many realized exactly what we need to unite. The irony that we used humans to get there only makes it sweeter."

I can feel Eden's pain, but worse, I can feel her strength draining. My mind desperately scrambles for a solution.

Avery stands slowly, like he's dealing with a rabid animal. My guess is he's trying to work some of his Fae magic to calm Kurt. "You will create nothing but division by hurting the Prime Alpha mate."

Kurt's eyes shift to Avery, but the bow never moves. "Stupid, sick old man. Don't you see that's the plan? You've lost the Glade, now there's only one more piece of proof to show these two were never meant to be our leaders." Determination suspends Kurt's face in the furious frown that has molded it. "I don't plan on hurting your daughter too much longer."

The next arrow flies through the air, skewering Eden only inches away from the last one. Only inches away from her heart. With lightning movements he has the next arrow notched.

I jerk forward, planning g on stepping between them, and Kurt jerks back the next arrow. I instantly hold myself in suspended animation. Kurt's cold gaze is very clear—if you move so do I.

In all this deadly focus, no one has noticed Dana. Dana is stepping to the side, moving away from Kurt. "Dad."

A ripple of anger flutters over Kurt's features. "Move back, Dana."

Dana pauses, her hands tangling in the edge of her shirt. "She turned Seth back to Were."

"And she can turn whoever she wants, but she still bleeds like a human."

I turn away from Kurt, risking the break in eye contact to look at Dana. She's wavering, which gives me a flicker of hope. "Dana. Eden is in pain. I need to help her."

I don't voice what scares me the most. My connection with Eden is faltering, which means Eden is faltering.

Dana's eyes fly to mine, the Channon hazel a turmoil of emotion. She opens her mouth to speak.

"Move back, Dana." Kurt's voice is low and deadly.

Dana looks at the three of us, Avery frozen, Eden injured, me desperate, then looks back to her father, the arrow pointed with his hunter's accuracy, waiting to shoot again.

"Now, Dana."

She takes a small step toward Kurt and my aching heart watches as his lips tip up in his rust-colored beard.

"There will be a turning of the soil." His face seems to set in stone. "That's when this starts."

He fires off the next arrow, and the gasp that slams through my ears tells me it found its mark. Eden's pain flares, and I use it to propel me forward, knowing there's no way I can stop the next arrow.

Kurt takes an extra millisecond to draw back the last arrow that extra little bit, his face a mask of satisfaction. This arrow will hit its target with as much force as the compound bow can create. There's no doubt in my brain that the others missed on purpose, Kurt is an experienced hunter. But for this one, the target is Eden's heart.

With a whoosh of air, he releases the deadly shot.

Avery roars the denial as my brain screams it. I stretch out my arms, hopelessly trying to change its trajectory. But even Were reflexes won't be able to stop this missile.

It's Dana's scream which drowns it all out. Closest to Kurt, shifting so she can harness the speed of Were, she launches herself to the left. In a split second, there's a new projectile seeking to cross the path of the arrow. The metal point must be the last thing Dana sees as it closes in on her eye.

Her death is instant as the arrow slices through her brain.

Dana's body drops, her human form lying lifeless on the ground.

The shock is so great that it takes moments for the relief to come crashing down. I kneel down, hands not knowing where to touch. Eden stares up at me, three arrows puncturing her chest. Blood blooms out like a deadly rose.

I hear Kurt move, but I don't care. Even when he roars his fury I don't turn around. There's only one thing that has my focus, I need to get Eden some help.

I take her by the shoulders but the minute I place pressure she gasps. Her forest green eyes fly open as a moan wrenches from her lips. I instantly let go, registering the blood that is cushioned beneath her.

"Eden, we...we need to get you to a hospital."

Eden swallows, the process looking painful and pronounced. She's diminishing before my eyes.

Kurt's voice, violent with fury washes over us. "What have you done?"

But I ignore him. Whatever he has to say is irrelevant now. Too much time has passed, too much blood has been lost.

I hear Kurt move closer. "That's two daughters you've taken from me."

I grace him with one glance, and one glance only. Kurt has bent over and picked Dana's lifeless body up. It's probably the most he's held her in her entire, short life. "You don't deserve either of them."

I turn back, not willing to lose another second with Eden. She's looking up at me, pained and confused.

Avery moves closer. "He's gone. He took Dana with him."

"We need to do something, Avery. It can't end like this."

Eden's eyes close and I jerk forward. "Eden!"

They fly open again, those pools of pain finding mine. "The baby, Noah..." A lone tear trickles down her face, then dropping to the ground.

I can't hold her. I can't stop this.

My heart is chanting her name, saying it will keep her here. With me. My hands, stained with red, flutter over her, around the arrows that are leaching her life, up to her frightened face. "I know, it's okay, she's strong."

A shadow of a smile flits over her face. "He was going to be just like his father."

Something fragments deep inside and I can't help the pain that overflows from my eyes. My hand strokes her cheek. Slowly her own hand comes up to hold mine.

Avery is beside me, but I don't look up.

His hand rests on my shoulder. "I can fix what I have broken."

What is he talking about? He can't fix this. Eden is dying, her blood coating my hands. I can feel our connection fading. It feels like it's decaying my soul.

Avery leans over Eden and her frightened eyes fly to his. "Dad?"

Avery's eyes close for the briefest moment, relishing the gift Eden just gave him. He opens them again, his hands coming up to cup her face. "Eden, I want you to know something."

Eden's eyes lock with his, her breathing short and pained. Her eyes search his face, not sure what she's looking for.

He rests one hand on her chest and wraps the other around the first arrow. "You should have known I was always there." With a fast yank, he pulls it out. Eden arches her back in pain.

"What are you doing?" I roar, launching myself at him. But Avery deflects me, and with a speed I didn't know he had, he wrenches out the next one. "Alexis should have known."

In a blink, the next arrow is out.

"Know that you were always loved, Eden."

Blood is flowing freely now, and I watch as Avery hastens his daughter's death. Ice explodes in my chest at what that means. Did he think he was doing her a favor?

Eden opens her mouth, and I feel my heart crack when

nothing comes out. The only thing that is warm now is the blood pooling around me.

"You learned before I did the power of connection, and for this reason, I am giving you this."

I'm about to push him away. These are Eden's last moments, and they shouldn't be about his absolution. But Avery leans down, touching his forehead to hers. His fingers brush behind her ear, then brush across his chest. He pulls in a deep, shuddering breath and brings his lips to hers.

There's a surge in the connection that was fading so fast, and for some reason that scares me more. I don't have time to register that Avery collapses beside her.

"Noah. I love—" She draws in a breath, back arching, pain lancing across her face.

"No." I dive forward as she collapses back onto the blood soaked grass. "No. No. No."

Eden's face calms, features relaxing, her breathless beauty replacing all the pain as her body loses consciousness.

"NO!"

PART V
EDEN

CHAPTER TWENTY-THREE

THERE'S A THRUMMING I HADN'T NOTICE BEFORE. IT FEELS LIKE IT'S deep beneath me, or maybe it's deep within me. My groggy mind drags itself from the sleep it was in, trying to place it. The low, rhythmic cycle isn't something I've experienced before. It's like a deep, throbbing heartbeat; measured and comforting. It makes my heart smile and my mind feel strangely content.

As consciousness finds me, so does the sounds of nature around me. Birds seem to be calling to me to join them in the sky, smaller furred creatures inviting me into their world. I marvel in wonder. This is a heaven I never imagined.

And then I feel Noah's pain. Stronger than any pain I've experienced, its piercing anguish stabbing me from the inside out, at the same time blunt force trauma is seeping everywhere. There's no fibre in my body that is safe from it.

My heart clenches, the desire to end his agony a driving force that has my eyes flying open.

"Noah." My voice is quieter than I had intended, my dry throat making it raspy and whispered.

But the drawn-in breath besides me tells me he heard it. I want to smile. Noah has been the one who has always heard me.

"Eden?"

His voice is raspier and more breathless than mine. Disbelief is all I can hear.

I swallow as I turn my head, wondering where I am and why I feel like this. Surely, I haven't fainted again.

My hands fly to my stomach. "The baby!" I shoot upright, my body feeling wet and sticky. Is that blood? Panic grips me. "Noah, the baby!"

But Noah is just sitting there, amazement dawning over his handsome face. "Eden?"

"Noah. The blood…" Doesn't he understand how serious this is?

Then it comes back to me. The pain. The arrows. Kurt.

My father.

Oh god, I almost…

Noah engulfs me in a hug just in time, because reality hits me like a sledgehammer. My arms clasp him back, holding him just as tightly and just as desperately.

Our connection seems to wind around us, drawing us in, reassuring us that our love is still whole. For some reason, it feels stronger, more pure than ever before.

Noah pulls back, one hand brushing back my hair. When his lips touch mine, my eyes flutter closed. We both need this affir-mation of life.

I rest my forehead on his. "But how?"

Noah jerks back. "Oh no."

He turns, and I see the body lying beside me. My father is stretched out on his back, eyes closed, face peaceful.

My hand flies to my mouth. "Oh god."

I'm by his side in a blink, lifting his hand in mine. It's cool and light, no sign of life weighing it down.

"Dad?"

My voice is trembly, and tears begin a steady stream down my cheeks. There is no denying that my father is dead. Grief lances through me, and I can feel myself reaching out, my heart calling out, but not knowing for what.

Noah is beside me in an instant, his arm wrapping around my shoulders. "I'm so sorry."

I take in the still body, not knowing how I feel about losing the father that I barely had.

Noah's eyes lift from Avery to mine. "He gave his life for you, Eden."

Always know that you were loved.

The tears keep coming and I don't stop them. The thrumming picks up and I pull back, confused. I look to Noah but his worried face tells me he doesn't feel it. I suck in a breath when the melody that has been with me all my life bursts into my head, somehow clearer and more poignant than it has ever been.

I brush my father's cheek. Avery didn't need to do this to show me that I was loved. I just discovered that he was telling the truth—he was always with me.

The melody picks up in crescendo and a breeze buffets my face. The thrumming has now become a rhythmic bass for the music, a cadence that all of nature knows.

"Noah, something is happening."

Noah looks around, the breeze tangling his hair, sensing the change. His arm tightens around mine protectively, eyes alert.

The first butterfly is a fragile mote of color. It flutters in and lands on the hand Noah has resting on my shoulder. We look at it, blinking in surprise.

More come, now birds and insects, anything that can fly, pouring from the trees, raining from above. The breeze finds momentum, seeming to spin like a whirlpool.

We both sit back when we see what is really changing. Avery begins to glow, a subtle, warm glimmer, but a glow nonetheless. The thrumming is almost a deep roar now, and my father begins to splinter. His Fae body fragments, small particles of shimmer separating with each pulse.

The moving mass settles around him like a breath.

Then the butterflies, birds, and fluttering insects each take a glowing piece and head for the sky. We watch, awed, as they disperse like a slow motion firework, spreading out over the horizon. Avery's soul is about to be dispersed over the earth he loved.

The melody dies with the breeze, but like Mother Nature, I know it will never be gone. It's a bittersweet grief which realizes that knowledge came with death.

I turn into Noah's arms and he holds me. We've lost the Glade and now I've lost my father. I bury in tighter. What's more, the Fae have lost their king.

"We have each other."

I look up, my eyes needing his summer sky warmth. "Which is all we started with."

Noah's smile is slow and beautiful. "Exactly."

I'm about to suggest we head home when a movement at the other end of the Glade has us turning.

The Phelans burst through the pathway, concern etched on all their faces. Adam is the first to spot us and he's by our side as fast as his long legs can cross the grassed area. I wonder how much his shrewd blue gaze takes in. We're here alone, but so much has happened.

Noah releases me and turns to his father. "Dad—"

"Holy gronkles, you're bleeding." Tara's hand flies to her chest, her hand reaching out to grasp Mitch.

I glance down at my chest. Three holes are all that is left of the arrows, the blood stain around it starting to dry. We must look a mess.

"I'm fine, really."

Adam squats down and picks up the arrows. "What happened here?" He looks at the arrows, their hollow metal tips glinting in the light. "These are hunting arrows."

Mitch steps forward, looking a little more closely. The fletches are a russet red. "We've seen these before."

Probably at the Channon household. Kurt liked to have his weapons of choice on display.

Tara gasps, her eyes flying to mine. I don't know how to put into words that her father just tried to kill me again.

Beth wraps her arms around Tara. "We knew this was going to happen again."

Tara's eyes scan me from head to toe, and then head to toe again. "You're okay?"

I nod. There are even less words for communicating that I only survived because of my father's sacrifice.

Noah puts a steadying arm around my shoulders. "We lost the Glade at auction."

Adam nods. "We know. Joe called us."

My eyes sting. "But there's more."

I feel everything in Noah tighten. This is just as hard for him as it is for me. "Let's head home. Eden needs to clean up and then we can talk. Some things have…changed."

I grasp Noah's hand, ready to leave. Technically we're trespassing, plus there's a lot we need to discuss. Tara is about to learn that she's lost a sister. I have to share that I've lost a father.

Noah shifts and I leap up, sinking into his white fur. As we head back to the auction site to drive home, I realize this is so much bigger than just those losses.

I can feel it in my core.

Everything has changed.

CHAPTER TWENTY-FOUR

FOR THE FIRST TIME SINCE THIS ALL STARTED, WE SIT AROUND THE Phelan table and everyone is silent. Even Stash and Caesar are quiet and unmoving. No one knows what to say. What's worse, everyone is worried there could be nothing to say.

Tara is grieving the loss of Dana, the sister who took the arrow aimed for my heart.

I am trying to come to terms with the loss of a father while trying to understand the gift he left behind. Since that moment in the Glade, the melody is never far away, my sense of connection with everything around me heightened.

But what has really silenced us is the communal mourning of the Glade, each one of us wondering whether the Prophecy can exist without it or the Precept Rock.

We know we're here because we need a plan...and yet silence reigns.

Noah repeats the action I've seen him do so many times since yesterday afternoon. He shakes his head as he looks at his family seated around him. "I could have sworn we figured it out."

United we conquer.

I grasp his hand. So did I. "Maybe we were trying to take the easy road."

Uniting Were and Fae had seemed so right. No bloodshed, no conquering those we are supposed to be uniting.

Adam nods. "Maybe. It seems Kurt was determined that this would be a war."

I never thought he would be the one to decide.

Mitch frowns, his own hand grasping Tara's. "And now he's lost another daughter."

Pack is everything to Kurt. We already know that the loss of Tara felt like a betrayal. The loss of Dana is only going to fan the flames of revenge. Would Kurt recognize that Dana died because she no longer believed what he is fighting for? I doubt it.

Noah sits up a little straighter. "He said something about a turning of the soil ceremony. That it would start then."

My phone vibrates in my pocket and I slip it out long enough to see that it's a number I don't recognize. I go to shove it back in, figuring ignoring it is the smartest thing to do. Hearing from a telemarketer about life insurance is the last thing I need right now.

Unless it's Orin returning my call. I left a message, asking him to come over, wondering how in the world I was going to give him the news.

I step away from the table and press the little green icon. "Hello?"

"Eden?"

I don't recognize the voice straight away, but I certainly recognize the accent. "Hello, James."

Noah glances at me, and the others follow. Both the name and my dead tone would have alerted them to who this caller is.

"My dear, I'm glad I caught you."

I consider hanging up. I'd prefer talking to a telemarketer. "I'm sorry, I can't talk—"

"This will only take a minute." James is talking rapid-fire. He realizes this phone call is going to be short. "I just wanted to convey that there are no hard feelings after the auction."

You've got to be kidding me. My finger comes up to press the button which will end this conversation.

"And Alexis and I would like to invite you to our turning of the soil ceremony this Thursday."

My hand drops, the cell phone almost following it. I tighten my grip. "What?"

"Yes, a celebration for the new beginnings this will mean." James seems pleased by my surprise, maybe taking the fact that I'm still on the phone as a good thing. "We're inviting the community and the media. We want everyone involved in this exciting venture."

Oh god. "James—"

"No need to RSVP," he announces jovially. "We just wanted to extend the invitation." He pauses. "We would love to see you there."

He hangs up and the phone goes silent.

I look up at the family all watching me. "Did you hear that?"

There's a chorus of nodding.

Mitch's lips flat line. "It will be a beginning all right."

Tara is looking pale, her hand curled protectively around her stomach. "They're falling straight into Dad's hands. Something this big is just what he wants."

Kurt was the one who helped Alexis buy the Glade. Kurt wants to prove the dominance of Weres, and what better place than an event with media?

Adam's face is carefully schooled as he looks like he's choosing his words. "The question is, what is he going to do?"

Noah and I look at each other. We both saw the need for violence on Kurt's face. We both heard his words. His plan was always to divide, and he was willing to lose the Glade to do that. My eyes widen. He's willing to kill to do it. I feel Noah's horror crash with my own.

Noah turns to the pack. "Kurt could use this as an opportunity to expose us and start his war at the same time."

Tara's eyes widen. "That's exactly what he would be planning. It's public, and there's a whole bunch of victims for the taking."

As we realize what we're about to come up against, each face around me becomes resolute. Adam grasps Beth's hand. "We know what we need to do."

We'll have to be there. We'll have to protect the people there to celebrate something they believe is good. We have to keep the Were secret safe.

Somehow, we have to stop Kurt once and for all.

Something shifts in Noah, and I turn to find his blue gaze on me. "You can't be there, Eden."

I frown. "Noah, we've been over this." This is not the time for him to be Mr. Protective. "We need to do this together."

But Noah is already shaking his head. "You're carrying our child. Tara can't be there, and neither can you."

The objection dies as his words hit me. Noah is right. I'm carrying the Prime Alpha heir, and although no one knows what that means, I can't risk being there.

I bite my lip because I can feel it trembling. "But it could be a bloodbath."

"I know."

"We're meant to be united."

Noah's face twists with pain. "I don't like this either. But there's no other way."

He's right, but it feels wrong. I know we need to be conquering, but without me there, we certainly won't be united.

Surely this wasn't what the Prophecy was asking for. Weres fighting Weres, humans the pawns as we battle to prove who is strongest.

Noah squeezes my hand. "We've learned that even apart, we're inseparable."

Mitch is rubbing his lip in that Phelan way. "Maybe we ask for some back up."

Noah's eyes light up. "Yes. We can ask the Tates, the Bardolfs, and the Lyalls. Everyone who supported the Glade. If we have the numbers, it might be enough to make Kurt think twice."

I look at Tara, who doesn't have her 'I'm convinced' face on. "Or it could act as a bigger red flag."

Adam leans forward. "I think many of them will want to be there anyway. They'll feel the need to see what is about to become of our most sacred space."

Worry chews at the edges of my nerves. This could either dampen the fire or stoke it.

But it seems the ball has been set in motion, because Adam stands. "I'll call John. We still need to deal with Daniel."

Mitch pulls Tara up with him. "We'll call the Bardolfs and the Lyalls. I'll try Nian but I doubt she'll leave her cabin."

Beth, pale and tense, stands too. "I'll make some soup for when everyone arrives."

Which just leaves Noah and me sitting at the table. I curl up, leaning into him.

Noah's arm wraps around me, warming me with the sensation of how well it fits. "You're hugging her again."

I look down to find my arm wrapped around my stomach. It feels like it's a little bigger every day. "I worry for him. The world we're creating is the world he'll be coming into."

Noah's kiss in my hair is soft and tender. "We're gonna make this right, Eden."

I push up, eyes desperately seeking his. "I think I should be there, Noah. Every other time something like this has happened, we've been separated. When Kurt challenged you to a Claiming, I wasn't there."

A frown creases Noah's forehead. "Well, you did show up anyway."

"And then at Council, we decided I'd come in later."

The frown gains some depth. "We've still won every time though."

I shake my head. "We won the battle. But the war hasn't ended."

Noah pulls back, the furrowing of his brow firmly entrenched. I can feel his tension, possibly frustration. "You know you can't be there Eden. I've already watched you die once, knowing it was two lives that were slipping away from me. There won't be a second chance."

I deflate. "I have to choose between our child or our pack, don't I?"

Noah's frown dissolves and he leans forward, warm hands cupping my face. "No, Eden, you don't. That beautiful baby you're carrying is our pack."

I close my eyes, willing the tears to recede. I don't know if it's more painful thinking about what could happen or knowing I won't be there.

When I open them I find Noah smiling, those soft eyes and tipped-up lips enough to lighten the pain. "Where is the girl who ran away at the first sign of conflict?"

That has me pausing. That Eden seems like a lifetime ago. My hand comes up to brush back that wayward hair of his. "She fell in love."

Noah sinks forward and I meet his lips halfway. I glory in the love that flows, in the sense of commitment and unity. Maybe I need to trust this.

"Thank you, Noah."

Although his summer sky eyes are laced with confusion, Noah pulls up that cocky grin of his. "I'm happy to oblige." He leans forward again, but I pull back.

"Because of you, I've become part of something..." I falter, some things are beyond words. "Unimaginable."

Noah's face relaxes, that glow of love which I've come to

depend on shimmering in his eyes. "You were the start of something unimaginable, Eden."

We kiss again, but the sound of Tara stomping down the stairs has us separating. And then the smell of onions burning hits us as Beth starts to make the soup. Having a family is a wonderful gift, unless you want some privacy.

"How about we head out to Grandfather Douglas? Let our daughter enjoy some sunshine."

I stand, not needing to be asked twice. "He prefers to relax under the shade of the canopy."

We're out the door before Tara can make it to the bottom or Beth can ask us to stir the blackened remains of the poor onion. We curl up against the trunk of the giant Douglas Fir, and I point out that his branches let through the sun but also provide dappled shade. "Even Grandfather Douglas isn't giving any hints as to the sex of this baby."

Noah chuckles. "We already know the answer."

Tucked into his side, I pull in a deep breath. We'll have a few minutes to have a break from the weight of responsibility before heading back in to face inevitability. There will be more phone calls to make, planning to do. But ultimately, on the day, it will be Noah who holds all the power. As Prime Alpha, he has the ability to change Were to human.

Noah tilts his head a little and I look up. He's concentrating, and I still. A moment later I hear it too. A car is coming down the driveway. Surely the Weres haven't arrived so soon.

We glance at each other, knowing our brief breath of grace is over. We both straighten in surprise when we recognize the car.

I reach out to grasp Noah's hand. "Noah, I have no idea how to tell him."

The hand surrounding mine tightens, telling me I can do this. "He's your brother. Your connection is just what he needs right now."

Orin climbs out of the car, his pale blond hair catching the light. We move forward, meeting him in the sunshine. It's hard to tell what Orin his thinking, he's perfected the serene Fae expression.

"Orin." I grab him in a hug, holding him tight. "I…"

Orin pulls back. "It's okay. I felt it. We all did."

Noah frowns. "You all did?"

"The Fae are as connected to each other as they are to the Earth. The loss of our King was felt by all."

Which explains the sorrow that seems to have compounded. Although it doesn't explain the melody or the rhythmic thrumming that now underscores it. Now isn't a good time to ask, but I hope Orin has some answers.

"I'm so sorry, Orin. He died saving—"

But Orin is already shaking his head. "This was what he wanted. My guess is he saw this as a redemption of sorts."

My eyes sting. "Yes, he did."

Orin's green gaze steadies, like he's trying to convey something. "He knew what choice he was making."

I open my mouth, feeling like that statement has layers. But Orin pulls back, sucking in a deep breath. "I'm actually here to extend an invite."

I frown, glancing at Noah, but he looks just as confused as I. Surely, he can't be here about the opening ceremony.

"We will have a crowning of the next Fae monarch. It is important that you be there."

Oh, Orin becoming King of the Fae. Again, I feel the many parts of me pulling at me. I'm not Were, not human, and I've never understood the Fae. "I would love to be there, but I can't go away right now, Orin."

Orin nods, like he expected that. "We plan to do it by the Glade."

A burst of surprise flares within Noah. "The Fae know of the Glade?"

"Mother Nature has many centers, hearts you could call them, and The Glade is one of them. That's why being there made Father stronger. I think he would have liked for this to happen there."

I chew on my lip. "When are you doing it?"

"We need to do it tomorrow."

"Tomorrow? Why so soon?"

Orin sighs. "Alexis is planning her ceremony in two days time."

Oh yes. How many more will be impacted by this? "And after that it will be gone."

"Exactly. We need a new sovereign, Eden. Everything is changing too fast."

Tell me about it. "I want to have Noah there."

Orin's face actually crinkles a little bit. "We've only ever had Fae at these ceremonies."

I arch a brow at him. "I wasn't supposed to bond with a Were either. Not to mention I'm only half Fae myself."

Orin's eyes smile. "You know you're far more than a Changeling."

"Which is why I need my mate there." I may not be able to go to the opening ceremony, but I can make sure we're together for this.

He sinks into thought, eyes staring at Grandfather Douglas' trunk. He looks back at us. "Bring your family."

My eyebrows hike up. "Really?"

"Father discovered our error. We remained separate, disconnected, and it diminished our power." He arches a blond brow. "Besides, I think it may be valuable for them to see this."

I turn to Noah, wondering what he thinks of this all. We need to prepare for the ceremony. At the same time, there is little we can do to ready ourselves for the approaching inevitability.

Noah nods and I can feel his curiosity. There is a lot we still don't know about the Fae.

Looking back at my brother, I nod. "It would be a privilege."

CHAPTER TWENTY-FIVE

DRIVING DOWN THE HIGHWAY, I'M GLAD THAT ORIN INSISTED I come to this. The tension of tomorrow is a solid weight in my chest, hard and cold and unmoving. Hopefully a Fae crowning can provide a brief distraction. With all of the Phelans coming, two cars were necessary. I took the opportunity to drive here early, needing some time to myself.

I slow when I see a great big truck up ahead. Bright orange, it looks like it belongs on a construction site. The breath that I suck in as I come closer hits the back of my throat with force. *She couldn't have...*

I pull over, eyes struggling to process what I'm seeing.

What should have been a wall of brown trunks and proud canopy is now gone. An entire strip of forest has been razed to the ground. Completely obliterated. The protective barrier that once stood between the Glade and the rest of the world is gone.

My hand covers my mouth but an anguished groan slips out. A broad road has been forged, a straight line heading directly to the place that has always been a secret. The bare ground looks violated, the air feels defiled.

What hits me in the the hardest is the knowledge that my own mother did this.

I creep forward, tires crunching over branches that were left behind after the carnage. In the distance I can see what no other human has ever seen.

The Glade looks bare and vulnerable, one side now an open wound. I pull over, knees weak as I walk the last few feet.

The Precept Rock stands where it's always been, but it's no longer protected. A handful of workmen are walking around, long tapes stretched out, lasers looking at where to level.

And one of them is my mother. Alexis is striding forward, smiling the smile of the satisfied. I think it's the first time in my life I haven't seen her in heels.

She spots me and the smile fades. After a brief pause, she changes trajectory. Stopping before me, I wonder what she can see on my face. There's too much horror and pain to be able to hide the emotions. My heart aches for the damage that has been done. "Why did you do this?"

Alexis's sigh is impatient. "How else were people going to get here? That rutted track that led to nowhere?"

"But—"

"What did you think was going to happen? The sooner we start on this, the sooner we see progress. Levelling this area is our first job. Then we look at digging the foundations."

"You're going to build it here?"

"Yes. James spoke to the builder. This natural clearing has great aspect." She takes a few steps forward, taking in the beauty she wants to desecrate. "And that cliff face back there will be a wonderful backdrop, like nature's own feature wall."

Nausea is climbing up my throat. I stride over to the Precept Rock, brushing back the long grass that protects its face. "What about this?"

Alexis looks at the stone, her face blank. "What about it?"

I wait for her to join me, which takes several moments. Alexis looks like she would prefer to walk away. Whatever the reason, she comes to stand beside me, staring at the proud monolith before us.

My heart sinks. "You don't see it, do you?"

"The rock? Of course I see it. I hope it won't be too hard to shift. I believe that's where we'll be putting the entrance."

I deflate. In desperation, I'd been willing to risk the secret of Weres, maybe even Fae, to show Alexis what she's doing.

But she can't see it. She's so disconnected, too self-absorbed. The most wondrous crossroad of where this could all come together is right before her, and she can't see it.

The weight that's been pulling everything down snaps. I recoil, the sensation a physical pain. "Never speak to me again."

Alexis narrows her eyes at me. "I beg your pardon."

"You heard me, Alexis. I don't want to see or hear from you ever again." Alexis' mouth opens in shock and it gives me a burst of satisfaction. I point my finger at her. "You made sure we were never close, deliberately pushed me away whenever you could. You probably wanted this all along." I turn and start to walk away. "Stay away from me. Whatever held us together is dead."

I head for the trees behind the Precept Rock, their calm comfort calling me. The severing of the connection should feel good. I'd hoped it would make me feel lighter.

But instead the loss seems to have lodged in my chest. It hasn't freed me like I thought it would. I almost turn around, wondering what Alexis thinks of the word I just threw at her. The melody seems to pulse in my head, tugging at my body. But now isn't the time for the connection to the Glade to power up. I need to get away from the woman who has tried to sabotage everything good in my life.

Deep amongst the trees I stop. The broad trunks surround me, reminding me that I'm not alone. I move to the closest one, resting my forehead against it. With my hand on the life growing inside me, I take a deep breath. It's shakier than I would have liked, but any tears that were thinking of spilling retreat. We have so much to deal with right now, I can no longer afford my mother any more energy.

I turn and rest my back against the solid wood. The melody seems to have quietened, maybe slowed. I have no idea what that means, but I simply focus on it, allowing its soothing chords to work their magic. The raw edges of pain slowly quieten.

Although Orin arrives not long later, by the time he's here I've shut it away. I've reached a place where Alexis can't hurt me anymore, and I tell myself that I'll learn to be at peace with that. I meet him at the edge of the Glade, not surprised that he knew where I was.

His face is pale, his green eyes shadowed with anguish at the destruction that greeted him. I pull him in. "I'm so sorry, Orin."

He holds me tight, giving as well as receiving the comfort we both need. "It has begun, hasn't it?"

I swallow as we separate, gazes drawn to the devastation that Alexis has wreaked. I think of the Prophecy started so many life-times ago, of Alexis and Avery and their love and their loss, of Noah failing to change. "I think this started a long time ago."

Orin falls silent and I can feel him contemplating my words.

At least the place is empty. Alexis and her workers have left, probably to celebrate what they achieved here today. It won't be long before she has a glass of champagne in her hand.

It's only then I realize Orin won't be able to have his cere-mony. The Glade is no longer a private cove for supernatural beings. "Oh no, Orin. How will you be crowned?"

To my surprise, Orin smiles. "Ah, sister. The Glade is far more than just a clearing."

I wait, but Orin doesn't offer any more than his enigmatic statement. I don't bother asking, knowing he's unlikely to elabo-rate. It looks like I'll have to wait and find out.

Instead, I use our few minutes alone to see if I can learn something else. "So, what exactly does the sovereign get to do?"

Orin tilts his head. "Basically everything you do now, but more."

"So calming animals so we can help them."

He nods. "From the smallest to the largest. But still more than that."

I think of the four Weres who tried to kill me and how I'd subdued them. I turn to him in shock. "It's mastery of all animals, isn't it?"

I try to imagine what that will mean for Orin. An ability to command any animal.

"When we have to." Orin's eyes narrow as he looks at me, seeming to give thought to his next words. "But it's even more than that. Fae are a conduit, a connection, between the earth and anyone willing to hear what she has to say."

"That's a big responsibility."

"Yes, it is. Too many people don't listen anymore. "

Like Alexis.

I look back at the road that now leads to the Glade. "He tried really hard, didn't he?"

Orin sighs. "Yes, he did. He achieved a lot of good too." Orin turns to me again, this time his eyes calm pools of green. "But I think he realized it was his legacy that would have the greatest impact."

I open my mouth to ask what Orin means by that, this time going to insist if he tries to sidestep an explanation, but two more trucks pull up beside ours. Noah and the others are here.

We greet them, joining our devastation with theirs. Beth has taken hold of Adam's arm like she needs the support. Adam looks like he wants to return the favor and raze whoever did this with his bare hands. Mitch and Tara are silent, both curled protectively around their unborn child.

Noah takes me in his arms, but I don't need the contact to feel what this is doing to him. It feels like a part of his own soul has been battered. I place a feather light kiss on his chin. "We'll stop this."

He nods; a short, sharp movement. "Yes. We will."

More cars arrive, and we all watch as three people climb out. Of varying heights and ages, they all have one thing in common —the length of their flowing long hair. As they approach, I see their next common feature. Green tilted eyes smile at Orin and then turn to me.

The melody swells and despite the destruction around us, I feel myself smiling. These are my people.

The first to step forward is a grey haired woman. "Welcome, Eden."

I hide my surprise that this woman knows my name. She introduces herself as Dawn, one of the five Fae Elders. The next is a short man, probably in his twenties, who says his name is River. Coral is the last one, flame orange hair framing her bubbly face. The same connection I feel to Orin ties me to these people.

They clasp Orin, murmuring their condolences. I'm not surprised when they call him Elder.

They all step back, faces expectant. I look to Orin. It seems we're ready to start his crowning.

Orin smiles his enigmatic smile and leads us into the trees. Noah takes my hand as we follow, his eyebrows raised. I shrug, just as clueless about what is going to happen. It's more of a novel feeling for him than me. I've spent the last year and a half discovering there are layers to our existence that most will never know about.

Orin stops once we're deep in the forest. Little sun filters through the dense canopy of pine above us, and the scent of resin is strong. Everything feels subdued and solemn. Orin and the others spread out, and I stand there, unsure of what I'm supposed to do. The Phelans seem to hold back, remaining at the rear where they can watch without obstructing whatever is happening.

I stand beside a particularly large pine, grasping Noah's hand tightly. Excitement and awe are beginning to bloom in my stomach. The melody is growing so powerful that it seems to be a live being within me, the thrumming pulsing so strong it connects straight to my heart. I look around, wondering how much the others can feel.

The Elders each glance at me and then at Orin. He nods and they fan out, each standing beside a tree of their own. I watch with bated breath, wondering what will happen next.

They all close their eyes and tip their faces up to the canopy and silence descends. I want to ask Noah if he can feel it, maybe even through our connection. I doubt he can hear the overwhelming beauty that the melody has become, but there's a sense of something accumulating, something coming.

I don't speak, knowing this is the time for silence. Instead I grasp his hand and move closer to him. Can he feel how right this is? It's returning something that I didn't realize had been missing. A powerful sense of hope is dawning within this space.

It's Noah's intake of breath that is the first thing to alert me. I follow his gaze and see that something is moving in the canopy above. If I could, I'd narrow my eyes to focus. But my whole face is open in wonder, wide with astonishment.

Small specks of glowing gold filter down. Within seconds they gain momentum, more of them appearing, rushing down to us. They trickle through the trees, flow down the trunks. When the thrumming seems to be a pulsating power beneath my feet, I look down. More flecks of fragile beauty, nothing more than particles of glow, are flowing below us.

Very soon, the same shimmery particles that flew away when my father died are cascading down the trees as more rush over the ground. They come together, swirling and dancing, and begin to coalesce together. I watch, eyes too scared to blink, as they start to form a circle. Flying and flowing, they move around us, creating a ring of light. Each of us, Orin, the Elders, myself and Noah, are encased in the magical halo.

The golden specks divide, and at five points around the circle they spear off. I watch as a star is created by their shimmering glow, with Orin and the three Elders all standing at a point.

It's then that I realize something—I'm standing at the peak of the star, Noah and I are the apex of this shimmering symbol. I gasp. The same symbol that is stamped behind my ear, that Noah has imprinted on his chest. It would have to be the same symbol each of the Elders have on their body too.

But why are we at the peak?

I feel Noah register it too and our hands tighten around each other. This is beautiful and profound and deeply mysterious.

The Elders lift their arms, faces defined by a glorious smile. It's the release the beautiful shimmer around us is looking for, and I feel the change. The intent to find their home.

The glorious motes seem to expand for a moment, like a breath being sucked in. I glance at Orin, knowing this is his moment.

But as the particles contract, as they begin to funnel, I step back in disbelief. The tree behind me becomes my spine as they flow toward me.

All of a sudden, I'm encased in glistening gold. The pieces that I now realize are far more than just my father, but the essence of generations of Fae, swirl around me like a maelstrom.

Noah releases my hand but I know I'm not alone. The melody, the very soul of the Fae, is surrounding me in its love. I can feel the Elders, the Phelans, my brother, the precious life growing within me, and my soulmate beside me. I can feel the trees and the life within and around them. I know if I tried hard enough, I could stretch this connection as far and wide as I want.

But instead, I raise my arms up, willing to accept this gift. Like a suit of gold, the particles come to rest on me, kissing me with their warmth. I draw in a breath when they sink down, dissolving into my skin.

Silence reigns as I realize it's finished.

I hold a hand up, unsure how it can look so normal. Turning to Noah, I try to find answers. Noah's face tells me whatever just happened was as fantastical and magical as it felt. His family behind him hold the same wide-eyed awe.

What just happened?

One by one, the Elders kneel. I watch in shock as Orin follows suit. I don't know what to say as they stay there, heads bowed. Do I kneel too?

Orin looks up at me, that calm smile of his starting in his eyes and blossoming over his face. "Elders of the Fae, I present to you, Eden. Our Queen."

PART VI
NOAH

CHAPTER TWENTY-SIX

WHEN MY MIND STARTS WORKING AGAIN AND I'VE TORN MY GAZE from the girl who just did the ultimate mind-blowing stunt, I turn to find the Fae have gone. Melded back into the forest, it's like they were never here. Without a word, my parents, Mitch and Tara head back to the Glade, probably needing to process what they just saw, but also realizing we need time to talk.

I turn back to Eden. "So...ah, wow."

Her smile is just what I was looking for. She glances down at herself, lifting an arm and turning it one way then the other. There's no sign of the glowing specks that had covered her. She looks around to find what I've already realized—we're alone.

She frowns. "They left?"

I shrug. "It seems Fae aren't big on pomp and ceremony."

"Did Orin say what I thought he said?"

I nod.

Eden was just crowned Queen of the Fae.

"But I'm a Changeling. I'm half human."

"And I was the Were who didn't change like I was supposed to at sixteen. I think the Prophecy doesn't care too much about blood lines."

That moment when Avery leant over her and touched her mark and his, must've been when he made the decision. Orin knew it too, Mr. I-Only-Give-Half-Answers had decided not to share that little nugget of news.

I'm so caught up in wonder at what I've just seen, unsuccessfully wrapping my head around what this could mean, that I don't hear them straight away.

At first it's only small animals, squirrels, voles, even a skunk. They materialize from the trees, coming forward. Eden kneels down, face alight with delight as she reaches her hands out. Noses brush her fingertips, heads stroke her hands. Their message conveyed, they move away. The birds are next, a massive osprey, a tiny humming bird and everything in between, they all swoop and flutter by her shoulders, their wings kissing her skin.

One by one, then by the dozens, they come to pay homage to their queen. From bugs to bears, they all come, touch their new monarch, their connection to the human world, and leave. I can't help my smile when I see a wolverine approach. He looks at me, and I'd swear his eyes widen with surprise. I nod, thanking him for letting me return to his queen's side.

My heart swells as I see the joy on Eden's face. No wonder it was such a struggle for her to accept she was one of us, because she never was. I can't believe we didn't see it—Eden was never meant to be assimilated by Weres. She was something that was meant to expand us.

I'm almost wondering if I should have left like the Fae Elders when Eden's hand reaches out. Like a fish on a line, I don't have a choice. I'll always come when this girl calls. I step forward, taking it, and she pulls me closer.

She pulls me into the circle of diversity that has been created, one hand holding mine, the other gripping the wolf pendant. The smallest are left now, butterflies raining their soft blessings, even some dragonflies flitting in spurts. I look down to find a lady beetle has crawled across our joined hands, now a brilliant red spot on my skin.

I look up at Eden and all I can feel is wonder.

Her smile is brilliant. "You're part of this now too."

They disperse as quietly as they came, blending back to their world. We stay kneeling amongst the pine needles. I blink. "Okay, so that was definitely a bigger wow."

Eden leans her head onto my shoulder. "Understatement."

I nudge her just a little. "So, I'm pretty sure a queen outranks an Alpha."

She raises her head, her look unimpressed. "We didn't notice who outranked who when I was a Changeling."

I stand, holding my hand out to her. "So, this changes things."

Eden gives me 'tell me about it' look. "The question is, how?"

She grabs my hand so I can haul her up, her other hand reaching out to the tree to steady her. I grin, because it seems my mate is already beginning to lose her center of balance.

But the grin fades when I see what that single touch has sparked. Three words appear across the trunk, silver and shimmery, like they've been branded.

Eden jerks her hand away and it disappears. We look at each other and then back at the tree. She raises her hand and slowly reaches out.

United we conquer.

Wide-eyed, Eden turns to the adjacent tree. The moment she rests her hand on it, just above her fingertips the three words flash.

United we conquer.

Running to the next one she tries it again. And just like the last, the words appear. She goes wider, this time finding an aspen further afield. I feel her excitement and curiosity—she's wondering whether it is just the trees that were somehow part of the ceremony.

But the words blaze again. *United we conquer.*

Eden comes back and stands before me, her smile radiant. I'm not even going to bother with the wow this time. There are only so many times you can say it before it becomes redundant.

I pull up a smile which probably matches hers. "Looks like the Queen of the Fae may be part of the Prophecy, huh?"

I lean down and kiss my girl, the one who has just learned her true potential.

The Prime Prophecy has just upped the ante again.

CHAPTER TWENTY-SEVEN

THE NEXT DAY, EDEN AND I ARE SITTING IN THE ONLY PLACE THAT can do everything that's happened justice. The sun is just peering over the treetops as we drop onto the thinking chair. Caesar curls up by her feet, Stash beside mine. We have a big day ahead of us —more phone calls to make and more money to raise. The sense that the grains of time are piling up on us is weighing everyone down.

Eden sighs, her head dropping onto my shoulder. I curl my arm around her as one of her hands comes to rest on my chest, right over the wolf tattoo, the other wrapping around her wolf pendant.

"I'm sorry, Eden."

She looks up, surprised and confused. "For what?"

"For trying to make you one of us. I should have realized that you weren't meant to be absorbed..." I brush back her hair. "You'll make us more, just like you made me more."

Eden leans into my hand, eyes closed. When she opens them, the emotion in their forest depths sucks the breath right out of me. "Noah." Her hand comes up to cup my face. "I've never belonged in the way I do with you. With Weres. I think this whole Fae Queen thing shows us that maybe Were and Fae are meant to be a 'we,' just like we are."

My lips brush hers, loving the feel of her, glorying in the emotion and sensation. How the hell did I get so lucky?

As I pull back, all I'm thinking is that yes, we've lost the Glade, yes, the hurdles have grown into insurmountable mountains, but it feels like we're building something. Forging connections that we never thought possible.

Surely that's got to count for something.

"Ahem."

I jolt back, instantly on alert. In part because I didn't hear the person approach, but mostly because I don't recognize the voice. I glance at the dogs, who surely should have heard this whilst I was busy, but Stash and Caesar are both sitting, tails thumping in the grass.

We stand, and all the tension must be getting to me because I find myself slightly in front of my mate before I realize it. Eden steps around as I register that we've met this guy.

I grasp her hand and squeeze it in apology. I'm thinking Eden being pregnant may not be so good for my protective tendencies. The brief look Eden graces me with tells me she gets it...but it doesn't mean she's okay with it. I smile, wishing I could kiss her.

Eden turns to our visitor, smiling. "Hello, River."

It's one of the Fae Elders who was at the crowning ceremony. Probably a little younger than my parents, he bows his head ever so slightly, his long braid slipping over his shoulder. "My queen, the Fae Elders send their congratulations and welcome."

Eden's blush is subtle but there nonetheless. "Please, call me Eden. And thank you, River."

I glance behind him, wondering why there's only one. Are the others unhappy with Avery's choice? River must notice, because he straightens. "Fae do not come together very often. Our shared features would raise too many questions. The others have returned to their homes. I was sent as a delegate."

I respect that they didn't send Orin. We know he's been glad to see his sister, but neither of us is sure how the other Fae Elders feel about Eden's newfound monarch status.

Eden nods. "I'm honored that Avery chose me."

And still totally floored by it.

"Avery was a man of great wisdom and foresight. He spoke of you often, of how much you'd taught him."

"He did?"

River nods. "He said you showed him it was time to do things differently." He angles his head. "He said things were changing. That new answers were needed."

Eden frowns as she takes this all in. "And what was his solution?"

River smiles that Fae smile. "I think it was you."

Eden falls silent. This is like the pressure and the expectations of the Prime Alpha all over again. I stay steady beside her, holding her hand, letting her know I'm here for her. I have a sense that River is here to find out what the new Fae masterplan is.

"We wanted to check, is there anything you wanted us to convey to the Fae?"

Yep, it seems so.

Eden blinks, and I can feel her surprise morph to anxiety. But I stay where I am, knowing that River is about to get a taste of the awesomeness of this girl. Her fears stopped holding her back a long time ago.

I watch as Eden's hand comes up to stroke her bottom lip. I doubt she even realizes she's doing it, but my chest almost bursts with pride. This girl is just as much a Phelan as she is Fae.

"Do you have a child, River?"

River looks away, then back. "I do. A daughter." He seems to swallow painfully. "We named her Hazel."

You've got to be kidding me. "Hazel?"

I glance at Eden. I told her the story of the sick little girl we met in Bowerman. After seeing what being in cities did to Avery, she was saddened, but not surprised, to hear about Hazel's frailty. Visiting Hazel is first on our to-do list once we're on the other side of Alexis' ceremony...whatever that looks like.

River notices our glance but doesn't comment on it. "Yes. We remain for the birth and the naming, and then we must leave."

Except Avery. He loitered in the background, unable to completely sever the ties with his daughter.

"Did you want to leave?"

River can't seem to hold Eden's gaze. He stares at the grass. "I understood the need for it."

That would be a no.

I can feel something building in Eden as she asks the next question. "Is it possible for the Fae to remain connected to their Changeling children and still maintain their secret?"

It's River's turn to blink. He grabs the tip of his braid and flicks it over his shoulder, pauses, then grabs it and brings it back around. I'm guessing that's some kind of Fae nervous tick. "We would have to keep our Fae abilities secret."

Eden nods. "Yes, you would."

I think of what it would mean if Hazel had a father, one that understood her. "But you could guide your children, help them harness the power of their abilities."

River looks at the two of us like we just suggested he should cut his hair. His eyes are wide and he seems to have been left speechless.

Eden smiles. "So many lines have been blurred since the Prime Prophecy began. I think it's trying to tell us something."

River twiddles the end of his braid. "It is risky."

I squeeze Eden's hand again. "We've discovered that. But like you said, Avery realized it was time to do things differently."

Which is one of the reasons he made his Changeling daughter Queen. We thought it was the fact that Eden blurred the lines that was the spanner in this Prophecy. When it's actually what the Prophecy has always been about.

We wait as River mulls over our words. He's right—it is risky. Weres know of Fae. There is now a human who knows of Weres. Things are definitely changing. And we're doing this all based on three vague words...united we conquer.

River's smile is nothing like the usual Fae smile. It grows and blooms bigger than you'd think was physically possible. It lights up his whole face, his green eyes practically becoming luminescent. "I will tell the others."

Eden nods, and I feel the relief flood her tense frame.

River turns away, looking eager to start sharing. "Thank you, my quee—I mean, Eden."

Eden steps forward. "River. How do I keep in touch with you and the others?"

River says nothing, simply looking at Eden.

Eden pauses. "Oh."

I realize that River just sent Eden some sort of message, like we do when I'm a wolf.

"Or you can send a courier."

There's another pause before Eden says that one word again. "Oh."

Interesting. It seems Fae have ways to keep in touch without the need for things like phones. That's certainly handy.

River is almost around the side of the house before Eden calls out to him again. He turns, looking at her in question.

Eden smiles. "I'd stop off in Bowerman on the way to seeing the others if I were you."

River's returning smile is so broad it tells us that's exactly what he was intending on doing.

I turn to Eden once we're alone again, pulling her into my arms. "Looks like Hazel will be growing up with a dad."

Eden's arms slide around my waist as she smiles up at me. "My guess is, she's about to get a whole lot better."

"I'm glad. She's a good kid."

Eden's head sinks into my chest. "I just don't get it, Noah. It seems to be one step forward, two steps back with this Prophecy."

I sigh, hands coming to squeeze her shoulders. "I know. It's like we've figured some things out…"

"And yet we've got something irrevocably wrong."

I rest my cheek on her hair, breathing in her wildflower scent. We've achieved so much, and yet lost even more.

And we both know that tomorrow is the day we discover exactly how right, or how wrong, we've been.

Eden pulls back as something dawns across her face. Her forest green eyes grab me and don't let go as she looks like the queen who got the cream. "Noah, I'm the Queen of the Fae now."

I raise a brow. "I noticed."

Eden is shaking her head in a 'I can't believe we didn't think of this sooner' way. "I could control Kurt and the others now." She swallows. "If I had to."

My mouth opens, then shuts. She's the Queen of the Fae, she can control any animal she wants. She can control as many animals as she wants.

Holy crap, in trying to kill her, Kurt has inadvertently created something far more powerful than he could have imagined. And even though Eden is pregnant, there is no one else powerful enough to contain the Weres that will be baying for blood.

She swallows, eyes pleading. "I have to be there."

Eden has already sensed my agreement before I say it. I'm glad I don't have to voice that it's underscored by the fear of what could happen to her…and the hope that this is what will tip the scales.

PART VII
EDEN

CHAPTER TWENTY-EIGHT

ARRIVING AT WHAT ONCE WAS A BEAUTIFUL, REVERED SPACE AND seeing what Alexis has done to it hurts like a wound that has been torn open again. I thought I'd come to accept it, but seeing the damage bares the pain all over again.

We arrive to find several cars are already parked on what used to be forest. We pull up next to them and pile out. Mitch and Tara came with us, while Adam and Beth drove in the other truck. Everyone is serious and grim as we survey what's ahead of us.

Alexis and James have two stands of bleachers along with a podium set up. I grit my teeth when I see the local news station has set up a camera. Recording what is going to happen here is the most dangerous thing of all.

The Precept Rock stands like a dignified sentinel to the right of the clearing, what used to be the head of this sacred area. The opening to the highway feels like it's bled out any magic this place once held.

A massive dozer is now the centerpiece. Hunkered down beside the podium, it's bigger than the one that was here two days ago. The turning of the first clod usually involves a shovel, but Alexis and James are obviously looking to make a statement.

Seth and Emily pull up, climbing out of their car and coming together almost instantly. They fit into each other like they don't plan on letting go.

Seth looks pale as he approaches us. Emily is tucked under his arm as they lean into each other. He nods at us before taking himself and Emily to the side. My hand tightens around Noah's, knowing there's nothing I can say that will make today okay.

More cars arrive, and I watch as Weres from all over the state park climb out. The Bardolfs, the Lyalls, some of the others from further afield. And finally, the Tates.

Maria rushes to my side, eyes already liquid before this has even started. Her hand presses over my now rounded belly. "How are you?"

"I'm well." Maria knows there's no way I can say I'm good. "You? How have things been?"

Maria looks down, face crumpling even more. "Daniel wouldn't listen to reason. He's basically under house arrest. "

Noah nods. "We will deal with that after all this is over. You did everything you could, Maria."

Maria's smile is tremulous but grateful. John wraps his arm around her shoulder and they head to the bleachers. Like all the Weres already there, they don't take a seat. They settle beside the metal stands, bodies taut with tension.

I'm not surprised when the Fae Elders arrive.

Orin inclines his head my way as they approach. "I spoke to River."

I glance at River, but it seems he's in Elder mode, because his face doesn't give anything away. I'd swallow if my mouth wasn't so dry. If Orin thought things were changing too fast before, what does he think of the changes I've already made? "And?"

His smile is small but there. "It will be a new direction for us."

I nod, not knowing what to say. Changelings will now know their parents—Fae will touch humans far deeper than they ever have.

Orin clasps me in a hug. "Avery knew what he was doing. We are now more intertwined than ever before."

I hug him back, letting his belief infuse me. "Thank you."

Orin releases me and the Fae head to the bleachers. Despite everything he said, they still look like they're heading to a funeral.

I glance around. It looks like Alexis and James are hoping to make an entrance once everyone is here.

Noah leans down to me. "Are they here?"

I close my eyes for a moment, connecting with my newfound powers. I can feel the Weres who are growing in numbers, all uneasy, many angry. The anger tightens the ball of anxiety that is lodged in my gut. I know they aren't okay with what's happening here, but their animosity makes me nervous.

Next, I register my fellow Fae. They're all hurting, taking comfort in each other.

The humans are the only ones who have some level of anticipation. How many would change their minds if they knew how important this place is? Or would they be like Alexis—too money hungry to care?

Then I feel them. They're further away, their burning determination scattered amongst the trees. I frown. "Four of them." My gaze flies to Noah. "One of them is Daniel."

"Looks like house arrest didn't work so well, huh?" He rubs his bottom lip. "There's less of them than we thought, seems this isn't such a popular idea."

"They're in the forest, not too far away."

Noah nods, then waits. There's one more Were that we need to locate.

But Kurt isn't with his little posse, and I'm not sure what that means. Why would he split up from them?

When I locate him I don't know how I didn't sense him first. His hot fury practically singes my consciousness. I slowly look up, not wanting to see him, but needing to know.

Kurt is up on the ledge, a russet red wolf stalking the edge one way then the other. Pacing from side to side, Kurt has chosen the place where he first attacked us to watch the ceremony unfold.

Noah follows my line of sight and his frown is ferocious when he sees him. "Bloody hell."

Kurt sees us looking, but it's me that he sets his canine gaze on. His loathing is a palpable force that spans the distance, but I'm relieved to find I'm not scared. Kurt is about to discover what his hatred is up against.

I look away, I don't want anyone else looking in the same direction I am. As long as the people here keep their eyes at ground level they won't see the unnaturally large wolf halfway up the cliff face. We need to ensure that the handful of humans here are never aware of Weres' existence.

Beth and Tara head for the bleachers, their job is to be interested humans. Adam and Mitch approach, ready to play their role in our plan.

Noah glances up at Kurt again. "So the others are in the forest?"

I nod. "To the east."

Noah's breath out is resolute. "We'll be back."

For the first time, a shot of fear spears down my back. I know he's the Prime Alpha with the ultimate power that any Were would be terrified of. He's stronger and faster than any of them. But he's also my mate. The boy I fell in love with, the one who I can't live without. I place my hand on his chest, over the mark that holds both Were and Fae. "Be careful."

Noah's smile is gentle, but also a little cocky. It's just what I needed to see. "I'll try not to trip on them."

I watch them walk away, three Alphas in their own right. Their broad backs and long strides say pride and strength, their thoughts say they are willing to fight for what is right. When I sense another presence I close my eyes for a moment, sending out a message. No harm in having a little backup.

I glance up at Kurt and find he's watching them too. Will he race down to meet them? Instigate the fight that is inevitable? For some reason I doubt it. Kurt is a coward, and facing the Prime Alpha when one drop of blood will mean he becomes human would be too great a risk. I shift my weight, my hand fluttering to my stomach then dropping. Realizing that he's probably going to stay up there intensifies the nervousness that keeps bubbling up. It means we haven't figured out what Kurt is planning to do here.

When I see Alexis approach, I turn away. On this day, as she puts into motion what will destroy so much, she needs to see that I meant what I said. Whatever semblance of family we had has been decaying for a long time. Now it's buried deeper than a coffin.

I don't wait to see what she thinks of it. Instead, I move to the second bleacher. Although it's not with Tara and Beth, I have a better view of the ledge. I need to see if Kurt is going to head down to meet Noah.

It means I don't see James walking toward me until he's before me. His smile feels wrong, and it reinforces just how clueless he is.

"We're delighted to see you here."

I realize he probably thinks this is some sort of tick of approval. "I'm not here to celebrate, James."

He glances around, acting like I didn't reply. If he wasn't spearheading such a terrible crusade, I'd almost admire his tenacity. "You didn't bring Noah?"

Noah is off trying to save your lives. I glance over at Alexis to find her staring at me, but not at my face. Alexis is taking in the swelling of my stomach that I can no longer hide. Her shocked eyes rise up to meet mine.

I look away before the shock can shift to whatever comes next. I don't ever want to see disappointment or disgust when it comes to the baby growing inside me. Although we never considered children, this child couldn't be more special or wanted.

I look back at James. "He's coming. He just had to look after something."

James smiles again. "Wonderful. This is going to be quite the show."

You've got to be kidding me. I turn away, wishing the distaste I feel wasn't there. "I really wish you'd listened, James."

For once, James doesn't have a reply. Instead he turns and heads back to Alexis. I don't bother to see what they have to say to each other. I have more important things to worry about.

Kurt is still pacing above, and I can feel that Noah is closing in on his prey. Although I know this all started long before this moment, I can feel it gaining momentum. Dominoes are being tripped as fate is propelled into motion.

Like he realizes it too, James steps up to the podium. "Thank you to everyone here, it's wonderful to celebrate this milestone with you all."

James' smooth English accent, his smile, feel like I'm at a supporters' rally. I would imagine most politicians would open with that line.

"Our eco-lodge has the potential to benefit many. We plan on fitting in with the existing typography and complementing the wonderful ecology that you all know and love." James sweeps his hands like some sort of magnanimous monarch. "Your community will benefit through the increased tourist trade, and our lodge will create jobs." He pauses, but James doesn't realize that most of the bodies here aren't human. There are few perspectives that want to clap at his words.

"This glorious area will be here for future generations as visitors learn of the power of conservation. This capacity for this project to have a significant impact is substantial."

I feel something move and I glance up. Kurt has stopped moving and it looks like he's listening along with the rest of us.

But unlike the Weres down here, whose anger is fanned by James' words, Kurt's mind feels like it's smiling.

I concentrate a little harder, wondering if I'm placing too much confidence in my ability to connect. Maybe I'm reading him wrong.

But the sensations I'm receiving from Kurt are a steady sense of satisfaction. It's like he wants this to happen.

Then I feel something else. Noah has been calm and focused since the moment he left with Adam and Mitch. But his senses have picked up, he's alert but also something else.

My breath catches in my throat.

Noah is on the hunt.

PART VIII
NOAH

CHAPTER TWENTY-NINE

THE MOMENT WE'RE DEEP ENOUGH IN THE FOREST WE SHIFT AND straight away I can smell their traitorous hides. My father and brother would have registered the same thing. There's four of them, fanned out, not far ahead.

We slow, spacing out so there are a few trees between us. I form the apex of our trio, eyes scanning the gloom as the smell becomes stronger. What little breeze there is, is working in our favor, but I suspect the element of surprise isn't going to last much longer. I scan the connection with Eden—she feels the same way she did when I left her—edgy but calm.

Good. I focus ahead. It's time to take out one of Kurt's foundations.

We slow as we stalk through the forest, closing in as much as we can. I focus my hearing beyond the trees around us—they seem to be staying put, probably waiting for the green light from their leader.

Looking at Dad and Mitch, we all nod. We've agreed how this will go.

I catch a glance of one of them through the trees. A light brown wolf, probably not much older than me, is straight ahead.

He's not anyone I recognize, not that it matters, I'm prepared to do what needs to be done.

The minute he smells us, he runs. I sprint forward like an arrow that was itching to be fired and take after him. He glances over his shoulder, and when he sees who's after him, probably more *what* is after him, his run becomes frantic.

I doubt Kurt mentioned there was a risk we'd make a pre-emptive move.

In the end, it doesn't matter how hard or desperately he runs, his pace is no match for the Prime Alpha. I close in steadily, knowing his fear of the inevitable is growing with each second.

As I come up beside him I see his wide, frantic eyes. I do it quickly, not needing him to anticipate the inevitable any longer. I snap my head to the side, jaw opening and coming down on his shoulder. A bit of pressure and the skin breaks. The moment I taste the metallic tang of blood I pull back.

The wolf staggers and trips and it's a human body that tumbles forward. The momentum he'd gained propels him over the pine needled ground, over and over. All I see is a young man tucking himself in tightly as I turn away. There are three more traitors to be dealt with.

The next one had time to think, which means he's chosen to run toward the Glade. He's probably figured that reaching the safety of people will keep him from his fate.

Well, he assumes he'll get there in time.

Powering between the trees, I use fallen logs as launching pads to gain even more speed. The wind is rushing at me so fast that I narrow my eyes. Within seconds I see him.

This one is a dark grey wolf, bigger but slower than the last one. This time I streak straight past him, cutting off his trajectory. Predicting his change of direction, I know he'll head east. He'll want to get back to his friends in the hope that there will be some safety in numbers.

He doesn't realize that with one down, he's number two.

Knowing I don't have much time, I swipe at his haunches as I overtake, slicing a thin streak of red on his thigh. This one lets out a yelp, his last as a Were, as he hits the ground like the other one, his pale human body slamming into a tree. I circle back long enough to see him push himself up and groan before collapsing again.

The third one hasn't moved far. He's either brave enough or stupid enough to think he can fight his way out. A mottle of greys, he's the biggest and possibly the youngest. He stands in the dappled shade, teeth bared and wild eyes determined.

The moment I breach the trees, he starts running. I drop my head, adding a dash of speed. Just like I knew he would, the instant we're feet apart he launches into the air. Mouth open, teeth snarling and exposed, he's looking to wreak some damage. I leap too, letting him think we're going to meet in mid-air. But there won't be a tussle for dominance; this traitor won't even get a snap in before I'm done.

Rather than aim high, I spear forward. The Were's eyes widen the moment he realizes we won't be clashing like he planned. Aiming straight for his underside, I twist. Like a slow spinning projectile, I pass under him, reach out and nip his underside, then land on my feet behind him.

The fast-moving nudge has the wolf tipping in the air, but it's a human who crashes to the ground. Pushing himself up, he looks down at his hands, realizes they'll never be anything but human again, and looks up. I straighten, disappointed that his choices brought him here, but unapologetic. When the hands ball into fists, I straighten even more, wondering if he has anything to say on the matter.

After a long moment he looks away, hands falling to his side.

I turn away, hoping I've hidden my disgust. His choices did this, not mine.

Tuning into my senses, I scan the forest around me. I can hear a muffled voice, Alexis, making some sort of speech behind me.

Good. It looks like I have time. I scent another but I quickly move on, it's not something that's important right now. Next, I pick up what I was looking for. Low, ominous growls tell me they're not far away.

I find the small clearing, only a handful of feet wide, and a pale grey and midnight black wolf standing at the edge. Daniel is lounging against a tree on the other side.

This was always the plan—I'd take out the others whilst my father and brother made sure Daniel didn't get away. This is the traitor who became Kurt's right-hand Were. His escape wasn't an option.

Although, we didn't bank on him shifting. He pushes away from the tree but remains at the edge. He's smart enough to know to keep his back protected. He's also smart enough to know I can't turn him unless he's a wolf.

I shift to human, too, as Dad and Mitch move in to flank my sides. "What's his plan, Daniel?"

Daniel's gaze is hard as he looks at me across the open space. "To do what needs to be done."

"This is no longer some game, you fool. How can you be okay with the prospect of so much bloodshed?"

Daniel shrugs. "Sacrifices have to be made. It's the only way that we'll show them."

"This is your chance to save lives, not take them."

"Survival of the fittest decides who lives and who dies."

I've had enough. I can no longer hear voices from the Glade, so it looks like the speeches are done. The time for talking is over.

"You either walk away human, or you don't walk away at all, Daniel. You choose."

Daniel huffs in disdain. "You don't have the guts to kill me." He glances at me, then the two wolves on my left and right. "It would be cold-blooded murder."

My heart hardens at what I have to do. This isn't something I look forward to living with, but this has to end.

I step forward. "An Alpha needs to make some tough calls." I straighten my shoulders, deciding to use his own words against him. "Sacrifices have to be made."

I hear my family beside me, two Alphas themselves, and realize I won't be alone in what needs to be done.

Daniel doesn't move, probably assuming we're bluffing.

From the shadows behind him, a shape materializes. A shape we scented minutes ago. A shape Daniel's human body didn't pick up on.

The grizzly rises up on his haunches, a towering mass of fur and fury.

I stop, and a flash of victory lights up Daniel's face.

I shake my head, almost wishing I could have done the deed myself. "You're about to find out that this is bigger than we all imagined, Daniel."

Confusion dulls his moment, the flush of victory short-lived and already dissolving. My guess is that all three faces across from him are looking up and past him.

Daniel turns slowly, and I wonder when the realization will hit. He either dies as a human or protects himself as a Were from the bear who has just made its decision. Except the moment he shifts, I'll be on him faster than he can pump out a heartbeat. And then he's human anyway.

By the time Daniel's turned, the bear is already caving in on him. That's the moment he decides to shift, it's probably practically a reflex.

But the realization is too late. Wolf or human, Daniel's fate is about to be consumed by the violence we can all see in the bear's eyes. He knows this needs to end as much as we do.

I look away as teeth and claws close in. Daniel's ending is fast, his gurgled scream swiftly cut off. I turn back in time to see the bear drag his limp, bloodied body into the darkness between the trees.

When the earth shudders, I look at Dad and Mitch. Their wolf faces are scanning, looking from where the bear just disappeared to the ground to me. No bear having his lunch did that.

We all hold still, feet planted into the soil that's still trembling. It feels like an earthquake, but we've never had an earthquake in these parts. We're nowhere near a fault line.

Looking at my father and brother, my heart contracts painfully. "We need to get back."

I throw myself forward, a wolf by the time my paws hit the ground. The three prongs of a trident, we sprint back to the Glade. The place where our loved ones are waiting.

A sliver of knowledge has my heart pumping painfully in my chest.

The Prophecy has always been about making the impossible possible.

PART IX
EDEN

CHAPTER THIRTY

THERE'S A POLITE ROUND OF APPLAUSE AS JAMES STEPS DOWN FROM the podium. Not one Were in the audience raises a hand. I wonder if James doesn't see or is deliberately ignoring the savage frowns that surround him.

Alexis certainly doesn't, judging by her smile as she steps up. I grit my teeth, not looking forward to having to listen to her words of self-congratulation.

"Thank you, James." She glances down at the cards she's holding and my eyes narrow. I don't think I've ever seen Alexis use palm cards.

"This project is not something I've undertaken before. But it was born of high hopes that it will do great things." Alexis looks up at those around her, but her eyes are unfocused. "It is an undertaking which will bring people together in ways they haven't before and build bridges that haven't existed."

I frown. What is she talking about? This project has been about nothing but a facade for her career-driven ambitions. By making them environmentally friendly she found a way to make them more palatable.

"But the only way to show that to you, is through action. For you to celebrate the outcome with us." Alexis scans the crowd, looks like she's going to acknowledge my existence, but then keeps moving. "So, without further ado, let us break soil."

A man who was standing beside the bulldozer plugs in a set of ear buds and climbs up to the cab. His head is already nodding to whatever beat his eardrums are absorbing before he's shut the door.

There's a rumble of engine and a blurt of smoke as the dozer starts up. The Weres around me seem to contract. This is like a terminal death—you know it's coming, and you think you're prepared, but when it's finally staring you down, you discover you really aren't.

The dozer trundles forward, a lumbering hulk of metal that very little could stop. Alexis is probably going to demolish another strip of pristine beauty just to make a statement. It's the only reason she'd have such a hulk lined up to do her dirty work.

I gave her the idea.

My eyes snap up to the ledge. Kurt is looking directly at me, knowing I heard his words. Even from this distance I can see his wolfish smile.

Why would you want to see something so important to Weres destroyed?

The enormous red wolf sits and I'm actually glad everyone is focused on the dozer. *Sacrifices need to be made.*

No. They don't. Anything that asks for the blood you crave is not what the Prophecy is for.

I feel his contempt slam across the distance. *I'm about to unite us in ways you have never been able. The subsequent conquering is inevitable.*

I feel when Daniel dies deep in my chest. The others didn't lose the thread that weaves us all together. It's a loss that didn't have to happen. It's a loss that hurts and angers at the same time. I glare at the driver of this train of death. *Your few supporters won't be helping you any longer.*

The wolf shakes his head. *They've served their purpose.*

What? My mind scrambles as I try to figure out what he means. Noah will be on his way back shortly, and he was never far away. Division of the Prime Alpha pair wasn't Kurt's plan. I look around, the dozer is moving in a straight line.

Directly to the Precept Rock.

Others will do it for me.

The Weres around us realize what's happening as I do. Several shout out for the dozer to stop. But he can't hear them—I barely can. His music and mechanical monster ensure he's cut off from the world around him. He won't feel the pain of the earth he's about to slice or that of the Weres he's about to lacerate.

James wraps his arm around Alexis' shoulder, turning her away from the crowd and toward what is about to unfold.

The bulldozer is a lumbering beast, its sights on the rock that has predicted it all. The gigantic bucket angles slightly down, like a surgeon aiming his scalpel. When it hits, my hand flies to my mouth. I wait for this venerated tablet of nature to crumble, knowing my hope is about to be crushed with it.

But the bulldozer comes to an abrupt halt like it just hit the side of the mountain rather than a rock the size of man. The earth shudders, like the rock's root is buried deep down. Everyone in the crowd is wide-eyed that the slab of granite hasn't been toppled.

What everyone else hasn't felt is that every Were's anger in the area spiked as the dozer connected with their beloved rock. They're all standing now, several have moved forward. They're waiting to see what the driver will do next.

I wait, breath imprisoned in my chest. A whole lot of anger is being held as potential energy at the moment. No one wants to know what happens if it is released.

When the earth's trembling doesn't stop, the humans stand too. Everyone is glancing at each other now, an acknowledgment that the rumbling is disproportionate. Even a deeply rooted rock shouldn't have the soil vibrating with seismic waves.

The bulldozer reverses, the driver doesn't seem to have noticed what he just triggered. I step forward, possibly trying to get ahead of the anger that is growing. Please let him keep moving backwards.

The dozer stops, idling on the grass. The driver moves levers before the engine revs again. The machine lurches, grass churning beneath its caterpillar tracks.

Oh god, he's moving forward again.

And this time, he's getting more of a run up. The dozer driver has been set a challenge—the motor growls louder as he picks up speed. The wave of fury swells with it. Not one Were here is going to be okay with what's about to happen.

The bulldozer hits the Precept Rock with a crash, and this time it feels like the very center of the earth roars with pain. I watch in horror as the proud rock, the holder of all Were law, fractures. Cracks spear through it like forked lightning, starting at the base and spreading out. Splitting and splicing, they reach the top. I gasp along with every Were in the Glade as it crumbles, toppling into nothing but a pile of ruptured rubble.

The bulldozer reverses, opening up the space around the pile so we can all appreciate what just happened. The driver cuts the engine, and I wonder if he can now feel what these actions have triggered.

The ground beneath us is shaking and rolling. I'm not sure if Mother Nature is shuddering in pain or trembling with anger. The people around me grab each other to steady themselves, minds starting to get scared. The Fae are no longer looking serene and calm.

It's only the Weres who seem to absorb the shaking. Maybe they were already shaking with fury.

I look up to find Kurt standing tall on the ledge. I can feel his smile in my mind.

This is what he wanted all along…

The Weres move forward, vengeance becoming a unifying concept. I step forward too, images of how this is going to play out splashing through my mind. These peace-loving Weres are taking this as a personal attack. One that needs retribution.

The shaking intensifies, like what we've just experienced was only a harbinger of what is to come. The trunks around me are shuddering, branches creaking, canopies shivering and rustling. The air around me feels like it's vibrating.

Behind me there's a creak of metal followed by cries of alarm. I turn to find one of the bleachers collapsing. People clamber off the staggered seats, rushing and screaming. Like a pile of pick up sticks, it collapses into a heap. Relief rushes through me as I see that no-one was hurt.

With a sudden shower of sparks, the camera that was filming this all pops and flares. The guy standing beside it yanks off his headphones, jumping back.

Some of the humans have already reached the conclusion that this is no longer a safe place to be. They run to their cars, reversing erratically in their rush to get out of here. Others are frozen, fear rooting them to the very soil moving beneath us.

I run to Orin, who has the Elders crowded around him. "Get them out of here!" I point to the people who are so flooded with panic that they're no longer moving. "They need to get out of here."

Orin and the others nod. They spread out, collecting the frightened bodies as they go. The humans recognize the calm faces that fill their vision as the lifeline they are. With soothing voices, the Fae take them to their cars.

I turn away, knowing that there are more intense emotions that I have to deal with.

Alexis and James stand by the podium, clinging to each other. In their disorientation and fear, they don't notice the bodies starting to move toward them. The sting of metal hits my nostrils and I know the Weres are about to shift. When they should be running for their lives, the Weres are closing in on the two humans who just destroyed their belief in a shared future.

One by one, they shift, until a mob of angry wolves are between me and those they blame for this.

Alexis screams and James pulls her to him. They look in horror at the mass of gigantic wolves who now line up before them.

I watch as Seth streaks from the left, shifting into his mountain of brown in the process. He runs into the space between Alexis and the Weres, claws gouging into the soil as he slides to a halt. He levels his gaze at his kin, head dropping, eyes warning them he'll protect these humans with his life.

The war that Kurt wanted is about to begin.

Weres against Weres.

Emily runs in, coming to stand beside Seth. She stands tall and trembling, one hand resting on his wolf shoulders as she shows them the unified defense they represent.

Weres against humans.

My heart feels like it's about to shatter just like the Precept Rock. I can feel Noah, sensing that he's not far away. But he won't be here in time. Not knowing what I'm doing, but knowing I have to try, I raise my arms and focus on their massive bodies.

Stop.

I feel their surprise, see one or two turn to look at me. Most are shocked and angered.

This isn't right. Weres don't hurt humans.

My mind floods with their cries of outrage.

They destroyed the Precept Rock.

Humans have showed us what they do with their power.

Now we'll show them what we do with ours.

I drop my arms, looking at these majestic beasts and knowing they're hurting. *Please stop.*

Several pause, looking between me and their target. Alexis

looks like pure fear whilst James holds her tightly in his arms. He would know that they will offer no protection if these gargantuan wolves decide to attack.

Seth and Emily seem to contract tighter, and I can feel Seth's heart thundering. He's hoping that the small barrier he represents is enough for the others to stop and think. There's no way he can protect Emily and the two frightened humans behind him too.

As the earth continues to rumble beneath us, Alexis crumples in James' arms. "Leave us alone!"

She wants us to move. Be careful what you wish for...

Does she even realize that she's caused this?

Stupid, clueless humans. They don't deserve to live.

Seth has lost his head, aligning himself with them. If he dies too, so be it.

No, no, no. I look up at Kurt. His mind is saying one thing. *Yes, yes, yes.*

"Get away from us!" my mother screams.

I raise my arms higher. *You will not attack them.*

They don't even bother to turn. The rolling of the ground seems to swell their anger. Alexis' absence of remorse only inflames their desire for vengeance. They have decided to destroy her in return for destroying the Precept Rock.

This is only the beginning.

I ignore Kurt, not even bothering to look his way. There's something he hasn't factored in.

Before I speak again, I move further to the center of the Glade. I hold my arms straight, palms out. Despite the shifting soil beneath my feet, over the top of the growling and my mother's shouts, the melody rises through me. I feed it, let it gain strength, I feel it connect with the pain beneath me, but also the potential around me.

"As the Queen of the Fae and your Alpha's mate, I order you to stop."

Every Were freezes, muscles locked in their threatening stance. The one at the head, the one who was the angriest, tries to step forward.

Only to find he can't.

He strains against the invisible bonds that hold him, but I don't let go. All they have to do is wait for the emotion to abate and they will see that there is more here than two humans who don't realize what they've started.

They'll learn that they've been manipulated, that someone was seeking to use their strength.

One or two try to turn, and I let them. They look at me, unsure of what this means, and I send them the energy of the melody. Maria is the first to take a step back, maybe realizing how close to being like Daniel she just became.

But several cling to the anger. They try to twist out of whatever is holding them. They want payment for their pain. I don't blame them. They have lost something that cannot be measured.

I stay there, the melody staying strong, knowing I can wait them out.

Without looking at Kurt I send him a message.

You have no idea what you've started.

PART X
NOAH

CHAPTER THIRTY-ONE

It's only a matter of time before the landslide begins. I can hear the rocks rattle and shift, feel them shear away from the rock face behind me. Dust fills the air, the smaller rocks reaching us first. The shaking and rumbling now comes from beneath me and behind me. I glance back to see Dad and Mitch not far behind, and the wall of powdered earth rising above behind them.

Panicked, I run faster. Most of the rocks will be stopped by the trees. But if there are any large pieces that gain momentum, then the Glade will be their final resting point.

As I reach the clearing, there's only one person I'm looking for.

I find Eden, standing almost in the center of the Glade, tall and unafraid. Alexis and James stand beside a pile of rubble, and my heart jerks painfully; that's all that is left of the Precept Rock. Between them are Seth and Emily, and the packs who came here to witness this.

I hear the first rock rumbling down the cliff face, looking over my shoulder to see it crashing through the trees and bowling them over like pins. There's nothing that can stop its trajectory. My mind does the math, acknowledging that Eden isn't in its path.

The roar that powers through the Glade isn't mine. Mitch speeds past me and I see what has his eyes wide with fear.

Tara, hand on her unborn child, is running. The boulder is powering through the Glade, and she's in its way. There's no way she'll outrun the rock that was thrown from the cliff.

Because Tara's pregnant and can't shift.

Go left! I want to scream, but my wolf throat has nothing but its own cry of denial. *Turn left, Tara.*

Realizing that its speed is greater than hers, Tara throws herself to the side. Her foot slips in the green grass and she stumbles. Hands reaching out even though there's nothing to grasp, she twists at the last minute, protecting her baby.

As she crashes to the ground, the rock rolls over her leg, coming to a standstill. The groan of pain is soft and low, but it reaches us all. Tara's eyes squeeze tightly shut, her back arched. One leg slips out, but the other has disappeared beneath the mass of granite which has come to rest on it.

Mitch reaches her a moment later, and then we're all there. Tara looks up at us, eyes pleading.

"We'll get it off, Tara." Mitch's voice is strained. "Before you can say fracking fish sticks."

I take in the mass of weight that we're going to have to move. It's going to be heavy, but we don't have a choice.

We all line up against the rock, shoulders hard up against it. Four Weres—my white, Mitch's midnight, Mom and Dad's shades of grey—take a position.

I'm not even surprised when Orin kneels beside her. He pushes back her hair. "We're here, Tara. We'll have this thing off in a moment."

Tara's eyes flutter open, looking up at us. "Jellybean?"

Orin smooths Tara's hair again. "You're going to be running after him in no time."

In unison we push. The granite digs into my shoulder and I welcome the pressure. We need to move this mountain of stone and we need to move it now. The boulder lifts a little and we all push harder. Tara groans as the pressure on her leg shifts, and I realize we need to keep up this momentum. If we don't succeed, this weight is going to crush her leg all over again.

Muscles trembling with strain, I shove harder. Mitch groans beside me and I know he's pushing with all his heart and soul. But the boulder sits on its fulcrum, taunting us.

I feel something nudge beside me and open my eyes to find John, a dark brown wolf, ramming himself against the rock. There's another as more Weres find somewhere to squeeze in. Even the Fae Elders push their hands through, wanting to add what little strength they have. We push again, and I feel it the rock lift another inch.

Almost there!

Until the next flood of earth tremors pulses beneath us. Like a wave, it pushes the boulder back at us, and we all contract, the weight pushing us down. My muscles strain like everyone else's would as we stop the boulder from crushing Tara further. As the ground settles, we push it back to its fragile pivot. Before we can push again, another crest hits us, and we take the weight. We don't have enough strength to overcome the surges and swells.

I look at Mitch, whose face is squeezed with effort. I don't know that we're going to be able to do this.

"Eden!"

I look up, and Eden's face matches the confusion that we both register. Although it's her name, it's not a voice we've ever heard use it.

Alexis is running toward her, one arm flailing as if Eden is standing on a road and a train is coming at her. "Move, Eden."

I look up and see what has Alexis finally using Eden's name. Kurt is no longer a wolf. It's man who stands on the ledge, a man holding a rifle.

Alexis grabs Eden by the shoulders and pulls her along. They both stumble as a bullet slices into the soil where she was just standing.

Orin's face is wild with fear as he pushes me. "Go to her!"

I step away and the boulder holds itself on the shoulders of the wolves who are now holding it. They contract as another wave pushes down. Even the addition of the strength of the Prime Alpha isn't enough to move the mountain of granite.

Torn, I start running to my mate.

"No!" James is racing to join them when he jerks back as if he's been yanked by a rope. He drops to the ground, one hand holding the bullet wound he just sustained to his shoulder.

Eden is righting herself, looking at James, then looking to me. Her green eyes are wide with fright, her face pale with foreboding. Everywhere everything is shaking.

I'm running toward her, desperation the drive that powers every step as I shout in my mind. *Head for cover!*

Eden grabs her mother's hand, looking around the clearing that was never designed to need somewhere to hide. Seeing the only place they can use, she runs toward the rubble of the Precept Rock, dragging Alexis with her.

They cower and I make a beeline for them. There's no way that pile, probably waist high on a human, will be big enough to protect a Were body, but I'm there in a second anyway. Being with my mate is all that matters right now.

Alexis screams for James, who rolls over on the grass. His hand holding his bloody shoulder, he looks at her. His voice is laced with pain but shouted nonetheless. "Stay where you are."

The gang of Weres that had accumulated seem to unfreeze, like puppets whose strings have been cut. A few step back, smart enough to start looking scared. Several set their furious gazes on James as he lies in the grass, injured.

Another wave of anger ripples through the ground. As I reach

Eden and her mother, I look up, wondering if this is going to be the end. I'm the only target Kurt has left.

Kurt is standing at the edge of the ledge, rifle raised, taking aim. I stand proud and tall, knowing we failed, but unable to regret the love that I discovered. Maybe Eden and the baby will survive this nightmare.

Maybe that's what the Prophecy had been all along.

I look down, wanting Eden to be the last thing I see, but Kurt seems to stagger, the rifle tip wavering. As one more surge powers through the ground, the ledge shears away.

I watch in shock as the shelf of rock slides down, at first with a short jerk, and then with a mighty yank of gravity.

I wonder if it's the knowledge that because of him Tara is trapped or that he's caused his own ending that flashes across his face as his body drops.

Nothing but a rumble of thunder heralds Kurt's fall to death.

PART XI
EDEN

CHAPTER THIRTY-TWO

Just like Daniel's, I feel Kurt's death.

It's like a severing of a painful, tortured thread. There's relief, but also regret.

But this is far from over.

As the earth feels like it's tearing apart, I realize Kurt is gone, his death brought on by his own greed, but he's left a legacy. Weres and humans have never been more divided. The bloodshed that has been avoided is still a very real possibility. If we get out of this alive, Weres will hate humans in a way they never have before. There's no way we can stop them now.

We've failed the Prophecy.

I curl one hand around a shard of rock, hating the metaphor that I'm holding. Crushed dreams, broken promises. Our future nothing but a pile of rubble.

I look out, Tara is now unconscious, her leg still trapped beneath a boulder. Mitch, Adam, Beth, and the others are still trying to move it, but the strain is starting to show. The weight crushing Tara's leg hasn't moved.

The Weres that I'm no longer controlling are looking like they're deciding what to do next. One or two step away, realizing they need to get to safety. A few are already focused on Alexis again. I'd say the rest will follow one of the two options. But even if one decides to attack, Noah will protect her, and the division will be complete.

James is looking at us across the distance. His face is dusty, his shoulder bloody. No, he's looking at Alexis. They're probably trying to understand what the hell is happening. And realizing they're unlikely to survive it.

I look up at Noah, hating the tear that has escaped down my cheek, but not bothering to wipe it away. He steps forward, his broad head coming down. Gently, reverently, he rests his forehead on mine. *We tried.*

I squeeze my eyes shut, not wanting more saltwater between us. *We really did.*

There was something we must've missed.

I curl my free hand into his thick, white fur. *I'm sorry.*

Noah's summer sky eyes shut for a brief moment. *No, I'm sorry.*

"I'm so sorry." We pull apart to find Alexis looking at us both, her own tears glittering down her cheeks. "I'm so, so sorry."

My mother's hand cautiously reaches out to me. My throat tightens painfully as her fingers brush my face and her palm cups my cheek. "Eden."

She turns to the massive white wolf beside me, her other hand reaching out. She pauses, the very air now a thunder around us, fingers trembling.

Noah holds still, gaze unwavering, as Alexis makes her decision.

"Noah," she breathes. Her arm extends, slowly but sure, until her fingers brush his fur. Just like she had with me, her palm cups his cheek.

"I wanted…" She looks back to me. "I wanted to love you." She shakes her head. "To show you that I love you. I'm sorry."

My tears are a waterfall now, not sure what I'm supposed to

do with this olive branch as the world is crumbling around us. I open my mouth, knowing it's not words lodged in my throat. It's the grief that we'll never know what this could have meant. I close it again, just looking at her.

We stay there in our circle, my hand on Noah, my mother touching us both when I feel the shard of rock vibrate in my hand. At first I ignore it, everything around us is shaking, the piece of granite in my hand is just an extension of that.

But then it warms, the vibration becoming a shudder. I pull back, holding it out. "Noah."

We all look down at the rock resting in my palm. It sits there for a moment before shivering again. The glow, to start with, is subtle, but it quickly gains strength. Within seconds it's a blossoming flower of light.

Noah and I look at each other, astonished. What is going on?

When the pile of rubble beside me begins to move, then glow too, I scramble back, taking my mother with me. Noah is a steely tower of protectiveness against my back.

The earth stops quaking. The silence afterwards feels absolute. There's no breeze rustling trees, no birds calling out in alarm, no voices shouting for revenge or for this all to end or wishing for forgiveness.

There's just the sound of rock shifting on rock as the radiance intensifies. I know everyone is watching, because there is no way you could miss the miracle that's happening before us. Brick by misshapen brick, the Precept Rock realigns and rebuilds.

Like a slow-motion reverse, the pieces stack up on each other, from the base up. The Precept grows, its fractures glowing then the dissipating as they seal. In the space of a few disbelieving breaths, it's whole again.

But this time, only three words are printed on it.

PART XII
NOAH

CHAPTER THIRTY-THREE

I SHIFT BACK TO HUMAN, TRYING TO WRAP MY MIND AROUND WHAT I'm seeing. The realization seems to hit Eden at the same time because she shoots upright and turns to me. I look at her, trying to comprehend what just happened.

We step back, looking around.

James stands as he holds his hand over his bloody wound. The Weres who remain shift back to human, their faces dusty and shell-shocked. The moment the earth stopped moving, my family finally tipped the balance on the boulder. Mitch is kneeling in the grass, holding a pained but alive Tara in his arms. The Glade is littered with shocked faces. Dust is loitering in the air.

But a single shaft of light spears down over one place.

The Precept Rock stands tall and proud, kissed by the sun, looking like nothing ever happened.

Except it's completely different. There are no longer five laws that Weres are to abide by stamped into its unyielding surface.

Stamped with authority, glowing with conviction, there's now one law, and one law for all.

United we conquer.

Alexis reaches out, her fingers tracing the letters. Her voice is a whisper as she reads. "United we conquer."

I turn back to Eden, knowing my disbelief echoes hers. Our hands reach out, smiles wondering if they can break out as we clasp the other.

My grin is gargantuan as Eden steps in closer. "We did miss something."

She blinks, eyes luminous and green. "Humans."

We say the three words together, three words that explain what just happened. "United we conquer."

This kiss is inevitable. When Eden's lips touch mine we sink into each other, arms coming around to hold tight. So much emotion floods me that I'm not sure my heart can hold it. It's her love and mine, it's our wonder and joy and devotion, it's the celebration of the future we just created.

We're wound so tightly together that when Eden's belly flutters, I feel it too. We yank back, both glancing down, breaths held to see if it will happen again. Holy heck, there it is again!

"Noah." Eden's voice is hushed with reverence. "He's letting us know."

I squeeze her tight, holding them both with all my heart. "Our baby girl is partying right along with us."

This time, the single tear that tracks down Eden's face is one I want to treasure. I take in her glowing face. "I think there's only one word that can capture this."

Eden pushes in close, whispering the word that keeps exploding in my mind. "Wow."

As sounds start to crowd into our beautiful bubble, I realize one last kiss is all we'll get for a little while. There are injuries to tend to and explanations to be made. As my family and hers, as Weres and Fae and humans, move in to honor what just happened with us, I lean down to gaze into her eyes. I adore, desire, want and need this amazing girl more than I could ever capture in words.

Luckily, our connection conveys it all. It means I can say the words that almost come close. "I love you, Eden."

Eden's smile somehow captures all those emotions and more. "And I love you, Noah."

PART XIII
EPILOGUE

EDEN

"Noah, you can't afford this."

Noah slips an arm around my waist, tucking the blindfold he just pulled off my eyes into his back pocket. "Not on Prime Alpha wages." His grin is cocky as he glances down at me. "Or in the Queen of the Fae tax bracket for that matter."

I look back at the clearing we stand before. Adam and Beth's house is only a few minutes walk away, Mitch and Tara's the same distance in the opposite direction. This is the land we we're planning on building our house on...eventually. Neither of us generates much of an income. With college part-time, our responsibilities take up the rest.

Except now there's earth moved, holes dug, and a stack of planks piled to the side. Someone has started building.

Noah steps around, swallowing my field of vision. His summer sky eyes are careful as he says his next words. "But Alexis can."

"What?"

Noah swallows. "Your mother and James designed it. It's ecologically sustainable, carbon neutral, and some other words that sound impressive. They wanted to do this for us."

I frown. "Don't you think giving us the Glade was enough?"

That was a memory which is forever implanted in my mind. We were at home, sitting under Grandfather Douglas. My belly was rivalling the size of a watermelon as we curled beneath the tree's expansive branches, reveling in the love and wonder that those movements had never stopped triggering.

We'd stood, well, Noah had stood and then helped me up, when we heard a car approaching. Then we'd frowned at each other when James had climbed out, coming around to open the door for Alexis.

They'd walked toward us, Alexis carrying a leather folder. Both had looked down but quickly recovered. It had only been a few of months since everything at the Glade, and yet our baby was already looking like I was nearing the end of my pregnancy. But then again, they'd already had so many assumptions about what is real destroyed.

Noah had reached out to shake hands with James, but I'd stayed put. Although hearing my mother speak my name had almost been lost in the enormity of everything that happened at the Glade, I'd heard it. It was her touch that completed the circle, that created the unity that had been needed to conquer the greed and hate that had been festering.

But I still didn't know what it meant for the two of us.

Alexis had taken a deep breath. "This won't take long. We wanted to make sure that you understood us when we said you could trust us."

James had nodded. "Seeing what we did, knowing what we know now...we didn't realize."

Alexis glanced down and away before looking back up. "I didn't listen."

Noah had waited by my side, knowing this was my olive branch to accept. I'd looked at them both. "Our lives depend on you keeping your knowledge of Weres and Fae secret."

Alexis' grey gaze hadn't wavered from mine. "We know. And

we would never endanger that. And to prove how important this is, we wish to give the land back to the rightful owners."

Stunned, Noah and I had just stood there.

James had shrugged a one shoulder shrug. "Besides, with the unexplained seismic activity that authorities have given up trying to explain, its land value has gone down significantly."

Noah had been the first to recover. "We'll pay."

Alexis was already shaking her head. "No, you won't."

James smiled as he shook his head too. "You don't pay for gifts."

Alexis held out the leather folder. Noah and I glanced at each other and then back. Feeling nothing but shock, I'd reached out and it had passed into my hand. Opening, all I'd seen were lines of black and white, legal jargon that I couldn't make sense of. But there in the center, had been our names. Noah Phelan and Eden St. James. Owners of the precious parcel of land that showed us the power of unity.

I'd looked up. "Thank you."

What had been the biggest shock of all was watching the undeniable blush that had crept up Alexis' cheeks.

Alexis and James had joined us for dinner that night. Alexis had smiled through Beth's charcoal chicken, Tara had spent more time smiling at the bundle she'd been nursing, whilst I'd said very little. Throughout the night, Alexis had looked at me often, but most intently when she'd told us that she was planning on establishing a company with James. Unity Holdings was planning on establishing eco-tourism locations around the world. The locations would be approved by all—environmental groups, local councils...Weres and Fae.

The many places of Mother Nature's heartbeats would slowly be preserved but also shared and celebrated.

I look back at the bare ground which was waiting for a home to be built on it. "Can we accept this?"

Noah's gaze settles on mine. "That's up to you. You know Mom would be happy for us to stay with them."

I think of Beth and how much she adores her growing family. The more the merrier seems to be her motto. Her joy at the arrival of little Joshua, a little over two now, is a shining example. He's almost as spoilt by her as he is by Tara and Mitch. Staying home and being the minder of her grandchildren as their parents attend college has been a labor of love.

I smile. "And we both know that's not because of our winning personalities."

I look around. I haven't been able to call Alexis Mom, and I'm not sure if there's a 'yet' at the end of that sentence. And this would be an undeniable way to weave her into our lives. But...

"I've seen some of James' designs. They're amazing."

Noah nods. "And I do worry that Ava thinks Mom's cooking is normal."

Like her name has conjured her, a blonde haired nymph runs at us on stubby, toddler legs. "Look, Mama!"

I look up to see Beth waving at us from the edge of the clearing before heading off.

Noah leans down to clasp our daughter as she throws herself at him. He lifts her up like he always does and she squeals with delight. Holding her up high in the air, her hair cascades down like corn silk as she beams at him "Daddy."

The true Daddy's girl that she is, Ava not only proved me wrong with her gender, but also learned how to say Daddy properly before Mommy. The peals of laughter that curl around us warm my heart.

From her perch, Ava holds out a small parcel. "Unca Orin," she announces proudly.

Noah lowers her, placing her in the grass. She plops onto her bottom, already intent on tearing it open. We both kneel down beside her, and I can't help but reach out and brush back her hair.

Far longer than any two-year old's should be, its wispy strands are already halfway down her back. Orin said that's normal for Fae children.

From the shreds of paper, Ava pulls out a native American beaded necklace. It seems Orin is back in the States somewhere.

It was hard to see him go, but I understood. He'd come to say goodbye the day after the Precept Rock had resurrected. I'd been standing there, not knowing how to apologize. I'd taken his birthright, even if it had been inadvertently.

He'd stood there, that hard-to-read expression of his firmly in place. "I knew what I was training you for, Eden."

"You did?"

He'd reached out a hand and rested it on the baby steadily growing inside me. "This was always bigger than just the Fae."

I'd given him a hug, already knowing he was leaving. "I'm going to miss you."

"I'll be back to meet my niece."

I'd rolled my eyes. "Not you too."

I should have realized he would know.

Ava holds the necklace up, her blue eyes wide with wonder. "Show Grandma?"

I smile. Although I haven't been able to call Alexis Mom yet, she's certainly Ava's grandma. That one word sparks a glow I've never seen in Alexis. It's the glow of a future I'm looking forward to being part of.

I take the necklace, a beautiful pattern of colored beads. "We can show Grandma when she comes over for dinner."

Noah slips his arm around me. "When we tell her the news?"

I smile up at the man who holds my heart, feeds my soul, and is the most wonderful father I could dream of. "We'll tell her she can build our house."

Noah lifts Ava again. "Did you hear that, baby girl?" He spins her around and her peals of laughter rain down on us. Bringing her to his hip, he engulfs us with his happiness. I lean in for a kiss, one that will be one of many, one that is unique in this moment. The moment where our future will be built from the ground up.

I feel a small hand pat my face, and I know Ava will be doing the same to Noah. She thinks it's hilarious to whack us with her baby palms when we kiss.

"Mama."

I pull back. Ava's voice isn't the happiness-filled melody it was a moment ago. Ava's tilted eyes are blue and watery. She wiggles and Noah places her on the ground, frowning a little.

Ava, the child who carries the namesake of my father, Avery, points to the cleared area she must have just noticed. "All gone."

She's talking about the vegetation that had been cleared for the house site. "Yes, Ava. This is where we're going to build our home."

Ava walks forward, but then her little body stops. "But all gone."

Noah moves forward to take her hand. "It's going to be a very special home just for the three of us."

Ava tugs him forward, and we cover the few feet to where there is nothing but soil. Although we're in a natural clearing, the thick carpet of grass has been scraped away to level the area. She squats down in the way of toddlers, frowning at the bare ground.

Noah and I look at each other. Ava has shown that she is as tough and resilient as the Were tattoo which is stamped behind her ear. Keeping up with her red-haired cousin, Joshua, even though he's already showing signs of Were height, is a personal challenge. But she's also shown that she's deeply in tune with the natural world too. It is forest animals who play with her in the backyard, birds who bring her flowers to distract her when she falls over. I doubt Stash and Caesar have ever devoted themselves so wholly to one little being.

"Sad, Mama."

I squat down next to her, Noah on the other. "We'll plant a very special garden once the house is built. How does that sound?"

Ava looks up, summer sky eyes sad and serious. "We fix?"

Noah strokes back the hair which falls across her face. "We definitely will."

Ava's smile is sweet and luminous, one that you can't help but return. I now have two favorite sights in the whole world. She looks back down, palm reaching out to rest on the soil. "We fix."

Noah reaches out to scoop her back up, but then pauses. Ava's looking at her hand, her stare intense but strangely serene. I have to stifle my gasp when I see what is happening.

Delicate fronds of green are pushing up through the brown soil. Like some sort of time-lapse documentary, the fragile grass unfurls and grows. And as Ava coaxes life from the scraped soil, as graceful green pushes up and through, I realize what is going to happen.

The Glade is the one place which visibly carries the scars of everything that has occurred. The track that Alexis cleared remains an open wound, the Glade no longer a hidden place from the eyes of humans. There have been no full moon runs since the earthquake. The Fae haven't wanted to use this particular heart of Mother Nature's to affirm their connection to the earth.

It is Ava who will heal it. The child who carries the fire of a Were, the calm of a Fae...and the passion and potential of a human. She will coax the forest to grow once again, and eventually enclose the sacred space.

Noah and I stand, arms wrapping around each other, as we watch our daughter work her magic. My mate arches a wry brow at me. "United, huh?"

I rest my head on his shoulder. "Who knows what we'll be able to conquer."

THE END

Ready for the next installment in the Prime Prophecy series?
Check out LEGACY AWAKENED!

AFTER THE PROPHECY THERE WILL BE
A LEGACY...

Noah and Eden's connection was prophesied to be a love that
would defy boundaries.

Now that very love will leave a legacy...

They fell in love long before they met.
Now the harshness of reality will be their love's ultimate test.

Ava.

The child of a prophecy.

Ava has seen a glorious white wolf in her dreams for two years. They've connected so deeply she's sure he must be real. She just needs to find him...

Hunter.

A protector at no matter the cost.

An Alpha from the age of sixteen, Hunter can't afford to find out if what he's seen out on the arctic tundra is more than just a lonely fantasy. Wolf numbers are critically low, and he's willing to do whatever it takes to save them.

They meet as a dangerous virus appears in the wolf population and poaching has become far more coordinated. It seems that some are seeking to hasten the wolves' extinction as the two desperately race against time to save them.

Battling a deadly disease, their responsibilities, and their own undeniable feelings, Ava and Hunter struggle to find the balance between what is right, what is wrong, and who to trust.

Ultimately, they are going to have to face the only possible solution - that their love may be the key to it all.

DISCOVER THE NEXT EPIC LOVE STORY HERE

http://mybook.to/LegacyAwakened

LET'S CONNECT!

Don't miss out on notifications and tasters of my upcoming books (I might be biased, but there's some awesome stories in the pipeline)! Subscribe to be the first to know and to make the most of any deals I have on offer.

https://www.subscribepage.com/TamarSloan

Every couple of weeks you'll get exclusive tasters of upcoming books, awesome offers and bargain reads, and an opportunity to connect (personally, I reckon that's the best bit).

There's also some cool freebies coming your way...

I'd love to see you over there.

Tamar :)

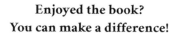

Enjoyed the book?
You can make a difference!

Reviews are gold for authors; they help with discoverability (one of the great challenges of being an author) and they let other readers know their time isn't likely to be wasted. If you enjoyed Legacy Accepted, please consider leaving a review on Amazon (or Goodreads). Even a line or two would be incredibly helpful.

Amazon | Goodreads

I look forward to connecting with you!
Tamar

ABOUT THE AUTHOR

Tamar really struggled writing this bio, in part because it's in third person, but mostly because she hasn't decided whether she's primarily a psychologist who loves writing, or a writer with a lifelong fascination with psychology.

She must have been someone pretty awesome in a previous life (past life regression indicated a Care Bear), because she gets to do both. Beginning her career as a youth worker, then a secondary school teacher, before becoming a school psychologist, Tamar helps children and teens to live and thrive despite life's hurdles like loss, relationship difficulties, mental health issues, and trauma.

As lover of reading, inspired by books that sparked beautiful movies in her head, Tamar loves to write young adult romance. To be honest, it was probably inevitable that her knowledge and love of literature would translate into writing emotion driven stories of finding life and love beyond our comfort zones. You can find out more about Tamar's books at www.tamarsloan.com

A lifetime consumer of knowledge, Tamar holds degrees in Applied Science, Education and Psychology. When not reading, writing or working with teens, Tamar can be found with her husband and two children enjoying country life on their small slice of the Australian bush.

The driving force for all of Tamar's writing is sharing and connecting. In truth, connecting with others is why she writes.

She loves to hear from readers and fellow writers. Find her on all the usual social media channels or her website.

CPSIA information can be obtained
at www.ICGtesting.com
Printed in the USA
BVHW041813010421
603947BV00015B/618